Corinne glanced at the sculptor's charcoal sketches which strewed the floor of the studio. 'You've only blocked in a rough outline of the bottom figure,' she said.

'Yes, the girl I use for that one can't come as often as the others.'

'I'll take her place,' said Corinne. 'And if you're so worried about models' fees, this one won't cost you anything.' And she stripped off a high-necked flowered blouse to reveal one of the fashionable new bust bodices.

'Corinne!' cried the sculptor. 'Stop that at once. I'm not in the mood. And anyway you're the wrong shape.'

But she had already reached behind her to unfasten the bodice and she wrenched the garment free, her full breasts bouncing lewdly as she reached out for him . . .

Lustful Liaisons

Anonymous

HEADLINE

First published in Great Britain in 1992
by HEADLINE BOOK PUBLISHING PLC

10 9 8 7 6 5 4 3 2 1

ISBN 0 7472 3710 7

Printed and bound in Great Britain by
HarperCollins Manufacturing, Glasgow
Typesetting by CBS Felixstowe IP11 7DR

HEADLINE BOOK PUBLISHING PLC
Headline House
79 Great Titchfield Street
London W1P 7FN

Lustful
Liaisons

Part One

City Lights

Paris - March, 1912

CHAPTER ONE

Six men in evening dress sat around the long table. Two, raffish fellows with bushy side-whiskers and a high colour, were in their thirties, the remainder elderly. All of them, to judge by the display of heavy gold watch-chains, jewelled cufflinks and diamond pins, were well-to-do. The atmosphere in the dimly lit room, winey with the aftermath of rich cooking, was spiced now with cigar smoke and the fumes of brandy.

In the centre of the table, a naked woman posed amidst a litter of empty champagne bottles, discarded napkins and coffee cups whose saucers overflowed with ash. She was big-breasted, fleshy about the hips, and not more than twenty years of age.

'Excellent!' the elderly man at the head of the table approved. 'Charles! you may instruct the musicians to begin.'

'*Bien, m'sieu.*' A waiter, hovering discreetly in the shadows, soft-footed to the far end of the room and vanished behind velvet curtains masking an alcove. Seconds later, the strains of a Mozart sonata, re-scored for violin, 'cello and flute, vibrated between the panelled walls. The girl on the table began to move.

Slowly at first, and then with increasing rapidity as the sonata's first theme was transferred from fiddle to flute, she oscillated her hips. The flesh of her calves quivered. She rolled her shoulders, snaking rounded arms this way and that.

When the second theme was introduced by the 'cello, she brought her legs into play, swivelling from side to side on her heels with her pelvis arched and her knees bent so that the slack bulge of her belly rotated.

Nobody could have called the girl beautiful. Her tawny hair was lank, the line of her jaw still softened by puppy-fat, her green eyes set too far apart. Her breasts, while firm enough, were slightly pear-shaped. But the body as a whole exuded an air of animal sensuality compounded by its presence in the richly furnished room, by the proximity of formally dressed men lewdly eyeing each curve of its shameful nudity.

It would have been an exaggeration to call the girl a dancer: her terpsichorean expertise would not have carried her past a preliminary audition for back-row *figurantes* at one of the lesser Montmartre music-halls. But she knew about sex. She had shown that, removing her outer garments and then her underwear in front of the velvet drapes with lascivious and studied abandon when she had been shown into the room twenty minutes previously. Now each movement of every muscle served to draw the onlookers' attention to the taut swell of a breast, to the darkly puckered skin of the areola surrounding its stiffened nipple, to a shadowed pulse in the crease of a thigh, to a scoop of naked waist or a fleshy hemisphere of the girl's bottom as smooth and firm and shiny as one of the cherries crowning the fruit bowl at the far end of the table.

The men around that table reacted differently. The one who had summoned the waiter sprawled back in his chair with his legs stretched out in front of him and a half smile on his lips as the ash lengthened on the tip of his cigar. Another of the elderly men sat forward, his elbows on the table, gazing with fascinated attention at the *mons pubis* gyrating above and within an arm's reach of his face. A third was breathing heavily, his eyes unnaturally bright and his forehead dewed with sweat in the lamplight. The fourth smiled slyly, covertly regarding his friends before he dared reveal any reaction of his own. One of the younger diners shifted awkwardly in his seat. His companion was affecting to be bored by the whole spectacle, but the knuckles of the hand lying carelessly in his lap were white.

Every one of them (the waiter knew with the unswerving certainty that experience in his trade brings) was already violating in his mind the nubile young woman whose body was so salaciously displayed before him, deeply penetrating the soft warm belly that trembled so temptingly near.

Languorously, as the violin and 'cello ushered in the sonata's slow movement, the nude girl raised her arms, lifting the big breasts with their ruby tips, revealing the tufted pits so reminiscent of that other furred chalice that lay enticingly between the moist slopes of her thighs. One of the watchers coughed nervously.

The girl bent her knees and turned around, spiralling slowly towards the littered table top with hands fluttering until she was almost sitting on her heels. In this position she revolved twice, staring with a mocking smile at each face as her own spun past. Then, with an agile leap, she sprang upright, spread her legs and leaned back . . . and for the first time the lustful onlookers were afforded a glimpse of those pink lips nestling among the hairs of the pubic triangle that seemed to each man to smile a secret, personal welcome to him. The girl smoothed caressing hands up over her waist to cup her own breasts. She massaged the heavy mounds, fingering them over her rib cage, tweaking the nipples and darting both hands down to tease the springy hair at the base of her belly. Her head swayed from side to side, tolling the lank hair behind her back like a silent bronze bell.

Abruptly the music quickened as the performers swung into the final movement of the sonata. The naked girl, almost immobile in her indecent self-absorption, sprang

5

to life with it. She pirouetted on one toe, kicking out with the other foot like a ballet dancer, so that the whole hairy furrow of her secret parts was open to the delighted gaze of the men around the table each time she spun past. A champagne bottle toppled over and rolled to the floor, leaving a fine white froth in its wake. One of the chairs creaked.

Strings ran up and down the scale; the flute trilled an obligato. Frenziedly, the dancer whipped her body into an orgy of motion. Arms flying, legs pistoned from each shuddering hip, she stormed up and down the table, stamping aside plates of *petit-fours*, wineglasses, a dish half full of trifle. Her torso writhed, sweat streaked the slopes of her breasts, the mane of hair thrashed forward to cover her face, then back behind her as she leaned away from her jerking pelvis. Finally, in time with the climatic bars of the sonata, she whirled around, bent double, to offer her transfixed audience a last glimpse of her now gaping femininity, and terminated the display, breasts bouncing, with a splits that slid to a halt in front of the man at the head of the table.

There was a moment's silence, and then a burst of applause punctuated by guffaws and an occasional 'Bravo!' The girl rolled over onto her back and lay among the ruins of the banquet with her knees drawn up. She was panting.

'Excellent!' the man at the head of the table exclaimed. 'Splendid!' He clapped again. 'But I see that our young friend has a part-portion of strawberry mousse adorning her person. Not too far, to be clinically specific, from that ridge of bone defining the pelvic girdle. Now which of you lecherous fellows is to be the lucky possessor of the tongue that removes it for her?'

The man seated on his left – a septuagenarian with thinning hair and a neat grey beard – chuckled. 'We shall draw for the privilege,' he drawled. And then, to the invisible waiter: 'Charles? You may bring the cards!'

* * *

The bearded man was the Comte de la Ferrière, an impoverished nobleman whose fortune had died with his rich wife – and who had, for some years now, been supplementing his meagre income by organizing, for a consideration, the kind of 'intimate theatrical spectacle' required to satiate the jaded appetites of his wealthier acquaintances. He was, in other words, a high-class ponce paid to stage obscene performances in private, recruiting for this purpose poorly paid dancers from the Montmartre night-clubs, midinettes and provincial hopefuls who had come to Paris expecting riches and ended up as waitresses in the men-only brasseries on the *grands boulevards*.

The man at the head of the table was – as his speech suggested – a doctor: a highly paid consultant at the newly established Villejuif hospital on the outskirts of the city. His name was Gaston Despierre.

Both the other two over-sixties were bankers. One of the younger men was the son of a prominent industrialist. His companion was a foreigner, an English engineer working for the design section of one of the new automotive manufacturing ventures. They were there at Despierre's invitation, following an afternoon skating with socialite daughters at the Palais de Glace.

A second girl had joined the young woman spreadeagled on the table. She was a little older, with short, dark hair, firm, pointed breasts and a wiry, muscular figure. It was a trim body, spoiled only by an excess of flesh below the hips: a slight softness to the skin of her rump, echoed in the blue-veined shadow pitting the creases that separated her bottom from the backs of her thighs. If the first girl was believably a dancer, her companion as clearly worked in some sedentary occupation. In fact she was a seamstress at the *atelier* of Poiret, the fashionable dressmaker.

But although she earned her living helping to clothe

the bodies of other people, she displayed no inhibition whatever in the exhibition before strangers of her own unclothed. Extending herself alongside the supine dancer, she supported herself on one elbow and allowed her free hand to wander suggestively over the young woman's abdomen, dabbling exploring fingers in the curls of genital hair, rotating the swell of belly from side to side and then swooping up over waist and ribs to contour first one breast and then the other. The dancer moaned softly and shifted her position. She drew up her knees still higher, then suddenly straightened both legs and turned towards the newcomer. One of her hands rose to stroke the dark girl's face.

The young Englishman was on his feet, leaning forward with his palms flat on the table, his eyes fixed on the tempting undulations of female flesh quivering so near to him. It was he who had drawn the high card which allowed him the privilege of licking the mousse from the dancer's love mound – only to have his hand slapped away when he tried to touch the secret place below.

Despierre pushed back his chair and strolled round the table to get a better view of the new girl's intimate parts. He saw, as she levered up her hips and straddled her partner, that where the dancer was hairy she was bare. The sculpted hollows of her armpits shone pink in the lamplight; below the sudden downward sweep at the base of her belly, smooth skin speckled with a trace of stubble split two fleshy pads whose shocking nudity served to emphasize the vulnerability of those creased lips – still firmly clasped together – that nestled between their twin embrace.

'Admirable,' Despierre observed. 'This time, De la Ferrière, you have chosen well. Contrast remains the *sine qua non* of the sexual ethos, and here we have it . . . most enticingly displayed. Am I not right, my dear Boudot?'

8

'Eh? What was that?' One of the bankers, surprised out of his lustful reverie thus directly addressed, started guiltily. 'What did you say?'

'I said sex relies for its success on contrast. Male and female, hard and soft – or, as is the case here, where female meets female, dark locks and light, big tits and little tits, flesh hirsute and shaven. You take my meaning?'

'Yes, yes, absolutely,' the banker said hastily. He licked his lips. 'You are undoubtedly right.'

The two younger men exchanged amused glances. It *was* amusing, watching the two girls together; it certainly whetted the appetite. It allowed the doctor to exercise his talent for orotund pronouncements and it probably helped to titillate the jaded appetites of the other older men around them. But what they were really waiting for was the promised feast that would follow this feminine hors-d'oeuvre, when lots would once again be drawn to determine who would be the first to lay hands on the hot flesh of the girls entwined on the table.

'Once I get in there amongst all that, *mon ami*,' the industrialist's son murmured, 'I promise you these old goats are going to have to wait in line while I savour my pleasure! Which of the two do you prefer?'

'The first one,' replied the Englishman promptly. 'I'm not sure that I go for the barber's pet!'

On the table there was movement now – an obscene coupling of flesh with female flesh, a writhing of limbs, a dart and plunge of exploring hands, a flick of tongues and a sucking of lips that drew sighs of ecstasy and finally small grunts and mewls of pleasure first from one partner and then the other.

'By Jove,' said the Englishman, whose name was Paul Mackenzie, 'your French girls really go at it, don't they!'

Bertrand Laforge smiled. The banquet, and its human dessert, had been set up by his father and Despierre – who happened to be his uncle – with the aim of stimulating precisely such a response from the impressionable young foreigner. 'You will not be disappointed by what follows,' he promised. 'The tawny one in particular – so I am told – is an expert performer.'

'I say, I say!' Mackenzie enthused. 'Actually, though, what *is* the form? Your guv'nor didn't go into detail.'

'Why, we shall draw lots again. And the holders of the two highest cards will take our entertainers behind the velvet drapes, where the resourceful Charles will have disposed of the musicians and installed a couple of convenient divans, don't you know.'

'What-ho!' said Mackenzie. 'And the unlucky four?'

Bertrand shrugged. 'The brandy is a Hine '84,' he replied. 'And there is a decanter of port from your countryman Monsieur Taylor that is quite exceptional.'

He clapped his companion on the shoulder and added: 'Plus, of course, the leftovers when the winners are through . . . for those who have the patience to wait!' He moved away to talk to Despierre.

The Englishman transferred his gaze back to the table, which was beginning to resemble the terminal stage of a Lucullan orgy. In their exertions, the two young women had knocked aside glasses, upset plates and smeared the polished wood with the remnants of a fruit compôte islanded with fragments of Camembert and half-eaten bread rolls. The shaven brunette, entwined lasciviously now with her fairer lover, wore like a damp badge on one breast a heart-shaped lettuce leaf.

Bertrand Laforge, leaning close, was murmuring in his uncle's ear. 'He does prefer the tawny one,' he said. 'We can rely on Charles to see that he draws the ace, can we?'

'Of course we can,' the older man whispered irritably. 'The boy got to lick off the mousse, didn't he?'

'Just double-checking, sir,' said Bertrand. 'Father is

so very keen to make sure that everything goes Mackenzie's way. The more he enjoys himself, the more, as the Americans say, we show him a good time, the more obligated he's going to be . . . and the more amenable he should be to any approaches we make finally.'

'Yes, yes, yes. Do you think I don't know? More than half my money's invested in your father's damned factory, for God's sake! You're squiring him around the high-class houses tomorrow, are you not?'

Bertrand nodded. 'The one in the Rue de Monthyon, I thought,' he said. 'And after that, perhaps a visit to Madame Kelly at the Chabanais.'

'Excellent.' Despierre favoured his nephew with a rare smile. 'That, after all, is what the perfidious English expect of Gay Paree, *n'est-ce pas*?'

'So they tell me. Though I notice' – he glanced at the three elderly men whose lecherous gazes were fixed on the coupling girls – 'there doesn't seem too much consumer reaction against the idea on this side of the Channel!'

'You make sure, then, that this particular *entente cordiale* continues,' said Despierre.

The young Frenchman grinned. 'It will be my pleasure,' said he.

Behind this sophisticated scenario designed to woo the foreigner lay the exigencies of the blossoming new trade in motor vehicles.

Laforge's new factory produced middle-range, medium-priced touring cars destined for the first time to appeal to the middle-class family market. The cars were comfortable and well-conceived – but so far there had been dismaying recurrences of problems affecting the reliability of the internal combustion engines that drove them. That was where the company owned by Mackenzie's father came in.

Mackenzie Senior produced a limited range of light-weight sporting vehicles – *voiturettes* or cycle-cars to the French – designed to appeal to the younger, monied owner interested in racing and hill-climbing events. They had nothing whatever in common with the touring Laforge. But there was a secret component in the manufacture of their motors that could well, from a metallurgic point of view, resolve Laforge's reliability problems . . . if the secret was known.

Thus the concerted attempt to win over Mackenzie's son, who worked in his father's design department.

What the conspirators didn't know was that Mackenzie too had problems. And that he believed one of the techniques used in the manufacture of the Laforge could iron those problems out . . . if he knew what the technique was.

Paul Mackenzie had been sent to France with instructions to ingratiate himself with the Laforge family and worm the secret out of them!

CHAPTER TWO

Two fiacres were drawn up by the pavement in the Rue St André-des-Arts, a narrow street in the Latin Quarter one block away from the river. The horses stood motionless, their heads hanging; above and behind them, the cabbies sat on their high seats and hunched into their oilskins, dreaming of warm summer nights. It was one o'clock in the morning and the March wind, blowing chill from the towers of Notre Dame, hustled scraps of paper along the cobbles.

One of the cabs had come from Maxim's in the Rue Royale, the other from La Cupole, the artists' rendez-vous in Montparnasse. Each had been given the same address and both were still occupied, though neither fare seemed eager to pay off his driver.

This was because the two gentlemen in question, each formally dressed with a tall hat and cloak, were still themselves occupied – though each in a different way – with the ladies they escorted.

The man who had hired the cab nearer the eastern end of the street had been trying, so far unsuccessfully, to seduce his companion for more than a week; the fare in the fiacre nearer the Buci market was attempting – equally unsuccessfully – to extract himself from the ul-tra-amorous embraces of his enthusiastic partner.

The two young women, whose escorts were unknown to one another, in fact shared an apartment in the same rooming house, No. 123 Rue St André-des-Arts. In the

13

six months since they installed themselves, they had gained quite a reputation in the quarter – for a number of different reasons.

Their names – Corinne Dubois and Camille Dufour – were strikingly similar to French ears. But, aside from the same address, every other thing about them was as different as could be.

Corinne was a true Parisienne, sophisticated and free-thinking; she worked for the society section of a morning newspaper. Camille came from a country town in Britanny and was employed as a seamstress in the studio of the fashionable couturier Paul Poiret. Corinne dressed extravagantly, almost immodestly, to attract the men for whom she had developed an appetite verging on the nymphomaniac. Camille, who was still a virgin, wore clothes decorous enough to please a bishop.

And, to underline the contrast and add spice to the gossip, the demure country girl was exceptionally beautiful, with exquisite boning and the shape of a love goddess, while the Parisian man-chaser was just a little overweight, with a bee-stung lower lip, slightly prominent teeth and thick-lensed spectacles.

In the café-bars of the Latin Quarter they were known as *Les Deux Du's* – the Two Du's – although the more sardonic denizens changed this sometimes to *Les Deux Doux,* the Sweet Couple. (It was an English sculptor who lived in the same house who remarked that beyond a certain point the bilingual wordplay was no longer valid: you could not, he said, extend the translation to the Two Do's . . . because only one did and the other didn't!)

The house itself, a narrow five-storey building dating from the 17th century, had an interesting history. It had once been used as a dormitory for the serving girls who worked as maids for the owner of a brothel operating in much larger premises next door. No. 125 still was a *maison close*, but now it was used principally as a house of assignation, where diplomats and wealthy businessmen could safely take an occasional *petite amie*, away from the limelight that was inescapable in such places as Maxim's or the Café de la Paix. There were, however, two resident prostitutes . . . in case friends of the present owner, herself a one-time street walker, found themselves at what the English sculptor termed a loose end. Discretion was in any case assured since No. 125 was built around a courtyard sealed off from the Rue St André-des-Arts by tall wooden doors beneath an entrance archway.

The man fruitlessly trying to seduce the untouchable Camille was Robert Laforge, *patron* of the newly established Laforge Automobile Company. He was a tall man, heavily built, with iron-grey hair and bushy eyebrows, a man whose smooth, cared-for face and determined jaw suggested a nature that was authoritative and unused to disobedience. Tonight was a check that was totally unexpected. Laforge had thought that an evening amidst the high-priced glitter of Maxim's, where the rich and famous openly paraded their costly mistresses, might tip the scales in his favour. Visible proof that what she thought of as sin could be fun, that 'vice' was not inseparable from gaiety, should, he reasoned, be sufficient incentive for the little hussy to re-examine her priorities.

He was mistaken. The scales remained obstinately tipped the other way.

Far from admiring – and thus possibly attempting to emulate? – the extravagantly costumed *Grandes Horizontales* and their boisterously joyful, champagne-drinking keepers, the chaste Mademoiselle Dufour was pleased to disapprove!

'I think they look silly,' she said unanswerably. 'All that flesh exposed . . . and all those gems sewn on to what there is of the bodice! There's too much body and not *enough* bodice, if you ask me. That's expensive material, that Dupion: it's a shame to hide it under a load of stones.'

'And the flesh, my dear? You do not approve of flesh?' Laforge asked, amused n spite of his frustration.

'It doesn't leave anything for their husbands to find out when they get married,' Camille objected.

'I doubt,' Laforge said, refilling her glass with champagne, 'that marriage is in the forefront of the minds of any of these ladies – unless it be marriage to a prince or at the very least a grand-duke.'

'Any marriage is better than a life of debauchery,' the young woman said primly.

Her own bodice, Laforge had noticed as soon as he called for her, was not designed to allow any putative husband even the merest hint of the treasures that lay beneath it. Softly draped over the bust in panels of contrasting green, it was open at the neck with a wide, laid-back collar – but the V-shaped gap was closed by an opaque insert of black moiré taffeta shaped around the slender column of the girl's neck and secured there by a black velvet band and a cameo brooch. The ensemble was completed by fringed, wrist-length sleeves and a long tubular skirt. No glimmer of flesh showed even below this, for Camille wore tightly buttoned black ankle boots.

In the cab on the way back to the Rue St André-des-Arts, Laforge deployed all of his considerable charm – and every stratagem that he knew – in an attempt to lay a hand, a finger even, on some part of the seductive anatomy so voluptuously hidden from his eyes.

He overdid the lurch imparted to his own body when the fiacre rounded a sharp corner; he shot out a hand to steady himself; he restrained the girl when the horse pulled up abruptly at an intersection and she shot forward out of her seat.

The warm weight of a breast – or, more exactly, the

layers of material that swathed a breast – brushing momentarily against the back of his hand was all the success he could count. And things were no better once they had arrived outside No. 123.

'I am most indebted to you, Monsieur,' said Camille, drawing her skirts about her, 'for an enjoyable, indeed an entirely instructive evening.' She reached for the tarnished brass loop that would open the fiacre's door.

Robert Laforge moved quickly. 'My dear,' he said, 'you must allow me to order the coachman to help you descend. In any case I would be most gravely lacking in courtesy were I not to alight and escort you to your door myself. But stay' – she was shaping to pass him, although the arm resting on the front partition still blocked her route to the door – 'we have to decide the time and place of our next meeting.'

She was obliged to sink back on the cushions. 'I was not aware, sir, that I had agreed to contemplate any such encounter.'

'Oh, but you must,' the industrialist urged. In the lamplight filtering through the cab's grimy window he saw that the fine-boned face was set in a somewhat forbidding expression, the eyebrows still superciliously raised. 'You must not, I beg of you, deny me the opportunity of spending a few more hours with a companion so enchanting!'

'You have, I believe, an enchanting wife, Monsieur Laforge.'

'Indeed I have. And it is precisely this,' he said smoothly, 'that allows me to suggest such a thing. For continuous proximity, you see, blunts in a certain fashion one's appreciation of the obvious. And it is only in the contemplation of something, of someone, equally alluring that one comes to re-appreciate – if you will permit me the term – the original.'

'That,' said Camille, repressing a smile, 'is a load of rubbish. And you know it.'

Startled at hearing so fragile and feminine a beauty express herself in such coarse terms, Laforge found himself momentarily at a loss. 'Come, come,' he stammered. 'Surely, my dear, you must realize–'

'I realize,' she cut in, 'that it is high time some cards were laid on the table. Let us stop playing word games, Monsieur, and be frank. Your sole object, inviting me to dine at Maxim's, showing off the scabrous behaviour of the high-class whores who frequent the place, is to seduce me. If not tonight then as soon as possible. Admit it now: your goal is my ... my virtue. You wish, as they say, to have your will of me. *Point final!*'

'Not at all, not at all,' Laforge spluttered. 'Nothing, I assure you, was farther from ... that is to say, naturally, that such an eventuality, such a delightful eventuality, were it ever to arise, would of course make me the happiest man alive. But, for the – ah – for the moment it is purely for the pleasure of your company as a dinner companion that I presume to invite you.'

'And Maxim's?'

'The wine is good; the food is passable. For the rest' – he laid a hand on her arm – 'why it was to flatter my ego, to be seen in public to have the honour of escorting so delectable a creature! And, incidentally, to show up the flashiness of those brassy women in comparison with your own beauty and grace.'

'A brave try,' said Camille. 'I salute the quickness of your mind. But I have to tell you–'

'Believe me, please believe me,' he pleaded, 'that I would never do anything in any way to hurt or offend you.' The fingers on her arm tightened, moved stealthily upward until the knuckles once again nudged a swell of breast. 'I am not a man to force himself, ever, upon an unwilling ... partner.'

'I have to tell you,' she continued imperturbably, removing that intruding hand, 'that I am not amenable to seduction. Tonight or any night.'

* * *

Fifty yards up the street, Patrice Delgado lay back against the cushions of his cab, pinned to the seat by the voluptuous weight of his companion.

Patrice was short, dark and wiry, with large brown eyes and a red-lipped sensuous mouth oddly at variance with his trim, lean frame. He worked as a music hall critic on the same newspaper as Corinne Dubois. It was not the first time that he had spent an evening at La Coupole with her, but – he told himself as he had at least a dozen times before – this was definitely the last.

Her wine-dark breath played on his face as her lips clung lasciviously to his own and her scalding tongue probed greedily between his teeth. He was minus two trouser buttons, and the hot clasp of her right hand, plunged between layers of his underclothes, encircled that part of him expressly designed for the gratification of members of her sex. Her left hand wrestled with the knot of his cravat. He jerked his head away.

'Corinne!' he panted. 'You must not . . . really, we cannot . . .'

'Of course we can,' she said fiercely. He saw the lamplight glint on her full lower lip as she freed her mouth to reply. 'You want it. You like it. I can *feel* that you like it as much as me!' The hand against his belly pumped the hardness aching his loins up and down.

'Twice already in the *vestiaire* of the brasserie!' he groaned. 'And now . . . No, really, a third time in less than an hour! Honestly, I cannot. In any case, here, beneath the street lamp, almost outside your own lodgings . . . suppose someone was to see, someone who knew you . . .?'

'Don't say that, Patrice. Nobody's going to flatten their nose against the glass and peer in at this time of night. And if they did, well, let them have a good time and enjoy it!' She shifted a little to one side. The cravat fell away from his neck. Her hand was beneath his shirt, massaging one nipple. The fingers of the other hand thrust, pulled, manipulated . . . and suddenly he felt the night air cool on the heated skin of his manhood. She had wrenched that part of him free of the tangle of garments.

Her wet lips traced the line of his jaw; her tongue darted in and then out of his mouth. 'I don't care what you say,' she murmured throatily, 'but I *know* you want me. What is this that I hold in my hand, after all?' Small teeth nibbled his ear lobe; the tongue spiralled moistly into the hollow above. 'Your soldier,' she answered her own question, 'refreshed after his rest, stands stiffly at attention awaiting orders, ready to answer the call of duty once more! He quivers, he is eager, I can feel him pulsing against my fingers as I stroke him. Come, place the faithful fellow' – she seized a hand resting on her broad hip and inserted it beneath her skirt – 'where a warm welcome already awaits him.'

Delgado shuddered. Despite himself, he sensed the fingers of the hand exploring. Advancing, touching, teasing, his fingertips slid over smooth skin, beneath the tight circlet of knicker tapes, up amongst curls of springy hair and the hot, wet clasp of female flesh. The flesh throbbed around his hand. He breathed the heady scent of a woman aroused.

Corinne's excited inhalation hissed between her teeth. With an inarticulate cry she rolled off him, onto her back, hauling skirts and petticoats up around her waist. She was in the throes, now, of her need; gone were the measured, almost playful tones of dalliance; naked lust shook her frame and the words tumbled from her lips in shameless abandon. 'Ye-es,' she gasped. 'Oh, *yes!* . . . put it there . . . let me have . . . I want it; I want you to . . . Ahhh, give it to me, Patrice; give it to me now!'

The young man himself was wordless. He was torn between two imperatives equally urgent. He had never intended the evening to be anything more than a casual encounter with a female colleague - finished, certainly, if things turned out right, by some interlude of an amorous nature. But he had not bargained for anything intense, and Corinne's lewd exploitation of their proximity, her voracious sensuality, frightened him as much by their unexpectedness as by the strings they implied. And yet . . . and yet . . . the hard, hot fingers wrapped around his rigid part were coaxing him, dragging him towards the secret, muscular grasp of that haven where twice that night already his proud ship had berthed to unload its cargo of desire. Her tongue again traced salacious arabesques around and into his mouth.

It was reason against emotion, head against heart. In this case the spirit was *un*willing but the flesh was not weak at all: the renewed ache in his loins which had started as soon as the cab stopped and she reached for him was now clamouring for release. And the engorged, supersensitive tip of his probing staff nudged creases of moist warm flesh that parted before his advance.

With a choked cry that was half ecstasy and half despair, Patrice flexed his hips and allowed himself to be engulfed within the heat of her belly.

Corinne arched her hips off the seat and met his penetration with fierce thrusts of her own. Her hands were clenched on the double swell of his muscled posterior. She crooned incoherent endearments into his ear as they settled down to a steady rhythm that eventually accelerated to bruise Delgado's knees against the thin carpet covering the floorboards.

The fiacre rocked on its cantilever springs.

Perched on his high seat up front, the cabbie sighed. He reached practised hands between the layers of oilskin swaddling him to produce a pipe and tobacco pouch. Shrugging philosophically, he began to smoke.

In the other cab, Camille struggled to free herself from Robert Laforge's sinewy grasp. Flattery, blandishments and special pleading having failed – and the girl herself having forcefully emphasized that she could not be bought like the coquettes at Maxim's – Laforge had finally resorted to physical action. His first attempt to seize her around the waist had been repulsed when she placed surprisingly strong, black-gloved hands against his chest and shoved him roughly away. Immediately afterwards, he swiftly changed position, half turning towards her with one knee on the floor and an arm on either side of her braced against the dusty seat back. But this move was as quickly countered when Camille ducked beneath one arm and slid away along the seat, leaving the industrialist staring at her skirts instead of the soft curve of her bosom. Now his hands had closed over her two wrists, drawing her closer.

His burning gaze bored through the gloom, fixed unswervingly on the pale outline of the young woman's face. 'Camille,' he said hoarsely, 'my dear. You must forgive me; I cannot help myself. You are so beautiful, so young, so fresh. I must . . . I can hardly . . .' He choked on his words, swallowed, and then continued: 'I long to touch you, to stroke, to caress. The thought of your tender lips, of those sensitive hands . . . I . . . it's driving me mad; I cannot sleep at night, thinking of you; all day long you fill my mind.'

'Monsieur!' Her voice was chilly, aloof. 'Monsieur, I beg of you . . .'

'A kiss!' Laforge croaked. 'That is all I ask; I demand no more. One tiny gesture . . . an earnest wish that perhaps, in the halls of your regard, one small niche may be reserved, a place that proves I may not entirely be forgotten–'

'*Monsieur!*'

'Oh, God,' the industrialist groaned, 'how I want you, and need you, my love!'

With a sudden powerful heave, he jerked her towards him, wrapping his arms around her back. The taut swell of her young breasts, squashed against the starched linen of his shirtfront, sent the blood racing through his veins. Sweat dewing his brow and upper lip glistened in the reflected lamplight. His fingers clawed the flesh cushioning her hips. His wet lips grazed the skin of her face. 'I pray you,' he whispered, 'be kind, be charitable to a man who—'

'How dare you!' Camille interrupted, really angry now. She could feel – disturbingly, even enticingly? – the hard ridge of his desire through the stuff of her skirt. 'Take your hands away. Let me go at once. *At once, do you hear!*'

And then, raising her voice because she was unable to break out of the embrace that was crushing her to Laforge: 'Coachman! Descend at once and open the door – and hurry because I wish to leave this cab!'

Perched on his high seat up front, the cabbie sighed. It was prudent, often enough on the night shift, to be a trifle hard of hearing. He lit a cheroot and shrank farther into his oilskins. It was the man, anyway, who was paying the fare, was it not?

CHAPTER THREE

Robert Laforge walked the seventy-five yards to the wooden gates walling off the courtyard of No. 125, Rue St André-des-Arts, with the collar of his topcoat turned up against the wind. The slam of the front door at No. 123 still echoed in his ears.

He had wasted another ten fruitless minutes wrestling in the darkness of the cab before the Dufour girl had finally eluded his grasp and flounced out into the street. The stinging slap on the face that had in the end freed her from his embrace remained as vivid in his memory – and as infuriating – as the humiliating concussion of the door she had slammed.

Now he was determined at least to satisfy the senses the little bitch had aroused, even if the experience would lack the savour of conquest that he craved. Beneath the large illuminated numerals of No. 125, he tugged a polished brass knob that jangled a night bell somewhere on the far side of the gates.

Footsteps. A Judas window slid aside. Eyes scrutinized the top-hatted figure standing beneath the street lamp. The window was shut and a pass door set in one of the gates opened. A porter in a black and yellow striped waistcoat with sleeves stood aside to allow Laforge to enter.

'Good evening, sir. Would Madame be expecting you?'

'No,' Laforge said shortly. 'But I have been here

many times before. I do not believe that she would refuse to receive me.'

'*Bien, M'sieu. Si vous voulez me suivre.*'

The servant led the way past a lamplit porter's lodge, around an illuminated fountain and up a flight of marble steps on the far side of the cobbled courtyard. A closed coupé with a liveried coachman and armorial bearings on its shiny doors stood beside the steps. The horse, a handsome creature as glossy as the carriage it drew, munched hay from a nosebag on the ground between its front feet.

Potted palms beneath a crystal chandelier flanked the glass doors under the portico. Inside, discreetly shaded lamps revealed leather armchairs, an Impressionist landscape in a gold frame, a white bearskin rug and a Negro figurine holding a brass tray for visiting cards in its ebony hands. A tall blonde woman of about forty swayed forward to greet Laforge as the porter bowed and withdrew.

'Monsieur Laforge!' she enthused huskily. 'What a delightful surprise!'

He looked at her with approval. She was statuesque, her well-corseted figure clothed in a tight-fitting evening gown of pink and grey striped satin. The neckline, cut daringly low, exposed two swelling slopes of creamy skin, and one tiny hint of that darker flesh surrounding her left nipple. 'The pleasure,' said Laforge, 'is entirely mine.'

He bent forward to brush with his lips the fingers of a white-gloved hand that she held towards him. Diamond rings blazed on each finger. The white kid, sheathing the woman's plump arm to a point well above the elbow, exhaled a faint, elusive perfume redolent of sandalwood and musk.

'You must come upstairs at once, *cher ami*, and we shall split a bottle of celebratory champagne,' she said.

'I can think of nothing I'd like better,' Laforge said truthfully.

At the far end of the hallway, thickly carpeted stairs curved upwards, illuminated every few feet by dimly lit niches that housed classical statuettes. Laforge could hear the sounds of subdued conversation above, punctuated from time to time by a woman's throaty chuckle. Somewhere in the distance, a pianola was tinkling.

He followed the blonde to the first floor.

A dozen years before, when she was a mere street-walker patrolling the Place Blanche and the gardens on either side of the Champs Elysées, she had been nick-named Milady by her professional colleagues, on account of the airs and graces she affected and the superior fashion in which she allowed it to be understood that, actually, she really came from a very 'good' family – perhaps even a noble one – but a family which had been brought low by the vicissitudes of a malignant fate.

A two-year association with a wealthy English sportsman, plus her share of a spectacular robbery plundering the tote at the Longchamp racecourse, had changed all that. But somehow the name had stuck. And today, several years after she had invested her money in the house of assignation in the Rue St André-des-Arts, none of her faithful clients would have recognized her by any other. Even – since she regularly paid her dues to the vice squad – in the police files of the Latin Quarter commissariat there was no record of her real name.

In any case, there was nothing illegal in running a brothel, was there?

Half a dozen men and a single woman graced the gilt convolutions of the spindly Second Empire chairs scattered around the comfortably furnished reception room on the upper floor. The first person Laforge saw was his son Bertrand.

The young man was standing alone with a brandy

balloon cradled in his hands. Startled, he turned slightly away as if to ignore the unfortunate coincidence, and then, on second thoughts, smiled and walked across to the older man with an outstretched hand. 'Father! What are you doing here? A joy in any case to surprise you as a fellow sinner in this den of iniquity!'

They shook hands, exchanging kisses on both cheeks in the French manner. Milady had crossed the room to order champagne from a manservant. 'Well, my boy,' Laforge said genially, 'it seems you are pilfering my lines as well as arrogating to yourself my favourite *divertissement*! *I* should be the one to express surprise . . . and ask *you* what the devil you are doing here!'

'Working late,' said Bertrand with a crooked grin. 'I am on company business!'

'Really?' Laforge's heavy eyebrows were raised. 'Might one ask–?'

'The Englishman, Mackenzie,' his son explained. 'You know Uncle Despierre asked me to, well, sweeten him up a little. This is one of the places I thought he might enjoy.'

'He is here now?' Laforge looked round the room.

Bertrand shook his head. 'Not tonight.' He smiled again. 'He is kind of hung over after the private party that De la Ferrière organized for us last night! No, I thought I would come by first, however, to satisfy myself that the place was suitable. If you know what I mean.'

'I know exactly what you mean. You wish to check the quality of the, ah, merchandise. Am I not right? Who did you have in mind?'

'I thought perhaps Nellie.'

Nellie was one of the two resident girls retained by Milady. 'An excellent choice,' Laforge approved. 'And doubtless you intend to, shall we say, sample the goods yourself first? Purely in the interests of objectivity, of course . . .'

'Of course.'

'. . . and to make sure that the dish offered to your guest is sweet enough for his taste?'

'Father,' said the young man, 'you are a mind-reader!'

Laforge clapped him on the shoulder. 'Maybe Professor Darwin was right and there is something to be said for heredity,' he chuckled. 'But if you intend to put tonight on your expense account, I shall want to see receipts!'

Milady, a graceful galleon under full sail, was bearing down upon them. She was preceded by a manservant with a silver tray bearing a bottle of Pol Roger in an ice bucket and three glasses. 'My dear friend,' she said to the industrialist, 'you must be sorely in need of refreshment. Come, sit by me and we shall drink to your recovery!' Subsiding into an S-shaped love seat, she flipped open an ivory fan and tapped the cushion facing her. And then, to Laforge's son: 'Bertrand – you may draw up a chair.'

She waited while the servant poured champagne and handed around the glasses before she added: 'Nellie should not keep you waiting much longer. Monsieur Champney is a man who takes his pleasures seriously – but, it has to be admitted, one also unusually aware of the passage of time: each minute of his life has its allotted place and none may be wasted.'

Bertrand grinned. 'So I hear. He is, you know, a friend – indeed a colleague – of the Monsieur Mackenzie who will, I hope, visit you tomorrow night. They both work in the design section of the automobile works owned by Mackenzie's father.'

'Really? What a small world!' smiled Milady.

The smile was reminiscent. She had herself contemplated marrying Hector Champney some years previously. He was a boisterous hedonist, at that time a passionate advocate of the Montgolfier hot-air balloon.

It had been a warm-hearted, if stormy, relationship.

Monsieur Champney was in everything an individualist, one of his idiosyncrasies being a belief that any man who spent more than two or three minutes consummating the act of love must either be craven or unskilled. 'Believe it or not,' he had said to her once, 'but some chaps take ages over this. Love, I mean. Go on for ages and ages. Fact. Sister of a fellow in my house at school told me. Must be hell for their wives; poor dears would be quite worn out. But there you are: some folks never think of other people.'

What Champney saved in time he squandered in energy, and it was the bruising resulting from this inverse ratio that finally decided Milady to escape the ferocity of his advances and return to Paris. They had remained friends, however, and the Englishman never failed to visit the house in Rue St André-des-Arts on his visits to France – 'sometimes for as long as a quarter of an hour,' as he once shamefacedly confessed to a friend.

Laforge Senior had been gazing with approval at the creamy slopes of his hostess's bosom. The scooped-out neck of the striped dress, he computed with his engineer's flair for figures, exposed either five-eighths or eleven-sixteenths of her generous breasts, whichever was the greater (although, regrettably, the crescent moon of darker flesh he had glimpsed on the floor below had waned as she sat down and was now sunk from sight below the lacy horizon). Perhaps later, when his son had withdrawn with the absent Nellie, he would permit himself the opportunity of discovering the precise proportion of those splendid attributes that her dressmaker had seen fit to reveal. It would at least be a more profitable pastime than propositioning some frigid little miss in a fiacre! Before he could voice his thoughts a couple appeared at the top of a staircase that led to the upper floors.

Hector Champney was tall, angular, with sandy hair and a fierce, reddish moustache. He was dressed in a rather loud check suit, and his bony wrists, downed with ginger hair, stuck out from the starched cuffs of his shirt.

The woman with him was about the same age as Milady. A crimson velvet dress that flared out below the hips swathed the upper part of her fleshy body. Her hair, which was very dark, was pinned up.

Nellie Lebérigot came from Brittany, a small town called Vannes, near the port of Lorient. Her father had been a fisherman, but after a succession of bad years had decimated the fleet, she had left home and come to Paris to seek her fortune rather than slave away 'in service' at some draughty country house. The fortune of course was illusory, and she was finally obliged to join the crowd of young girls, several hundred in number, who paid twenty francs a month for the privilege of parading their charms around the notorious *promenoir* of the Folies Bergère – a huge open space behind the theatre stalls which was in fact the city's largest shop window for the sale of sex.

In the hierarchy of prostitution, the Folies *promenoir* was already several steps up the ladder. Marchand, the theatre manager, insisted that every girl wore gloves and a hat. If a girl solicited too often in the same clothes, he would advance her money to re-equip herself. And he was adamant that his *filles de joie* never sold back the flowers and candy bought for them by admirers, or received any sort of commission from the bar once presided over by the busty blonde immortalized by the painter Manet.

As a result, the girls at the Folies gained a much higher reputation than the whores who sat in the garden of the Moulin Rouge or the hatless hussies patrolling the Boulevard de Clichy. Many of them, Nellie included, soon found that they could transfer their business to the less arduous territory of a *maison close* or high-class brothel. Milady, who had known Nellie during her days as a street-walker, was quick to recruit her when she opened her own house. She was a jolly girl, with a snub nose and smiling eyes . . . although, to be sure, her expression was dazed rather than amused as she trod down the stairs behind Hector Champney.

Apart from the Laforges, the five other men in the reception room, all of them in evening dress, were clustered around a ravishing woman with green eyes and chestnut hair who was lolling on a chesterfield among the gilt chairs surrounding a bright log fire. Their murmured conversation ceased as Champney and the girl appeared, and their heads turned towards the staircase. Once again Robert Laforge heard the low, throaty female chuckle he had noticed on his way up to the room. 'Who is that?' he whispered to Milady. 'The latest acquisition to your stable?'

'Heavens, no!' she replied. 'I wish I was that lucky. That is the Comtesse van den Bergh.'

'Not the famous . . .?' Eyebrows raised, he left the sentence unfinished.

'The same.' Milady flicked a glance at the woman, whose voluptuous figure was sheathed in jade green taffeta. 'She comes here from time to time – as she does to the Chabanais and No. 14 – on what I might call a talent-spotting expedition.'

As she cited two of the most luxurious of Paris's high-class brothels, Laforge gave a low whistle. 'And it's true, what they say . . .?'

'Madame la Comtesse likes her vice – as they say – versa!' Milady nodded.

Dagmar van den Bergh was in fact one of the leaders of the notorious *Amazones* – the fashionable lesbian cult whose members, booted and top-hatted, could be seen every day riding in the Bois de Boulogne or exercising their Russian wolfhounds in the gardens of the Luxembourg palace.

'Well I certainly wish I was one of her vices . . . or

that I possessed the kind of talent she would like to spot!' the younger Laforge said enviously.

'You be content with what you have, young man,' said Milady. 'In any case her tastes veer, as I say, towards her own sex.'

'In Maxim's,' said Bertrand's father, 'they say that she is not always content with a single . . . partner.'

'Dagmar is adventurous,' Milady conceded. 'She has even, if the gossips are to be believed, flavoured her amorous pursuits with the addition, occasionally, of a bashful youth - whose seduction serves simply to prove to her current love the sexual supremacy of the female.'

'Then there is always a hope . . .?' Bertrand began.

'But it is only when the mood takes her,' Milady continued. 'And her moods are . . . unpredictable . . . to say the least.' She looked again at the Comtesse, who was fitting a Russian cigarette into a long black holder.

The green eyes, slitted, gazed out from beneath heavy lids as one of the men struck a wax vesta and held the flame to the cigarette tip. Dagmar van den Bergh stared across the big room at Nellie, smiling a small secret smile through curls of blue smoke. A white gloved finger beckoned imperiously.

Nellie glided over to the chesterfield.

'By Jove, that was good!' Hector Champney crowed, striding up to Milady and slapping his thigh. 'Does a fellow a power of good, what, a touch of the old *amour*! Wish I had the time, old thing, to nip across and see your gels more often. Haw!' He uttered a short bark of laughter.

'I was surprised you felt able to spend so long this time,' Milady said drily. 'More than twenty minutes!'

The irony passed the Englishman by. 'Have to take a breather, you know,' he said. 'Need an intermission. My age. I mean like between the acts. Haw!' Once again the snort of mirth.

The Laforges, father and son, exchanged amused

glances. 'Do you mean . . .' Robert started. 'My dear fellow, forgive the indiscretion, I beg you, but are you saying that you – er – pleasured the lady twice in that time?'

'Well, of course.' Champney was astonished. 'The dear things expect it, after all. Don't they, duckie?' He dug Milady's padded ribs with his elbow. 'Never do to let 'em down, what?'

Milady laid a hand on Bertrand's arm. 'I fancy you might do well to mount a rescue operation,' she said, nodding towards Nellie and the Comtesse. 'If your pleasure runs to anything more than another glass of champagne, that is.' He nodded in turn, rose to his feet, kissed her hand, and left them.

'Mind you,' Champney was droning on, 'I'm not saying a second helping comes amiss chez-Hector! Chap can't really pretend to be an altruist when the jolly old appetite's involved. Haw!'

'I'm not sure that I really like her,' soft-voiced Nellie confided to Bertrand when they were alone in a room on the floor above. 'I mean, she's very sweet, and all that. A girl likes to be flattered, to be made a fuss of. But there's something . . .' She shrugged plump shoulders. 'I dunno. It's not just that I know she's les. Many of us girls are, too. It's . . . I can't put it into words.'

'She makes you feel . . . creepy?'

'Not at all.' Nellie shook her head decidedly. 'No, it's more . . . well, to tell the truth, dear, she makes me feel that if I did do . . . what she wanted . . . then I might, well, actually enjoy it! And that *is* a bit spooky. Come round behind and help me with these hooks, will you?'

The room was richly furnished, with a deep-pile carpet, heavy drapes that were lined and interlined, a polished dressing-table and wash-hand stand in bird's-eye maple, and comfortable chairs upholstered in expensive brocades. Brass fire irons gleamed on either side of the logs burning in the grate.

The chambermaid who had brought hot water to the *toilette* cubicle had turned back the covers on the soft-sprung, muslin-frilled brass bedstead. Now Nellie sat on one side of the feather mattress, unpinning her dark hair so that it fell almost to her waist.

Bertrand stood before her, conscious of the constriction at his loins that was thrusting out the crotch of his tight black evening trousers. 'My goodness,' he said, 'let's forget about the damned Comtesse! You really are the most luscious . . . I cannot imagine why I never came upstairs with you before!'

He had in fact visited the house in the Rue St André-des-Arts a number of times, on some occasions – as was customary in most of the better Paris brothels – merely to drink with friends or joke with Milady, on others to satisfy his sexual needs. But in the latter case it had always been with compliant young women he knew socially or with the other girl retained by the brothel-keeper – a slender, almost wiry brunette named Lily Leblanc, whose armoury of tricks and teases and amorous techniques had been acquired on a visit to the Far East.

'It's good for a young gentleman to turn this way as well as that,' Nellie said politely. 'They say variety is the spice of life, don't they? And Lily has told me you're a very *nice* young gentleman too, so I'm glad you did decide to come with me tonight.'

Since Bertrand had unhooked the back of her dress, she had unbuttoned the bodice and he could see between the edges of crimson velvet, above the black lace corset that hugged her waist, that her breasts were large and perhaps a trifle soft. But the skin was smooth as silk, and the sight of those mounds of flesh swelling out above the corset made the agonizing tightness constricting the young man's loins more acute than ever.

If Mackenzie wasn't grateful for ever more, having this delicacy put his way (Bertrand thought), then he wasn't the enthusiast he claimed to be!

Nellie had shrugged out of the sleeves of her dress, and the velvet now lay pooled around her waist as she sat on the bed and strained the satin-covered busks of the corset together so that she could free the hooks from the eyes and unfasten the front of the garment. 'Mercy!' she exclaimed, allowing the whale-bone inserts to spring apart and expose the pale flesh within. 'What a relief! It's still a bit of a struggle, you know – but ten years ago the busks were steel and there was no opening in front, only yards and yards of lacing behind. It took twenty minutes, sometimes, to get the thing off. And that was only if some kind gentleman offered to help!'

'I would have been . . . most happy to oblige in such a charming task,' Bertrand said in a hoarse voice, all thoughts of the Englishman banished from his mind by the proximity of her body and the faint, exhilarating scent that rose from her perfumed skin.

Nellie smiled. 'You could still loosen the laces a little, if you like. That will make these pesky hooks easier to fasten when I put it on again. In those days' – she mused as he knelt behind her and busied himself at the back of the corset with trembling fingers – 'nobody would look at you if you had a waist anything over twenty inches. There was a music-hall star called Polaire, a singer, and she could lace herself down to fifteen and three-quarter inches! Can you imagine: *fifteen and three-quarters!* When she toured America, the producers of the show offered huge sums of money to anyone in the audience who could produce a smaller waist than that. But nobody ever claimed the prize. All the same, they say the tour wasn't really a success.'

'Maybe she didn't sing very well,' Bertrand said.

'She was a good singer. I heard her more than once

at the Folies. And at the Moulin Rouge. Maybe a tiny waist wasn't as important as we all thought.'

'The important thing about a waist is that it should be like yours.' Looping out the final length of lace, he lifted the corset away from her and placed his two hands on the soft warm pads of Nellie's hips.

'Monsieur is gallant!' She leaned back, tilting her head so that one damask cheek rested against Bertrand Laforge's face. 'But – so I have been told by other gallants – I have attributes, still hidden perhaps, that could claim an equal part of your attention. Could do so almost at once, I judge, if my interpretation of a certain hardness, a rigidity pressing into my bare back is not incorrect!' She gave a low laugh and twisted to face him.

Bertrand's breath hissed in. The breasts, splendid in their nakedness, the rosy points already erect and quivering, were squashed against his shirt-front, just above the waist.

He felt the smooth weight of the breasts against his palms; the nipples were hard against his thumbs. Drawing away a little so that he sat on his heels, he feasted his eyes on the statuesque nude rising phoenix-like from the tumbled flames of the red dress. He plunged the fingers of both hands between the waistline of the dress and her belly, feeling the curve of flesh cool against his knuckles.

She laughed again, a conspiratorial chuckle that promised a lifetime of shared wickedness. Her left hand brushed the taut bulge of his desire, expert fingers tweaking open the fly of his trousers. 'Oh, my!' she exclaimed. 'What an eager fellow we have here! Let us give him some air, so that he can breathe more freely . . . and perhaps look around him a little to see what life has to offer?'

She thrust aside shirt-tails and layers of underclothes so that the vibrating proof of his manhood sprang into view. 'Oh, my!' she enthused for the second time. 'There's a good soldier – at attention, and ready for orders!' She gazed with approval at the veined and throbbing length she had produced, ran feather-like fingers up the shaft to flutter around its engorged tip, and then wrapped her whole hand around it so that she could draw him to the edge of the bed. She moved aside, relinquishing her grasp, and stood up.

The velvet dress dropped to the floor. Bertrand stared with mounting excitement at a froth of linen and silk and broderie-anglaise that fell in a white cascade from the young woman's naked waist. 'You may unfasten the buttons and tapes if you wish,' she said.

Wordlessly, he leaped to the floor, the nude proof of his sexuality spearing obscenely from his trousered loins. On his knees, he reached up to the first of the petticoats concealing Nellie's drawers. She stood with her leg slightly apart, watching with a quizzical smile as he unthreaded and unbuttoned. A layer of frou-frou shushed to the carpet, and then another. By the time a third had joined the red velvet dress, Bertrand's plundering hands were trembling and the unmistakable outline of her hips and thighs sculpted the remaining garments.

A silken shift swished down, and then he was fumbling at the wide black ribbon that tunnelled through the linen waistband of the drawers to be secured with a bow on each hip.

Once loosened, the drawers slid easily over the hipbones and past the swelling orbs of her behind, though he was obliged to exert more pressure to drag them below her spread thighs.

There were more tapes just below the knee. And then black stockings ringed with red and shiny black ankle boots with cuban heels.

One of the tapes was knotted, and it seemed to Bertrand an age before he could free it. But at last the drawers had joined the rest of the clothes around Nellie's feet, and he was able to gaze in rapt admiration at the splendour of the white body rising from them: slender legs soaring to the dark triangle furring the mound at the base of her belly; a taut bulge of flesh that swooped into a pliant waist and then the rose-tipped swell of breasts; parted lips in a face framed by black hair.

With an inarticulate cry, he wrapped his arms around her hips and advanced his own face towards the softness of her belly.

Nellie laughed and pushed him away. 'Not so fast, friend!' she admonished.

'I've had enough Champneys for one day! Take off your clothes like a good boy and wait while I nip into that cubicle there. I'll expect to see that soldier on parade when I return!' She stepped out of the tangle of garments and walked with swaying hips toward the shower curtain. Bertrand caught his breath at the sight, between the stockings and the dark spread of her hair, of that insolently twitched bare rump.

With feverish haste he tore off his clothes and flung them over a chair.

Water was still running in the cubicle when he heard a knock on the bedroom door. He was lying, naked, on his back on the bed, his male pride, stiff with anticipation still, arrowed towards the ceiling. Before he could answer, Nellie called from the shower: 'Come in, come in!'

The door opened and a maidservant in a starched cap and apron entered. She carried a silver tray on which a bottle of champagne and two glasses were ranged. She laid the tray on a bedside table, paying no more attention to the young man's nakedness or the obvious state of his sexual excitement than if he had been a casual customer at a sidewalk café ordering a bock.

Expertly easing the cork from the bottle, she poured the sparking wine, sketched a curtsey, and said: 'Compliments of Milady, and she hopes you enjoy your evening.' She went out of the room and closed the door.

Before Bertrand could express his astonishment, Nellie was back. She still wore the stockings and boots.

'Admirable!' she smiled, glancing at the tribute to her beauty that stood like a flagstaff above his hips. 'I commend your subordinate for his sense of duty.'

He could not take his eyes from the downy triangle at the base of her belly. 'Not so much a subordinate,' he said in a strained voice, trying to fall in with her jocular manner, 'as a . . . a *staff* officer, shall we say? It is he and not I who is becoming insistent upon action!'

'In that case' – Nellie sat beside him on the bed – 'we had better start the operation before any more time is lost.' She reached out a hand still wet from the douche and seized his hardened member.

Bertrand gasped at the touch of those cold fingers on his hot, distended flesh. He could feel fire searing through his loins. From the bulbous, engorged head of his weapon, along the whole tight length of the shaft and then deep into his belly, his every nerve was quivering with desire. 'My God,' he choked, 'you're so . . . so absolutely . . . I must, I have to . . .' He raised himself on one elbow.

She sprang nimbly up onto the bed and pushed him back on the pillows. 'Not yet,' she ordered. 'Later perhaps. For the moment, since we seem to be playing soldiers, I have a mind to take up position with the cavalry.'

He stared at her, uncomprehending. She grinned mischievously, pushing herself upright and then standing nakedly above him, with one narrow, booted foot placed on each side of his waist. Wide-eyed, he riveted his gaze on the dark hairs masking the furrow between her thighs, at the sweep of belly curving away above, and the twin breasts hanging heavily from her rib-cage. Drops of water from the douche still dewed the lower hairs, and a pearl of moisture which had nothing to do with tap water gleamed between the pink lips nestling in the heart of that furrow.

He started to say something, but she bent forward from the waist and placed two fingers over his mouth to silence him.

She bent her knees then, lowering herself slowly in the direction of his upstanding male stem. She parted the lips with a licked forefinger, crouching to lower herself farther still so that the swollen head of the shaft nudged aside the wet hairs to touch her flesh.

Bertrand groaned, arching himself up to meet her so that the hypersensitive tip eased itself between the moistened lips, and then slid its whole hot length into her as she at last sat, straddling his hips.

The scalding clasp of her flesh slid down his shaft, sheathing him as tightly as the finger of an oiled glove.

He caught his lower lip between his teeth, holding his breath as she began to move, rising and falling in invisible stirrups, riding him like a steed with her hands on her hips, a slight smile twisting her mouth when he reached up with both hands to fondle her hardened nipples.

The sensation was exquisite. As the blood coursing through Bertrand's veins appeared to flood inexorably towards the very centre of his being, every nerve in his body too concentrated its reflex in the hard-fleshed stem on which the rider was impaled. He lay in a trance of ecstasy, watching enraptured as Nellie's mouth fell half open and the expressions contorting her face settled into a single animal gaze of naked lust.

He began once more arching his pelvis up off the bed to meet her thrusts, but she shook her head, removed his hands from her quivering breasts, and leaned forward again to stretch his arms above his head. 'Lie still,' she whispered. 'I'll tell you when. For the moment this is my ride!'

The movement had started, as it were, as a walk. But now it accelerated into a trot that jolted the young man's breath from his lungs each time she thudded against his hips. Soon he was grunting to the rhythm of a canter.

Bedsprings beneath him creaked in protest when the canter was transformed into a gallop.

For several minutes, Nellie continued at this break-neck pace. Then suddenly, as the pistoning of her fleshy hips reached a crescendo, the rhythm faltered, became sporadic . . . and the muscles of her belly convulsed while she gasped out a low, crooning release.

Beneath her, forbidden to respond with his normal muscular thrusts, Bertrand had sensed more and more the excruciating pleasure of his entire sensory perception concentrated upon that part of him engulfed within his partner's loins. Now, as she shuddered with diminishing vigour above him, he was on the verge of spurting up into her the gushing proof of that sexual need he had so long held in check. But she tore herself away from him and flung her shaking body on the bed with her legs spread wide. 'Now!' she gasped. 'Oh, now – do it to me! Take me now, my darling boy!'

Snatched down from the crest of a wave, he rolled over onto her with a hoarse cry, the evidence of his lust throbbing more painfully than ever.

His lips lowered to the pink buds tipping her breasts. His hands clawed wider her parted thighs, fingers dabbling lasciviously within the hot, wet entrance to her secret place.

Her whole body was still trembling. 'Come, lover, come!' she breathed.

Groaning with desire, he lowered himself between her legs and allowed her hand to make the introduction he craved. Her hips rose to meet him as he thrust . . . and they settled at once into a reciprocal rhythm rapidly increasing in intensity until a second peak was scaled and the young woman gasped out yet another release while Bertrand at last fountained his own tribute into her receptive body.

At the top of the house, the pianola, which had been playing ever since he first came in, jangled suddenly into silence.

When he returned to the reception room an hour later, Bertrand said to Milady: 'I shall certainly insist that my English friend visits you tomorrow. But I must make one thing clear: his pleasures are to be strictly on my account. So far as Monsieur Mackenzie is concerned, Nellie will simply be a girl he met socially over a drink – a girl seduced into bed by his manly charm!'

Milady smiled. 'It shall be as you say.'

'I will settle the bill next time I come,' Bertrand promised. 'And that will be soon, I assure you! . . . Oh, by the way: my father has gone home, I suppose?'

She smiled again, a more secretive smile. 'I fancy he may be staying awhile yet,' she said.

In the far corner of the big room, the log fire had burned down. The Comtesse van den Bergh was on her feet, with one of the remaining two escorts about to wrap a silk shawl around her shapely shoulders.

Nellie was standing nearby with a glass of champagne in her hand.

'In the Avenue Kléber,' the Comtesse said, handing the young woman a gilt-edged visiting card. 'The big house on the corner. I shall expect you at four o'clock.'

CHAPTER FOUR

Tom Crawford, the English sculptor who lived at No.
123 Rue St André-des-Arts, was fond of boasting that
he was the only *artist* to be found in the whole quarter-
mile of the narrow street; apart from Milady's brothel
at No. 125 and two cheap hotels near the Buci market,
the remainder of the inhabitants being shopkeepers of
one sort or another, or artisans. Two café-bars, a restaurant
and a number of small businesses – a haberdashery, a
milliner's workshop, a grocery store – were to be found
on one side of the street; a butcher, a baker, a cobbler
and a wine merchant on the other.

Crawford's apartment was on the ground floor. He
had acquired it from a bankrupt pastrycook, turning the
room at the rear, where the ovens had been, into his
studio. Separated from this by a curtained arch was the
old shop, which was now his living quarters.

Unusually for the Latin Quarter, the sculptor was a
nordic type – a muscular six feet with a thatch of pale,
straw-coloured hair and light blue eyes. As a student he
had worked with the Fauvist painters Vlaminck and
Van Dongen. More recently, his abstract work had been
influenced by the Cubists Braque, Picasso and Juan
Gris. But the market for pure form, especially when it
concerned an artist unknown to the general public, was
limited. Crawford was in fact engaged that month on a
purely commercial job: a figurative group commissioned
by Robert Laforge, who planned to instal the finished

work above the gateway to his factory. Basically the group was a variation on the Three Graces theme: a trio of nudes symbolising Speed, Silence and Security, the slogan coined by the industrialist's advertising department for the Laforge motor car. The naked figures were twined around a giant letter S – which would serve, in the case of literature printed with an engraving reproduced from the group, as the initial letter covering all three words.

Crawford hated the job, and despised himself for doing it. This made him bad-tempered and irritable, apt to shout at his models, and frequently drunk. But he was unable to disguise the fact that his work was nevertheless extremely good. He was at present working in his studio on the *maquette* – the plaster model that would later be reproduced, over-life-size, in Carrara marble at a stoneworks near the Bois de Vincennes, south-east of Paris. Laforge was dickering with the idea of commissioning a miniature version of the group, to be cast in silver and used to adorn the radiator caps of his cars.

On the morning after Laforge's visit to the brothel next door, Tom Crawford was in a particularly bad mood. He had spent half the night at La Coupole and he had a hangover. In addition to that, one of his models was being difficult – and one had not shown up at all.

Crawford had strong views on models. He had strong views on most things and was not slow to express them. 'Don't moralize to me about models!' he had roared in one of the café-bars a few nights previously. 'There are only two points of view on that subject: that of the prudes and that of the know-alls. "Oo, my Lord!" say the prudes. "Artists and models! What lechery, what lust! With naked women, what can you expect?" To which the know-alls, the intellectuals, reply: "Rubbish! The Artist's eye is totally impersonal: he sees his model only as an object, as light reflected off a surface, as interacting planes in space!' ''

'Well let me tell you' – he shouted, silencing someone who was about to speak with an angry glare – 'let me tell you: it's the bloody prudes are right! Artists do chase their models around the studio! At least every one I know does. They don't see them as interacting planes, or light reflected off anything: they see them as tits and bellies and quims, which is what they are. They see them as cunts they hope to get into on the bloody day-bed!'

Someone else shouted something from the far side of the bar.

'All right, all right,' Crawford yelled. 'So the work comes first. But only after the initial pass has been made and a status quo established, in most cases. Even so, I'll have you know that sex treads pretty close behind!'

In his own life, the sculptor was a good advertisement for his precepts. But he wasn't thinking of sex today. For the tenth time he wished he had decided to lay out the money for professional models.

Sophie and Sylvie, the first two girls he talked into the job, were unreliable for two reasons – Sophie because she spent a lot of time auditioning, usually unsuccessfully, for dancer's rôles in music-halls and night-clubs; Sylvie because she worked at a dressmaker's *atelier* in the afternoon and evening. They were in fact the two girls who had put on the after-dinner sex show for Paul Mackenzie's benefit at the request of the Comte de la Ferrière.

They had earned their money there. But they were less effective as models: movement was their strong point, rather than immobility.

The third of the Three Graces was Nellie Lebérigot – and she, although she sat well enough, was unreliable because of the exigencies of her employment at the bawdy house next door . . .

Crawford sighed. He took a swig from a half-full litre bottle of red wine that stood on the floor beside the trestle table on which the half-completed *maquette* was posed. He glanced at a charcoal sketch of the group pinned to an inclined drawing board and shook his head.

The models were placed on, in and around a seven-foot capital S made from canvas and plywood. The head and shoulders of Sophie, the tawny-haired beauty, appeared above the letter, so that her remarkable bosom could rest on the upper slope of the curve. Sylvie's slender, shaven body was curled into the semicircle below, with Sophie's legs draped over her shoulders and her hips canted towards the artist. Nellie, the heaviest, was folded into the lower semicircle, facing the same way in the 'Lotus' position.

But Nellie had not turned up today, and that was making difficulties.

'For God's sake, Sylvie,' Crawford fumed, 'can't you organize yourself into some pose a *little* like the one we arrived at yesterday?'

'I'm exactly as I was yesterday,' Sylvie said sulkily. 'I know because of the pain I suffer when I twist this bloody leg the way you want it.'

'Bollocks. You had your whole dam' pelvis facing much more this way. That was the whole point of shaving your cunt. Just flesh, no pubic hair.'

'You don't need to be coarse. Anyway, I can't support myself this way without Nellie's shoulder to rest my heel on.'

'Well, Christ almighty, we'll put a chair-back or something under your foot! I mean it's not a fucking photo I'm taking: I don't have to include every damned thing just because it's *there*.'

Five minutes later, with the chair-back in place, he flung down a handful of wet clay and swore again. 'You moved your *leg*! I'm working on the crease at the bend of the knee, and now I can't even *see* it!' He gulped down more wine.

'All right, all right.' The girl jumped down from the letter's embrace. 'I'll pack it in altogether if you're going to be like that. Anyway I'm tired.' She walked dispiritedly across the room and flopped down on the studio couch.

Sophie climbed from her perch and joined her.

'Oh, come on!' The artist was suddenly contrite. 'Come on, girls. You can't let me down now. I'm working against time; you know that. I'm paying you, for God's sake. I'm sorry if I spoke out of turn, but this job's really important to me.'

'Not so important to us perhaps,' said Sylvie. 'If it was, you'd be paying us more.'

Before Crawford could reply, her friend leaped into the centre of the bed and stood upright, marking time a little with each leg to keep herself erect on the springy mattress. 'Maybe,' Sophie said slyly, 'there are more . . . *interesting* things to do?'

'What . . . what do you mean?' The sculptor frowned, confused.

The tawny-haired girl altered her stance. She balanced with her legs apart, slowly rotating her hips, so that the reddish bush softly curling over her pubic triangle oscillated lasciviously from side to side. At the same time she shrugged alternate shoulders dreamily in a swaying rhythm that shifted the two breasts with their hardened nipples in a lewd and private dance.

Sylvie caught on at once. She lay back on the bed, supporting herself on her elbows, and deliberately opened her thighs to expose the creased pink lips smiling from her shaven loins. Above her taut little belly and her pert, pointed breasts, her mouth smiled too.

'What the devil are you two playing at?' Crawford demanded angrily.

Sylvie glanced at her shamelessly displayed loins,

and then up at her companion's bobbing breasts. 'Some folks call it love!' she said.

'Look, stop it, will you?' Crawford protested. But both girls were staring at the tight trousers sheathing his crotch. Unmistakably, a hardening bulge was manifesting itself at the top of his thighs.

He shifted uneasily from foot to foot, absently wiping the clay from his fingers on a damp cloth. Sylvie looked up suddenly and their eyes met. She smiled again, slowly, salaciously, sensually. She freed one arm, resting now on a single elbow, allowing her hand to roam over her belly, kneading, stroking the slack flesh, the lewd fingers sliding ever lower until they pinched up the shaven skin just above her outer lips, all the while holding Crawford's gaze with that knowing stare.

Beside her, tawny Sophie stood shaking her body, jiggling the tight curves of her breasts as she raised beckoning arms above her head, threshing her hips this way and that to swing the bronze curls covering her sex as suggestively as a Turkish belly dancer – a pointer and a complement to the hairless loins of her partner.

Abruptly Sylvie threw back her head with a sudden explosion of expelled breath, spreading apart those outer lips with the forefinger and second finger of her exploring hand to reveal the dark-fleshed oval within.

Between them the two naked girls worked in perfect harmony, the one teasing, tempting, seductively provoking desire, the other indolently signalling where the tension fired by that desire could be released.

Yet again the sculptor cursed. His arousal was now complete; a small dark patch of damp marked his trousers at the tip of the lengthening bulge. Despite himself be became aware of a trembling at the base of his abdomen. The urgency of his need, warring with the demands of his mind, was paining the whole rigid extent of his shaft. 'There's at least two more hours work we have to get through this morning,' he protested. 'At least!' But his voice lacked conviction.

'You work twice as fast when you're in a good mood, when you're happy,' Sophie said. 'That gives us one hour together before you start again, no?'

'I'll be happier when you two bitches are back posing again, the way I pay you to pose,' stormed Crawford.

'All in good time,' she soothed. 'But first, why not *have* a good time?' She lowered herself to the oriental bedspread covering the mattress and stretched out, on her back, beside her friend. With both hands, she smoothed the swell of her belly, to thread questing fingers through the mat of springy hair below. She caressed herself, spreading apart the two pads of flesh shielding the entrance to her secret place.

The sculptor was staring, bemused, unable to take his eyes from the twin shrines of sex so indecently exposed. He was breathing hard and there were drops of perspiration on his upper lip.

Sylvie was still gazing meaningfully at the ridged outline thrusting at the top of his trousers. She half opened her mouth, sliding out a pink tongue to lick the curves of her own upper lip. 'Come over here, Tom,' she said throatily. 'You know you want to.'

'I do *not*!' Crawford sounded panic-stricken. 'I tell you I have no–'

'You mean that's not a cock standing there below your waistband?' Sophie cut in derisively. 'What have you got in your trouser pocket, then? A rolling pin?'

Before he could reply, the two nude girls moved swiftly, springing from the bed to drop on their knees in front of him, each with one arm around his waist and the hand of the other at his crotch.

He gasped, struggling to escape their grasp as they jerked open his fly and slid marauding fingers in among his underclothes. Sophie wrenched aside shirt-tails and dragged down the drawers beneath; Sylvie grabbed the pulsing proof of his desire and drew it out into the open.

The erect penis was no less than six inches long, ridged with veins at each side and a purplish-red at the cushioned tip.

Kneeling, the slender, dark girl positioned herself so that her pouting lips were level with this gleaming knob. She looked up at Crawford from under her eyebrows. She favoured him with a mischievous grin. And then, holding the shaft between finger and thumb at its thickened base, she advanced her head and opened her mouth.

Tilting her head on one side, she put out her tongue and licked, with a trembling, fluttering movement, the whole length of the urethral canal distending the underside of the organ.

Crawford shuddered. His pelvis convulsed and his hips jerked involuntarily forward. His breath surged out once more in a hoarse gasp.

Sophie had worked trousers and underwear down to his ankles from behind. Now she thrust a hand forward between his thighs and clutched the two hairy globes hanging in their sac of flesh below the shaft. She moved the glands within the sac, stroking and cradling the wrinkled skin of the pouch.

At the same time, Sylvie drew back her head, stretched her lips wide, and swayed forward to take the whole engorged penis head into the hot wet cavern of her mouth.

It was more than Tom Crawford could stand. His frustration, the pent-up desire he had tried for so long to suppress, boiled over into an explosion of action.

Kicking the clothes away from his ankles, he disengaged himself from the kneeling girl, bent forward to seize her under the armpits and picked her up bodily to stride towards the bed. He flung her onto the mattress. Then, with a wordless cry, he kneed apart her thighs and threw himself on top of her.

He entered her savagely. The throbbing, velvet head of his staff tore between outer and inner lips and plunged into the scalding clasp of the flesh beyond.

Sylvie's exclamation was half surprise, half pain. But she responded at once – and with enthusiasm, arching her hips off the bed to meet his long strokes with energetic thrusts of her own. Soon they were reciprocating with the precision of a well-oiled machine. Her small pointed breasts, their tips rock-hard now, were crushed against the woollen shirt sheathing his muscular chest. Her legs, slender and shapely, spread wider still and snaked up and over to lock behind his hips. Her breath, shorter with each thudding stroke, became hoarse and ragged.

For some time Sophie stood by the tangle of clothes on the floor, one hand on her generous hip, watching the brazen spectacle on the studio couch with an approving smile. But finally the immodesty of the sight, the sounds of flesh slapping wet flesh, the grunts of lust that accompanied the exertions of the entwined couple stirred tremors of desire in her own loins. She strode across swiftly and hoisted herself up onto the bed beside them.

As neatly as if it was a rehearsed technique – as indeed it was – she positioned herself on her back immediately behind her sosie, her crotch just above Sylvie's head, her spread legs draped over the short brunette's shoulders. She reached forward then with both hands and seized the blond locks of Crawford's hair, pulling his head towards her.

Because he was a tall man he could, without in any way compromising his penetration of Sylvie, stretch far enough to place his head above the tawny dancer's pubic triangle. Without relaxing her grip, she pushed his face down into the bronze curls.

Crawford groaned. His mouth opened. His lips closed

on flesh. His tongue snaked into wetness and warmth and the soft, sliding folds that concealed the tiny bud whose nerve ends could trigger such paroxysms of delight.

The tip of the tongue located the bud and Sophie uttered a sudden squeal of pleasure. The tongue worried the rubbery button of flesh, pushing it from side to side, rotating it, pressing it hard back into the cavity.

The girl's hips arched up, spasmed, and started to jerk up and down on the mattress. She squealed again, gasping out unintelligible words.

Crawford's mouth sucked avidly at the fleshy folds, his tongue eager to lap at the erect bud as it projected between the inner labia. 'Oh God! Oh *yes*!' Sophie panted. 'Lash me; *whip* me with your tongue! Do it, do it!'

He redoubled his efforts, aware suddenly that the acceleration of his lingual attentions was being matched by the pounding of his hips between the scissored grip of Sylvie's thighs.

The brunette's whole slender body stiffened. A high, wailing cry choked out from the back of her throat. She climaxed in a series of shuddering waves, drumming her heels on Crawford's back to force him deeper into her as the ridged muscles of her love canal tightened on his pistoning shaft.

Crawford's hands clenched on Sophie's breasts. His pelvis bucked and the nerves of his loins contracted to spurt, at last, a deserved tribute into the depths of Sylvie's receptive belly.

Nellie Lebérigot pushed open the heavy oak front door of No. 123, Rue St André-des-Arts. She walked down the short dark passageway, past the worn stairway that spiralled upwards, and fished in her reticule for the key to Tom Crawford's studio. She unlocked the door and let herself into the apartment.

None of the three occupants of the studio couch noticed her come in.

Crawford was as naked as the two girls now . . . as much of him as was visible anyway. He lay on his back beneath them, only his legs and the pale thatch of hair on his chest apparent among the tangle of limbs above him.

Sophie, her thighs spread wide, squatted astride his hips, with that part of him expressly designed for the gratification of the opposite sex deeply buried within the tawny bush clothing the lower part of her loins. At the other end, kneeling on his shoulders, Sylvie was positioned in a similar fashion over his face with no more than the tip of his chin showing below her shaven mons. The chin was moving.

The two young women were leaning forward, each with her arms around the other, their breasts hanging, their mouths working as they greedily kissed. Crawford, his upper arms pinioned by the dark girl's knees, had tucked his elbows into his waist and reached up his hands to fondle first one and then another of the four nipples swinging above him.

The whole tableau was moving, the component parts combining to establish a seductive, dreamy rhythm, female hips rising and falling, tongues interlaced, bellies expanding and contracting, all powered by the muscular heaving of the man beneath.

This complex choreography of naked flesh was complemented by multiple groans and gasps and muffled, wordless exclamations, themselves combining to form a single ecstatic hymn to the forces of desire.

For some while, Nellie stood watching the display, standing with one hand resting on a curve of the huge letter S that was the centre-piece of the group that Tom Crawford was supposed to be sculpting. There was a half smile on her lips, a knowing gleam in her eyes. Perhaps she was wondering whether the letters E and X should not be added to the initial.

The tempo established by the trio entwined on the bed was accelerating. Fleshy hips rose and fell faster. The breasts were bouncing. Lips sucked more fiercely and the gobbling motions of the sculptor's chin became swifter than ever. If that part of Crawford's person buried in Sophie's belly had indeed been designed for her gratification, then the designer – judging from the expression on her face – could congratulate himself.

The communal groaning produced by the group was reaching a crescendo.

The young man was the first to succumb, arching his pelvis up with a sudden convulsive thrust as the love juice squirted from his loins. And this in turn tripped the hammer of Sophie's release: feeling the hot liquid spurt within her, she threw back her head and squealed with delight. At the same time the threshing of Crawford's tongue provoked a galvanic shudder that shook the whole of Sylvie's frame. Tearing herself away from her girlfriend's embrace, she uttered a high, keening wail that died away in a diminishing series of gasps while her belly spasmed uncontrollably above the prone man's head.

It was some minutes later – Crawford was levering himself out from under the two exhausted girls – that Sylvie became aware of the silent figure standing beside the S. 'Nellie!' she exclaimed. 'I'd no idea . . . When did you come in? How long have you been here?'

'Long enough,' smiled Nellie.

Crawford sat up and pushed the blond hair from his eyes. Flushed and glistening, the proof of his virility, still not entirely deflated, lay along the sturdy muscles of his thigh. 'We thought you were not coming,' he said, his breath still labouring after his exertions on the bed. And then – seeing Nellie's glance linger on his tumescent maleness, and determined, once he had given way, to ride as it were the whole course – 'Now that you *are* here, why not join us? You know you French enthusiasts say: '*Jamais deux sans trois!*' Good things and bad things always come in threes. Well, there's also Third Time Lucky, isn't there? Sylvie and Sophie and me already struck lucky twice; how about taking off those clothes and making it a full house?'

'Who's talking?' Nellie demanded. 'The King of St André issuing his Order of the Day?'

Crawford grinned. And then, always eager to play on words, he added: 'You know what they say about the monarchy: it never reigns but it paws!'

'Not in the case of *this* subject,' Nellie said briskly. She wrapped her duster coat more tightly about her and firmly tied the waist belt. 'You pay me to pose for you: that entitles you to *look* at my body. If you want to *use* it, you come next door to No. 125 and pay the going rate!' She nodded to the two naked girls and swept out.

CHAPTER FIVE

The *Société Anonyme des Automobiles Laforge* was based at Le Bourget, a few miles north of Paris. The offices, accounts department, design centre and presidential suite were housed in a small château set in five acres of wooded parkland just off Route Nationale 32. Workshops, stores and the main factory building had been constructed on the site of a farm belonging to the property. The factory where the finished vehicles were assembled had been designed by Peter Behrens, an Art Nouveau graduate of the *Deutscher Werkbund* which later produced Mies van der Rohe, the architect Le Corbusier, and Gropius, of the Bauhaus school.

It was a clean, modern building, devoid of unnecessary ornament, with tall arched windows and a gallery beneath the single-pitch glass roof. Stamping, pressing, drilling and all work requiring powered machine tools were carried out in the shops and forge behind this block. Engine components, body panels and accessories were then bolted to the chassis in the Behrens complex. A spur from the main railway line to the north-east delivered work sub-contracted to foundries and ironworks in the industrial area near the Belgian border.

Paul Mackenzie, whose father's lightweight sporting cars were handcrafted in a couple of sheds in a London suburb, was impressed. He had been lunched royally at the château by Robert Laforge and his son, and was inclined to marvel at anything he saw. He stood with the two men in front of a glassed-in timekeeper's office at one end of the assembly shop gallery. Below them, blue-overalled workers trundled in trolleys loaded with parts from the foundry. Craftsmen and mechanics then added these to the six half-completed cars lined up in the centre of the shop floor. At the far end of the spacious building, tall sliding doors sealed off the loading bays for road and rail delivery.

'We restrict ourselves at the moment to three models,' Laforge Senior was telling the young Englishman. 'All of them built on the same chassis, with basically the same engine.'

Mackenzie looked over the gallery rail. The cars were large and heavy – four of them with high, angular, squared-off saloon bodies, the remaining pair fitted with unfinished, bathtub-shaped, open tourer coachwork. 'And the third model?' he asked.

'A stripped-down semi-racer, with the engine "breathed upon" by our technical wizards,' Laforge explained. 'But we only make them to special order. The profit margin is too small to have them lying around in showrooms.'

Mackenzie nodded. 'The sporting public has been slow to appreciate the possibilities of the motor car,' he said. 'My father finds the same thing. Only a minority of rich eccentrics seem interested.'

'Ah, but your dad's voiturettes are in a different bracket,' Bertrand Laforge cut in. 'What do they weigh? A thousand pounds? And you've got small, quick-running engines. Those damned *berlines* down there' – he gestured at the unwieldy saloons below – 'turn the scales at two tons! The chassis alone weighs half that. So even with no more than two seats, a bolster tank and a bonnet to cover the motor, our racers are already at a disadvantage.'

'But even with those giant castings, surely the power curve–?'

'Oh, the engines are powerful enough,' Robert Laforge admitted. 'But, as I say, with all that weight to shift, and six litres of displacement with a maximum rpm of two thousand two hundred . . .' He shrugged and left the sentence unfinished.

The Englishman nodded again. 'My father believes that the future of the power unit, certainly as far as sporting performance goes, lies with the small, efficient, high-revving motor that delivers a lot of horsepower for its size.'

'That's all very well,' Laforge said, 'but a unit like that . . . what are you talking about? Something of the order of four thousand rpm?'

'Five thousand five hundred, actually.'

'Very well. A mechanism turning that fast is going to throw one hell of a strain on its moving parts. I mean, we ourselves tried . . .'

He broke off, intercepting a warning glance from his son.

'Perhaps our guest would care to take a closer look at what we do have on the floor,' he said smoothly. He took Mackenzie's arm and steered him towards the iron ladder leading below.

His father had been about to touch on the problem whose solution – they hoped – could be wormed out of Mackenzie during the young man's visit to Paris. And Bertrand considered the time was not yet ripe. There was a lot more spadework to be done before this particular fruit could be plucked.

For the Laforge designers and engineers had indeed experimented with a lightweight high-speed motor. But they had discovered to their chagrin that it suffered – to a more advanced degree – from the same lack of reliability that plagued their production engines: an unpredictable tendency for the big-end bearings in which the crankshaft ran to break up. A fault which, apart from immobilizing the car, involved the owner in very expensive repairs.

The Mackenzie sports cars, despite their abnormally high engine speeds, did not suffer from this defect.

This was because the crankshaft bearings, instead of being the normal tin-based white metal, were made from a new alloy on whose composition Mackenzie's father was notably reticent.

If the secret of this material were theirs, the Laforges reasoned, they would be able to retool for a smaller, higher-speed, more reliable power unit which would improve the marque's public image and reputation, reduce the big cars' overall weight, and at the same time reduce their excessive consumption of fuel.

Paul Mackenzie, they reckoned, might – if sufficiently sweetened – be persuaded to part with the secret. He was an impressionable young man, eager to be in the swim, socially conscious, and quick to appreciate any action that would contribute to his self-esteem or drum up admirers ready to pay tribute to his intelligence, perspicacity, charm or talent. The Laforges were in a position to pander to each of these priorities.

Mackenzie stood now beside the most nearly complete of the Laforge saloons. He enthused over the finish of the gold-lined green bodywork ('A primer and nine coats of hand-applied coach paint,' Robert Laforge boasted), examined the highly polished brass carriage lamps attached to each windshield pillar, and tested the deep-button leather upholstery of the two tub seats in the driving compartment.

He stooped down then, peering between the painted wooden spokes of the artillery wheels, looking up beneath the extra-wide, flanged mudguards. 'You have some kind of undercoat, there above the springs and axle,' he said.

'Yes, yes,' Robert Laforge said hurriedly. 'Now I'd particularly like you to see the shop where the touring hoods are manufactured.' He led the way to a recess at right angles to the main shop floor, where women in overalls sat threading twine through sail needles and the air was heavy with the peardrop odour of acetone proofing the cutout canvas panels.

'We thought it wise to employ a limited number,' Laforge said, 'before this wretched suffragette movement that's bothering your country catches on here.'

'Although,' his son observed later, driving their guest back to Paris, 'there are more interesting ways to employ a woman, in my opinion, than having her sew together strips of doped material!'

'And more interesting occupations for her,' Mackenzie agreed, 'than chaining herself to railings, throwing herself beneath a horse, or shouting for the vote!'

'As I trust you will find out tonight, *mon ami*,' chuckled Bertrand. The car – a canary yellow tourer that was attracting admiring glances from the crowd thronging the fruit and vegetable market – was rumbling slowly down the Rue St André-des-Arts. 'There! The place with the courtyard and the big gates! That's the – uh – club I suggest you visit tonight. I regret that I cannot myself be with you, but members' guests are always welcome.'

Mackenzie swung around in his seat to look at the building.

'You will remember it all right,' Laforge said. 'See, the number 125 is there in big numerals above the arch. They will be illuminated at night.'

'It's very kind of you,' Mackenzie began. 'I don't know that I should–?'

'Nonsense, nonsense. You are in any case expected. Just ring the bell and give my name and your own to the concierge. He will take you in.'

The car emerged from the narrow street and rolled across the Place Danton. Laforge parked by the fountains. He switched off the motor and climbed down. As the Englishman was stepping onto the wide running-

board, a tall, straw-haired individual wearing a floppy
bow tie and a broadrimmed hat halted by the brass
radiator and raised both arms in greeting. 'Bertrand!
My dear fellow!' he said in English. 'Just the man I
want to see.' He shook hands vigorously. 'The fact is . . .
well, it's really more a matter for your Pa, but I was
wondering whether . . . not to put too fine a point on it,
I'd appreciate a couple of days grace on the *maquette*.
Would it, do you think, be a totally disastrous tragedy
if I delivered at the *end* of next week instead of the
beginning? I'm having a spot of trouble with – er –
with the models, you see. And you know how unreliable those little bitches are!'

'I shouldn't think it would be the end of the world,'
Bertrand said, laughing. 'Shall we say artistic . . . li-
cence? I'll have a word with the old man and let you
know.' He turned to Mackenzie. 'Oh. Forgive me. Paul,
this is Tom Crawford, the sculptor who's working on
the group destined to become the emblem of the glori-
ous Laforge, the automotive dynasty whose watchwords
are silence, security and sex-for-all! . . . Tom, meet
Paul Mackenzie, whose father builds expensive racing
cars.'

As warily as two dogs sniffing each other's rumps,
the two men evaluated each other's comportment, social standing, tailors, haircuts and self-esteem, the way
the English do when faced with a compatriot abroad.
Then Mackenzie nodded briskly and held out his hand.
'How do you do?' he replied.

Crawford took the hand and shook it. 'How do you
do?' he replied.

Neither question received an answer.

'Who are the models for our badge?' Bertrand asked
the sculptor.

'Semi-professionals.' Crawford told him. 'Sylvie and
Sophie, a seamstress and a would-be dancer; and Nellie, who works at the next-door–'

'Yes, yes. I know the lady,' Bertrand interrupted brusquely. 'Well, if you think you can complete the preliminary work by the end of the week . . .'

Not for the first time, Mackenzie wondered about this inconsistency in the young Frenchman's character. Normally an easygoing, hail-fellow-well-met companion, well-mannered and politely spoken, he was nevertheless capable, for no apparent reason, of abrupt behaviour that verged on downright rudeness.

He had cut off his father when Laforge had been about to say something on the subject of crankshaft bearings and experiments made at the factory. He had been equally curt, driving into the city, when Mackenzie himself had for the second time mentioned the undercoating beneath the mudguards of the cars on the production line. Now he had arbitrarily interrupted Crawford.

The affair of the undercoating – Paul repressed a smile – had been understandable; even the father had been evasive about that. For it was precisely to discover the secrets of this that Mackenzie had been sent to Paris. Wet roads and muddy hill-climb tracks had created terrible rust problems with the flared wings and spartan, pressed-steel bodywork of the Mackenzie roadsters. But whatever the conditions – and on the northern French *pavé* they could be awful – Laforge cars never showed any sign of rust at all. So it was, after all, reasonable that Bertrand should be cagey about this important asset of the marque.

But what could there be concerning the model called Nellie that he wished to hide from his guest?

'Now if only' – Bertrand was saying – 'we could get hold of models like those two . . . !' He gestured towards two young women crossing the square.

Mackenzie followed his gaze. He saw a slender blonde with an exquisitely boned face, arm in arm with a slightly fleshier dark girl who wore thick-lensed spectacles. The blonde wore a small felt hat trimmed with two feathers and a plain, long-skirted brown suit as severe as a riding habit. Her companion, who was hatless, was dressed in a flowered, tight-waisted garment whose *décolletage* would have been considered immodest even in the evening.

'Why don't you try?' Bertrand said to the sculptor.

'With those two?' Crawford laughed aloud. 'They live on the top floor of the same house as me!'

'You know them then? So why not ask them to sit to you – it's correct to say sit *to* you, isn't it, and not sit *for*?'

'Yes, it is. But I wouldn't dream of it.'

'Why ever not? They both look rather beautiful to me, especially the fair one.'

'Mademoiselle Dubois and Mademoiselle Dufour – the lady of the wood and the lady of the oven,' he translated for Mackenzie's benefit. 'But, alas, there is no fire in the oven of Mademoiselle Dufour – your fair one – and the wood of her friend kindles too close for comfort!'

'Very droll,' said Bertrand. 'And in plain language?'

'The pale one is as cold as an iceberg and the other's too hot to handle.'

'But if you were just asking them to model . . .?'

'Listen' Crawford said, 'if I was to ask Dufour *to take off her clothes* in the sacred cause of Art, she'd curl up inside her sensible shoes and die! If I asked her friend, she'd have mine off as well before I could get to the door!'

'And what do these ladies do,' Mackenzie asked, 'except scare off sculptors?'

Crawford grinned. 'Miss Hot is concerned with *La Mode*; she writes for a newspaper. Miss Cold, like one of my models, is a seamstress, but rather a special one: she is employed by your namesake, Poiret.'

'My namesake?'

'*Paul* Poiret. More famous, and more daring, even

than Worth or Paquin . . . look, there she is now! That's about as close as you'll ever get!' He pointed across the square.

No. 123 was at the corner of the Rue St André-des-Arts and the Place Danton. It was flanked, in the square itself, by a single-storey pavement café with a striped awning. Above this the blank side-wall of the building rose five floors to a chaos of ancient tiles and chimney stacks and dormers, between two of which a small railed balcony had been wedged. And on the balcony, watering a potted shrub from a brass can, was the blonde girl they had recently seen crossing the square.

They say love at first sight is an illusion. If so, as far as Paul Mackenzie was concerned, it was the most successful conjuring trick in history! From the moment he laid eyes on the fragile perfection of Camille Dufour, on the gracefulness of her walk and the smile on her lips, he was smitten.

Now, with the added bonus of a second sighting – even if it was a distant one – he determined with all the dedication of the young that, come what may, he would engineer an introduction to this beauty. He would meet her, he would invite her, he would wine and dine her, he would charm her, and . . . he would at this point permit his thoughts to go no further than that.

They had, however, already noticeably brightened a day that had dawned both windy and dull. Since they had climbed out of the Laforge, the sun had sailed into a patch of blue sky and silvered the budding leaves on the plane trees bordering the square. And against that blue, elegant behind the iron railing, was the heavenly silhouette of Mademoiselle Camille Dufour.

He glanced momentarily at the big yellow tourer with its wide flanged wings. Who could think of rust on a day like this!

CHAPTER SIX

Nellie Lebérigot paid off the cab outside the archway that led to the mansion in the Avenue Kléber. On the far side of the arch, pink and white camellias in stone urns surrounded a cobbled courtyard overlooked by severe classical façades dating from the period in the previous century when the *Préfet*, Baron Haussmann, had transformed Paris from a mediaeval to a modern city. A smart brougham with a gold coat of arms on each of its polished maroon doors stood by the flight of steps that led to the portico.

Nellie crossed the courtyard. She was a little worried, a little awed by the size of the house, a trifle apprehensive at the thought of this invitation from a grand lady who was also a notorious lesbian, almost ready to regret her own daring in accepting it. But she couldn't resist the lure of wealth; the temptation to see how the rich lived was too strong. And, after all, they couldn't *force* her to take part in any kind of orgy, could they? It was all experience anyway!

The coachman standing beside the brougham touched the brim of his uniform hat as she climbed the steps. She nodded, wondering about the life her hostess led. There had of course been a Comte van den Bergh once, but he had returned fifteen years ago to his native Belgium and his banking interests in Liège, leaving – so the gossips said – the house in the Avenue Kléber to his wife, plus a huge sum of money each month on the understanding that she stayed out of his life. Nellie reached out a white-gloved hand and tweaked the highly polished brass bell-pull set in the stonework at one side of the portico. Somewhere far away, below in the basement she supposed, there was an answering jangle.

Now that she was here, now that she had taken the irreversible step and rung the bell, she was assailed by doubts more immediate than speculations on her hostess's sexual behaviour. What about her dress – the new green velvet with the hobble skirt and the tightly buttoned bodice that pushed up her breasts? Would it be all right? Who else had been invited to the Comtesse's salon? What time should she be expected to leave?

The double doors were thrown open by a liveried footman.

He led her across a black and white marble checkerboard hallway, up a staircase with a brass rail, and across a landing flanked by classical busts on plinths. He paused by tall white double doors with panels picked out in gold, knocked once, then leaned forward to open both doors. 'Mademoiselle Lebérigot,' he announced.

For a moment Nellie stood stock still, confronted by what seemed to her a room full to bursting with haughty and overpowering women.

Dagmar van den Bergh hurried forward with outstretched hands, her auburn hair shining in the light from crystal chandeliers. 'My dear! How *delighted* I am to see you! How very kind of you to come!' She kissed Nellie on both cheeks and led her into the centre of the room. 'I must introduce you,' she said, 'to all my friends . . .'

In fact the big drawing room was not all that crowded: apart from the Comtesse herself, there were no more than five guests. They were presented as Mademoiselle Gabrielle Dorziat, the Baroness Gisela von Zwickenheim, Madame Marie-Ange Foucault de la Roquette,

Mademoiselle Gertrude Margarete Zelle and Madame Agathe Laforge.

Nellie already knew Dorziat, at least by reputation. She was an actress, reputedly a leading *Amazone*, whose picture was seen frequently in the society magazines. She had appeared with Bernhardt and was now said to be working with the comedian Max Linder on one of the new cinematograph films.

The German Baroness was buxom and blonde, about forty years old. She wore a black riding habit and shiny black boots. Discreetly dressed, each of the two married women hid their features behind enveloping veils which fell from the brims of their oversize hats to fasten around the neck.

Margarete Zelle, Nellie thought, was something of an enigma. She had a thick body with small breasts, but the face beneath the fashionable turban she wore was fascinating – thick, straight eyebrows, a long, well-shaped nose, and a mouth that curled up provocatively at the corners. The expression in her dark, slumbrous eyes was a continual challenge. 'She is a Dutch-Indonesian,' Dagmar van den Bergh confided in a whisper. 'Her mother was Javanese. She dances, you know, rather in the style of Isadore Duncan – mostly at private parties, but I believe she once appeared at the Moulin Rouge.'

'She looks interesting,' Nellie said, accepting a *tisane* of rosemary in a cup of eggshell Limoges porcelain.

'Oh, but she is! Especially at those parties!'

The Comtesse herself was dressed in a stunning ankle-length gown admirably designed to set off her beautiful hair and green eyes. It was short-sleeved, with ruffles at the neck and a huge bow just below the bust to mark an absurdly high waist from which a tubular skirt fell in wide sage and cinnamon stripes. Nellie knew it was a model dress from the house of Paquin because she had seen it illustrated – a design by Georges Lepape in the

Gazette du Bon Ton fashion review.

'I think your dress is marvellous,' Nellie said truthfully. 'You look like the spring we are all waiting for!'

Dagmar van den Bergh flushed with pleasure. 'You are a dear,' she cried. 'I am so glad you came. Come, we shall talk together later. For the moment, I have to play the hostess. Do, I beg you, take a sandwich or a pastry.' She gestured towards the far end of the huge room, where a waiter in a white jacket presided over a table covered in a starched white cloth. Beyond the plates of tiny triangular sandwiches and the tiered stands of *patisserie*, french windows looked down on a walled garden. Through the gaps in a stone balustrade garding the balcony outside the windows, Nellie saw stone urns planted with daffodils and crocuses, a paved walk flanked by classical figures on plinths, the branches of three chestnut trees not yet in leaf. Allowing the waiter to hand her a plate carrying a diminutive chocolate eclair, she turned back to face the room.

Ladies in ball gowns and military ancestors in dress uniform stared down at the gathering from gold frames on the walls at each side of a marble chimney-piece. A fire burned in the brass-barred grate. Behind the tapestry-covered chairs and settees on which the guests sat, Nellie saw glass cases loaded with Dresden and Sèvres, an antique commode piled with art books, two marquetry tables crowded with snuff-boxes and a collection of animals in jade. She walked primly across and sat down beside Madame Laforge, who looked the least formidable lady there. ('She is very unhappy,' Dagmar had confided. 'Her husband is rich – he fabricates motor carriages – but he has lost interest in her.')

The woman was perhaps fifty years old. She wore a check duster coat over an expensive wool suit. Shadowed by the veil, her face looked puffy and discontented, although the features were pretty enough. Her body was large and soft.

In fact the afternoon was not the ordeal Nellie had feared. Agathe Laforge made polite conversation on banal subjects – the viability of the new *métro* subway stations south of the Ecole Militaire; the price of foodstuffs; the effect of the pacifist ideas of the Deputy Jean Jaurès on the growing fear of war with a belligerent Germany.

Later, when the conversation became general, indignation was expressed at the cost of clothes, at the taxation laws, at the news that dinner at the Café Anglais now cost six francs instead of four. 'It is intolerable,' pretty, dark, doll-like Marie-Ange Foucault de la Roquette complained. 'Even in the country one cannot exist on less than forty thousand francs a year, and the wages of servants are counted in *hundreds*!'

Nobody made any suggestions, proper or improper, direct or indirect, to Nellie. She wondered why she had been asked. She wondered, too, perhaps because her own existence was so much concerned with flesh, how these pampered women behaved in the intimacy of their own homes. How did all these scented breasts and bellies and buttocks react to the touch of alien hands, male or female? Did they cry aloud when a tongue located their secret buds? Did they sweat when they shuddered in ecstasy? Did they crave the hard thrust of a man? How often did their own fingers, plunging through thick curls to the folds of warm flesh beneath, bring them sweet relief?

Although she surprised the Baroness meditatively staring at her several times through slitted eyes, Nellie was only asked what she did by one person. Gertrude Margarete Zelle strode across, about an hour after her arrival, and squatted down beside her chair. 'I dance,' she said, staring directly into Nellie's eyes. 'What do you do for a living?'

Thus abruptly accosted, Nellie could not shrug aside the question. Nor was she prepared to answer it truthfully. Relying on a part-time job she had had when she was working the *promenoir* of the Folies Bergère ten years before, she replied: 'Nothing more interesting than a seamstress, I'm afraid: I help decorate the creations of the theatrical costumier, Landolff.'

'Oh, but that is *very* interesting!' the Dutch-Indonesian exclaimed. 'Ever since Monsieur Diaghileff bought the Russian ballet to Paris in nineteen-nine, we have all been *mad* about the eastern accent! And as for the theatre . . . ! It must be fascinating, working on those costumes: all those swirls of colour; all those glittering sequins and stones!' She herself wore an exotic Javanese gown.

Before Nellie could frame a suitable reply, Dagmar swooped down and carried Gertrude Margarete away. Mme Laforge, with whom the dancer had apparently arrived, was about to leave. The motor was waiting below.

When Nellie herself left a few minutes later, Dagmar walked with her to the head of the stairs. 'It was kind of you to come,' she said in answer to her guest's polite thanks. 'I do hope you were not too bored.'

'Quite the contrary,' said Nellie. 'I found your friends . . . fascinating.'

'In that case' – the Comtesse produced a small-format newspaper titled *La Fronde* – 'perhaps you would care to read this. It is a feminist review, edited, written and produced entirely by women . . . for women.'

As Nellie murmured acknowledgements, she added: 'And you must come to our meetings sometime.' She smiled. 'We, the so-called *Amazones*, that is. At Renée Vivien's "Temple of Friendship" in the Rue Jacob.'

Framed by the long V-neck of her dress, Dagmar van den Bergh's splendid breasts, rounded and peach-bloom smooth, swelled on each side of a deep cleft just above the big bow at her unnaturally high waist. Nellie could scarcely take her eyes off them. To make conversation, she said: 'Thank you, I should like to. Sometime. What an interesting person your Dutch friend is.'

'Gertrude Margarete? Yes, she's a new addition. We find her . . . captivating.'

'She told me she was a dancer,' Nellie said. 'But I must say I can't recall seeing her name on a poster or a playbill.'

'Oh, but you wouldn't,' Dagmar smiled. 'She doesn't use her family name: when she works as an entertainer, she calls herself Mata Hari.'

CHAPTER SEVEN

Dressing for the evening, Nellie wondered for the tenth time just why the Comtesse van den Bergh had asked her to come to the salon in the Avenue Kléber. Because, as an admitted sapphist, she was physically 'interested', certainly. But, apart from the vague invitation to visit the lesbian club in the Rue Jacob as she was leaving, no mention had been made of this. And there had been no advances of any kind. In any case, Dagmar van den Bergh herself was a frequent visitor, a favoured guest of Milady's – as she was at several other high-class *maisons closes* in Paris. She had even, in some of her more disreputable moments, hired rooms there to entertain men as well as women! Efforts to seduce Nellie could therefore be made – had already been made more than once – at the house in the Rue St André-des-Arts.

Was there a possibility then that she had been asked to the Avenue Kléber as it were 'on approval' – as an item of merchandise to be inspected before any firm offer was made? And if so by whom? Someone, clearly, who would be shocked to descend into the demi-monde of brothels and sex that was saleable.

Merchandise she was, of course; or at least her body was. The Comtesse knew she was a whore. How many more of the ladies at the party did? The German Baroness probably, who Nellie suspected of being an intimate of their hostess. There was something knowing in the way she had looked at her. None of the others, she thought.

Except perhaps the enigmatic Dutch dancer – what did she call herself? Mata Hari, wasn't it? But her knowing look had been purely physical, person to person, rather than professional. It was a look Nellie knew well: it meant, I want you, whoever you are, and whatever the consequences.

She chuckled, hooking herself into the corset which had so stimulated Bertrand Laforge the previous night. What would the sad Madame Laforge have thought if she knew her tea-party companion had spent several hours in bed with her son less than twenty-four hours before!

Nellie made sure that the tapes securing petticoat and drawers were not too tightly knotted (although to dispense with those garments altogether would banish half the mystery, and thus half the fun, for the client). She eased herself into the dress that Milady had chosen for this particular charade.

It was an ivory-coloured sheath in heavy silk brocade, with two layered overskirts of the same material beaded with oriental designs in dark crimson and jade. From the wrist to the neck, and from the neck to the top of the low-cut, high-waisted bodice, semi-transparent, gunmetal organza shadowed the bare skin and endowed Nellie's firm flesh with a secret, untouchable air. To complete the illusion that she was a lady of leisure who had just 'dropped in' to a club for an apéritif with friends, there was a loosely draped silk overblouse with white fur collar and cuffs. She settled this on her shoulders and went downstairs, wondering what Bertrand Laforge's pigeon would be like.

He could have been a younger brother. He was the same height, with the same carefully tended side-whiskers and similar cheeks tinged with the pink of youth. He had a firm chin, a wide, generous mouth and steady grey eyes. Nellie liked him at once.

She was sitting at a low table in the bar that led off the first-floor reception hall when he arrived. The outdoor overblouse was thrown over the back of her chair and she was nursing a glass of champagne ('It looks better, dear, more convincing, if you're already drinking,' Milady had said. 'I'll put it down at half price when we make up the month's accounts').

It was a quiet evening. Dark, pert Lily Leblanc, in full equestrienne attire, tapping a plaited riding whip against the heel of her boot, was being severe with a fair-haired young man sporting an immature moustache. Two elderly sportsmen in evening dress sat with a couple of showgirls from the Parisiana music-hall. A uniformed police inspector was drinking a *fine à l'eau* at the bar, and a group of army officers stood exchanging pleasantries at the foot of the staircase that led to the rooms above. Over the low murmur of conversation and the occasional clink of glasses the eternal tinkle of the pianola filtered down from the top floor.

Milady sailed into the bar with one beringed hand on Paul Mackenzie's arm. She was wearing black, with a solitaire diamond surrounded by sapphires brooched above the generous bosom of her high-necked dress. The young man was getting – Nellie was amused to see – the full social treatment.

'. . . such a joy, *cher Monsieur*, to receive someone of one's own class,' the big blonde drawled. 'One has so often, alas, in these days, to open the members' list to persons of little culture and low background, when one would so much prefer to restrict entry to the quality. However' – she sighed, shrugging her shoulders so that highlights slid over the black dress as her breasts rose and fell – 'it is a matter of business, you understand. And in these days one cannot afford . . .' She left the sentence unfinished.

Nellie repressed a grin. The young man spoke good enough French, but she imagined he would not be sufficiently familiar with the nuances of the language to identify the Marseillaise dockside accent that gave the lie to so much of Milady's high-flown rhetoric.

'You are a member of White's Club in London, no doubt?' she was saying. 'No? The Carlton, then? . . . no matter. Any friend of the Laforge family–'

She broke off, affecting to notice Nellie for the first time. 'Mademoiselle Lebérigot! How very nice to see you again! It is always a pleasure when our lady members favour us with their charming company . . . Now, I must present to you our new – er – honorary member, Monsieur Paul Mackenzie, from London.'

'Enchanted,' said Nellie, languidly holding out a gloved hand.

Paul took the hand, not sure whether he was supposed to kiss it or shake it. He compromised by bowing, raising the hand halfway to his lips, and then standing back. 'I am delighted to meet you, Mademoiselle.' he said stiffly.

The barman, well briefed, was signalling. 'Goodness! You must excuse me: I am wanted in the office!' exclaimed Milady. 'Forgive me if I leave you two young people on your own for a minute.' She hurried away.

Nellie drained her champagne glass and set it on the table. Paul cleared his throat. 'Perhaps,' he said. 'That is . . . would you permit me to order you another?' It seemed to be expected of him.

'That would be very kind,' said Nellie. She smiled. And all at once, looking down at the seated young woman, he realized how extremely seductive the bare flesh looked beneath the soft folds of organza sheathing her shoulders and bosom. 'Do sit down,' she invited, after he had raised a finger to summon the barman.

He sat, a little awkward, a little unprepared for a tête-à-tête with a glamorous member of the opposite sex so soon, with so little lead-up; at a loss, momentarily, for a signpost, a direction in which to steer the conversation.

'Your club,' he offered eventually, 'it seems very nice ... I mean the members – a pleasant cross-section ...' He looked despairingly around the reception hall. 'Those officers there: are they Zouaves?'

'Spahis,' Nellie said. 'Zouaves are infantrymen. These are officers in charge of cavalry recruited from native troops in our North African colonies.'

He nodded. 'Very impressive uniforms.' Swallowing, he stared at the pale blue tunics, the gold braid, the encrusted insignia of rank and the wide red stripes on the men's trousers. He turned abruptly and said with an earnest expression: 'Talking of which, I have to tell you that I think that's an absolutely stunning dress!'

She laughed. 'I am flattered ... and flattery is always more enjoyable when it comes from a handsome man.'

Paul flushed. Before he could reply, the barman sat an ice bucket containing a bottle of Krug demi-sec on the table. He sprung the cork, poured two glasses of champagne, and went away.

Nellie raised her glass, thinking it was time, maybe, to jolly along a little this rather shy foreigner, to nudge the conversation more towards the bedroom where she was being paid to take him; to emphasize the rôle of a woman of the world overcome by his manly charm. She said: 'And still talking of clothes, I imagine that evening jacket *must* have been cut by an English tailor? In Savile Row perhaps? ... Ah! I thought so. Nobody but the English can build suits like that: it shows off the breadth of your shoulders and the narrowness of your waist without ever approaching the flashiness of so many continental clothes or the vulgarity of the purely physical.'

Paul didn't know what to say. He drank his champagne and poured more for both of them. It was odd, he thought, that he experienced no inhibitions whatever at a licentious stag party with paid female 'entertainers', such as the dinner he was taken to some nights ago by Bertrand Laforge . . . while a lady, on her own, who was both attractive and alluring, left him almost tongue-tied.

The conversation continued haltingly. He drank some more.

The woman – what was her name? Lebaron? Lebérique – really was extremely seductive! As she leaned towards him, smiling with her eyes, he was unable to take his own eyes away from the dull gleam of those two proud swells of flesh half seen through the flimsy material at the top of her dress. Infatuated though he was with the vision of the girl who lived on the corner of the Rue St André-des-Arts, that was all in his mind; he had not even met her yet. But this young woman was real, was flesh and blood, was within reach of his hand . . .

Nellie took the champagne bottle from the bucket and upended it over their glasses. Paul signalled the barman to bring another.

Lily Leblanc and her escort passed the table on their way to the staircase that led to the upper floors. 'I am truly vexed with you,' Lily was saying. 'Your behaviour is unforgivable!'

'Mistress, I apologize,' said the young man. 'Humbly. I am very sorry.'

'You will be sorrier,' the equestrienne promised, thwacking the riding crop against her thigh. She prodded him up the stairs.

At Nellie's table, the subject of clothes, and fashion in general, had come around again. 'We are luckier now than we were even a few years ago,' she said. 'In nineteen hundred, long corsets pinched in our waists and cruelly compressed our busts and hips. It was like

82

being imprisoned in a steel tube!' She laughed. 'Jean Cocteau – one of our promising young poets – once said, "To undress one of these women is a costly enterprise which it is advisable to organize well in advance, like a house removal"!'

Paul smiled. 'But you say things are better now?'

'Oh, yes. Confined like that it was virtually impossible to use the new *métro* or sit comfortably in a motor carriage. Even in fashion there has to be progress. And we have to thank couturiers like Paquin and Poiret for a looser line altogether. You see' – she shifted her haunches on the chair seat and lifted her arms to raise her generous breasts – 'we still keep a short corset to trim our waists, but above and below we are free!'

He nodded, picking up the second bottle to pour. The reply he wanted to make refused to form itself into words.

'There are still difficulties, just the same,' said Nellie. 'For some of us. Or so it seems.' She picked up a folded newspaper that was lying on an empty chair and turned to an inside page. 'This might amuse you. It is written by a *chroniqueur* who concerns himself with what we call *mondanités* – with society life.'

She folded back the paper and read aloud:

' "On certain afternoons, in certain half-deserted streets, one sees women with happy, fulfilled expressions hurriedly searching for a cab . . . to take them back to their own carriages, complete with coachmen and footmen, which have been waiting for hours outside a department store with several exits. Usually, they carry a parcel, hastily wrapped and tied with string, which they try to hide: the corset their lover hasn't had time to re-lace!" '

'I wish I had the chance to re-lace *your* corset!' Paul blurted out.

He flushed to the roots of his hair. He hadn't even known that he was going to say it! Appalled, he swallowed the rest of his champagne.

'Before you could do that,' Nellie said softly, 'you would have to have unlaced it first.'

He stared at her, wide-eyed. 'You m-mean . . . that could be p-possible?'

She looked down demurely, smoothing spread fingers over the silk covering her thighs. 'I think it might be arranged.'

'B-b-but how? When . . . and where?

'This is . . . a residential club. I keep a room reserved here for . . . for the occasions on which I decide to remain overnight in the city.'

'And this is one of them?' He could scarcely believe his luck.

'What do *you* think?' She raised her head suddenly and stared straight into his eyes. 'And to your second question – don't your countrymen have a saying: there is no time like the present?'

Nellie rose to her feet and picked up the overblouse. In truth she was a little tired of jockeying this engaging young foreigner along, tempting him to make a proposition he would doubtless consider immodest. Still – she stifled a sigh – it was after all what she was being paid for. She called to the barman: 'Jules, you may send the remainder of this bottle up to the Blue Room. Oh, and by the way, you might as well save time later and add another one to it.'

'*Bien, Mademoiselle.*'

Paul was fumbling for his wallet.

'On my account,' Nellie added with a wink that only the barman saw.

'Oh, look here . . . I mean I couldn't possibly,' Paul began. 'I insist–'

'My dear man.' She laid a hand on his arm. 'I have to tell you that–'

'Please. I really cannot allow–'

'Surely you must know club rules,' Nellie interrupted

again. 'Non-members are forbidden to pay for refreshment. It's the same everywhere.'

Once more the young man blushed. He swallowed. 'Well . . . if you are sure. I mean I really don't like . . . you must let me return the compliment another way.'

Nellie glanced across the reception hall. Milady, who had been joking with the officers, had discreetly retired to an anteroom where she saw them rise from their table. The officers were drifting towards the bar.

'I know *exactly* the way you can return the compliment!' Nellie said. She took his hand and led him to the stairs.

CHAPTER EIGHT

The drawers, which were of white linen, ended in ruffles of Chantilly lace some inches below the knee. Tapes securing them there and at the waist were the same colour as the scarlet corset Nellie wore. Beneath the loose drawers, a close-fitting undergarment with an open crotch hugged her shapely hips and thighs.

Paul Mackenzie had drunk a lot of champagne, and there had been wine with his solitary dinner at the Café Anglais earlier. He scarcely remembered climbing the stairs and he had no recollection of the thickly carpeted upper hallway or the buxom chambermaid who brought hot water into the room. He slumped into an over-stuffed easy chair and dizzily watched the gilded mirror, the prints of horsewomen in the Bois, a commode of birdseye maple, the brass bedstead, spinning past his head. He was, he realized, not only a trifle tipsy but also fuddled, squiffed, twinkled, inebriated, the worst for wear and pie-eyed. Not to put too fine a point on it, he was drunk.

It was the heat from the coal fire that had driven the fumes of alcohol to his head, he decided, squinting at the flames. Two ice buckets and two bottles of champagne stood on a low table near the bed (were there really two, or was he seeing . . . ? No. Panic over. One was half full, the other unopened). He didn't remember the waiter bringing them in. He remembered Nellie – dear, generous Nellie – insisting that she remove that beautiful dress herself. There had been something about that filmy stuff which hid her flesh so seductively tearing too easily. Fine lawn, lacy petticoats swirled around her ankles. Hadn't he pulled them slowly down *himself*?

She stood above him – he was on his knees; how odd! – with her legs astride and her hands on her hips: black boots, white drawers, red ribbons, the tight corset red again, pale dreamy flesh, and then back to black for the hair. He was saying something but he couldn't hear what it was.

She moved a hand to ruffle his hair. She smiled. She said something he didn't quite understand, but his hands had risen obediently to fumble with the scarlet tapes.

The waistband sagged. His hands were claws, dragging the material down, unsheathing the swell of hips, the thighs – alabaster, did they call them? Marble columns? These thighs were warm flesh, musky with woman scent, tingling with the hint of some forgotten oriental perfume, dabbed on long ago. Between the tights, the tightness of the undergarment, the gusset, the gap, with a curl of dark hairs thrusting through the white.

The material ripped as he pulled them down after the drawers.

The garments jammed; he could move them no further.

'Below the knees, Paul. The knees!' Suddenly her voice was crystal clear. The room swam into focus.

He had forgotten to untie the lower tapes.

Paul hesitated, feeling foolish. Hoist them all up again? Ask her to hold them while he . . . ? No! The nearness of that soft belly was too much. What was it the poet Mallarmé had said? A snowy slope leading down to a new forest drawn by a master hand, where the mossy nest of a goldfinch could be found? He lowered his face towards the dark triangle of hairs.

'Paul!' She was laughing. 'Let *me* handle my clothes

for the moment. After that I shall be free to deal with yours. Meanwhile, why not make yourself comfortable, sir? Perhaps at least you would care to remove your jacket, no?'

He realized with a start of surprise that he was indeed fully dressed. What else had happened – or hadn't happened – during the puzzling time the room had been whirling around him? Again feeling gauche, perhaps even a little ashamed, he stripped off his jacket and piquet waistcoat, and kicked away his shoes. He began to untie his white cravat.

The bed, the coal fire, the items of furniture, were firmly in place now. He felt a clarity of vision, an icy coldness that left him totally in command of everything: the night, the room, his own actions. Even the damned pianola, still playing somewhere above, could be silenced if he put his mind to it.

Nellie was standing by the curtain that closed off the corner where the douche and lavabo were situated. She was wearing nothing but the boots, black stockings and the red corset. Of course, he had promised to do something about that, had he not?

Flames crackling in the grate sent shadows prancing across the walls of the dimly lit room. What shadows? The shadow of a man sitting in a chair, for one. His shadow.

He was sitting? Yes, he was. That again was curious. He lay back with his legs stretched out, wondering how the glass of wine came to be in his hand. Nellie knelt between his knees, her hands busy about the buttons fastening the fly of his trousers. The constriction, the agonizing tightness martyring his loins – why had he not registered it before? – was all at once released.

Cool air, hot air from the fire, played on the superheated skin of his most private part. The distended flesh throbbed gratefully under her touch.

He stared down at her. She was smiling, the dancing

89

firelight reflected in her eyes as she fondled and massaged the rigid proof of his desire. But her mouth was half open, the lower lip glistening, and she was breathing hard.

She stood up suddenly, leaving his maleness to project lewdly through the gap in his trousers . . . and then, seizing his ankles as though they were the shafts of a wheelbarrow, she pulled him off the chair and onto the floor, finally dragging the trousers off him altogether.

He lay in his shirt and underclothes, struggling to push his own drawers down over his hips. Before he had freed the rest of his genitals, she was crawling over him, swift hands ripping open the shirtfront, knees between his knees, her winey breath playing warm on his flushed face. 'Oh, you,' she breathed. 'Off with the rest of them, quickly! I want you on the bed! Now!'

Was this abrupt flood of lust just one more facet of the rôle she was playing of the young society matron seduced by the charms of a foreigner? Was it an automatic weapon from the arsenal of her sexual expertise, triggered by the familiar situation in the familiar room, deployed like a conditioned reflex as part of her professional strategy? Or was she genuinely aroused by the proximity of this handsome and virile young man, unable to keep her hands off him because of the yearning trembling through her own loins?

Nellie never knew. She too had drunk a great deal of champagne. All she knew at that moment was that something had been unchained within her, something that craved satisfaction – and the craving could only be satisfied by the inclusion within her body of that throbbing and engorged part of him which had first stimulated her desire.

She leaned over him, panting, full breasts hanging and thighs trembling as together they wrestled off their remaining garments. Once he was naked, she flung herself on the bed and pulled him down beside her. He was fumbling for the scarlet corset, trying to lever her on to one side so that he could get at the laces, when she said sharply: 'Not now! You can do that later: now I need you in front of me. Here! Come!'

She reached for him, drawing him close. Her eyes closed and her mouth opened. Against his muscled frame he felt the whole long, smooth length of her – the firm swell of calves, cool fleshy thighs hard against his flaming hardness, a slack curve of belly and then, after the satin, leather and whale-bone severity of the corset busks, soft shifting breasts squashed against the hairs on his chest. Her arms wrapped around his shoulders; her nails dug into his back.

Suddenly emboldened, Paul shifted his position, leaning over her with a knee wedged between her thighs, his palms against her breasts. She was breathing in short, hoarse gasps. He lowered his head, closing his lips on her half open mouth.

The reaction was electrifying. Her tongue, hot, wet and trembling, leaped to meet his own. Her hips thrust fiercely up off the bed. Her chest heaved and the thigh nearest him was jammed savagely against his aching staff.

Cheeks hollowed, mouths sucking, gobbling, greedily clinging, they kissed passionately, the two tongues, muscular and wiry, probing and entwining in a frenzy of desire.

For an instant, Nellie released his back. She reached up and unpinned her hair, still kissing him, and then drew momentarily away to shake her head violently. The freed hair tumbled about her shoulders in a dark tide.

With a harsh, wordless exclamation, she held up her mouth, demanding his lips and his tongue again.

The hard mound at the base of her belly ground against him. She parted her thighs, sliding one hand between their bodies to grasp his swollen member. At once he eased himself across and lowered both his legs between hers.

The hand tightened, coaxing, pulling. Knuckles, wrist and forearm moved beneath the weight of Paul's taut, flat belly. He gasped, the hypersensitive, satined head of his wand brushing through hairs, bludgeoning warm flesh, stirring the sweet wet folds . . . until suddenly, with a final push from his partner's fingers, he was home. The head thrust aside the clinging embrace of those secret lips and was swallowed in the scalding clasp of her innermost throat, the whole, hard, quivering length of him engulfed.

He bunched the muscles of his behind, driving in even further, penetrating to the hilt. Nellie arched up to meet him and he groaned aloud. Her damp fingers clenched on his shoulderblades and the nails raked his skin.

Within seconds they had established a reciprocating rhythm as precise as the thudding of a beam engine, as positive as the powered thrusts of a locomotive's connecting rods.

Soon Nellie was rolling beneath him, wrapping both legs around his back, pummelling his spine with her fists as her head thrashed wildly from side to side on the raven carpet of her hair. She drummed imperative heels on his backside, willing him even deeper within her heaving belly. Unintelligible cries forced their way through her clenched lips.

Paul's upper lip was dewed with perspiration. Sweat ran in the hollow of his back and dripped down his ribs to mingle with the moisture on her own skin where their bellies sucked and slapped.

He had no idea how long it was before the gathering tension within him reached a point at which the exquisite agony of his need imposed a hesitation in his rhythm; his thrusts, although stronger than ever, became sporadic, jerky.

He felt as if every nerve-end in his body had displaced itself to quiver in the depths of his loins. His staff felt like a rocket ready to explode. At the same time, the young woman was mounting suddenly, swiftly to her own release.

A deep shuddering started somewhere far inside her. The movement became more powerful, accelerated; the ridged muscles of her love canal contracted; her heels locked behind Paul's back and her thighs clamped ferociously against his waist. Then her whole pelvis convulsed and she gasped out her climax in a long, slow, crooning Oh-oh-oh-oh-*Aaah!*

It was enough to make the Englishman himself spend. The wave of excitement, of tension, on which he had been precariously riding, reared suddenly up, speeding him with it, curled dizzily over . . . and broke with a thunder about his ears as he squirted the testimony of his delight deep into the darkness within her.

Later, much later, after the hot showers and the last bottle of champagne, they found time for the delicacies and the subtleties that haste and the desperation of their shared need had denied them – the stroking, the caresses, the kissing and the murmurs of endearment.

Still later, after Paul had realized that he was deliciously, soberly still awake and aware and there were still several hours of the night ahead, there was another bout of lovemaking of the energetic kind . . . a bout which involved the use of an upended armchair, the maple commode, and finally a pile of cushions in front of the fire on which he laid Nellie face-down so that he could shaft her from behind.

Strangely enough, the very last thing he did before he tumbled into a deep and untroubled sleep was in fact the first thing for which he had originally been coaxed upstairs – the unlacing of the scarlet corset!

CHAPTER NINE

Paul Mackenzie was crossing the Place St Michel on his way to the new Métro underground railway station when he saw Camille Dufour for the second time.

She was emerging from the narrow canyon of the Rue de la Huchette with a shopping basket full of groceries. It was still quite early and a thin drizzle was falling, gusting across the open space in the squalls of east wind spilled between the twin towers of Notre Dame. Clearly the young woman liked to do her marketing before she went to work for the famous couturier – Paul somebody, wasn't it? – the sculptor had told him about.

Mackenzie himself was suffering from a massive hangover, the dull ache in his head and the unacceptable tremors of liver and stomach only partially relieved by memories of the titanic bouts of lovemaking that enlivened the night he had spent with the voluptuous Nellie in the club off the Rue St André-des-Arts. He had been both flattered and thrilled by the encounter with a *mondaine* woman so expert and adventurous. It had indeed fulfilled every fantasy, each romantic notion he had cherished about Paris and the Parisienne: reality had for once lived up to the dream.

Sensuality, abandon and pure lust had filled his sexual horizon in the company of such a mistress. And yet, the moment he laid eyes on the pale hair and classic features of the girl who lived next door to that club, his sights narrowed; his field of view could encompass no more than a single image. Nellie Lebérigot and her innermost, most intimate secrets were forgotten.

How could he engineer a meeting with this delectable creature?

Why had he not insisted, when he first saw her, that the sculptor call her back and make the necessary introduction?

Was there any way he could scrape an acquaintance with her now, this very minute?

Camille was hurrying. She had turned up the wide collar of her light tweed redingote and ducked her head to keep the drifting rain out of her eyes. The feathers decorating her pert velour hat were already bedraggled. Now she was threading her way between the streams of cabs, drays, buses and motor cars flooding south from the bridge that led to the Ile de la Cité and the fashionable Right Bank. She walked a little unsteadily: the shopping basket was clearly heavy.

Should he run after her and offer to carry it?

He shook his head. Even if she accepted, there would be no way he could further the relationship: respectable young women did not accept invitations, still less make assignations, with strangers who accosted them in the street – however helpful, however courteous the stranger. Such a man could be some kind of confidence trickster, a tout, or even a character connected with the white slave trade. Besides, such a thing simply was not done.

Pretend to trip, then? Lurch against her – gently, of course – in the effort to avoid sprawling on the wet pavement? *Then*, while apologizing profusely, offer to relieve her of her basket?

No again. Similar objections. Much too obvious a ploy: any intelligent girl would be suspicious at once.

Then what – Paul was already running out into the roadway, his feet slipping on the wet cobblestones – what on earth *could* he do? Because he was determined that, this time at least, he must do something.

For a moment Camille was lost to view. From beneath a cape-cart hood fastened to the front mudguards with long straps, the driver of a Daimler-Benz tourer shouted abuse at him. An errand boy on a bicycle swerved wildly; behind him another chauffeur honked. Then a two-horse omnibus, coming from the other direction, pulled up suddenly outside the café and disgorged a crowd of American and German tourists.

Paul splashed through a puddle and leaped for the sidewalk.

He was already too late: the girl was at the entrance to the narrow street where she lived. As he watched, helpless, she unlocked the door of No. 123 and went inside. He was still thirty yards away when the door closed.

This time Camille did not come out onto the fifth floor balcony.

Later that morning, Bertrand Laforge and Tom Crawford met in a wine bar on the Quai Voltaire. It was still raining, and the grey slate turrets and roofs of the police headquarters on the Ile de la Cité shone silver above the sluggish swirl of the river. Beneath the central arch of the St Michel bridge a tug appeared, towing a string of barges loaded with coal.

'Filthy weather, even for March,' the sculptor remarked, sipping a tall glass containing hock. 'Deuced awkward if it keeps in and ruins the party.'

Bertrand's eyebrows raised. 'What party is that?'

'Oriental costume ball. Didn't you know? That dressmaker fellow, Poiret, is pushing the boat out at the end of this week. Camille, one of the girls upstairs, works for him – and she's going to try and wangle me a couple of invitations. Think you'd care to go?'

Bertrand was drinking a Byrrh apéritif. He drained the conical glass and set it on the small round marble-

topped table they were sitting at. 'It might be an idea.'
And then, remembering the Englishman he wished to
impress: 'I suppose there'd be no chance of getting a
couple for *me*?'

Crawford shrugged. 'They say the guest list is set at
two thousand, believe it or not! Unless they print precisely that number, no more and no less, I'd think it
wouldn't be too difficult to fiddle an extra one or two.
I'll do what I can.'

'Many thanks,' said Bertrand. 'I'd be obliged.'

'You'll be more than obliged if it comes off,' the
sculptor told him. 'Because it's to be a *masked* costume
ball . . . and there'll be more crumpet there than you
ever saw in your life! Hot crumpet, beautifully buttered, eager to take advantage of the anonymity con-
ferred by those masks!' He laughed boisterously, holding up a finger to summon the waiter.

Outside, beyond the closed booksellers' stands strung
out along the rainswept Quai, a river steamer hooted,
heading for the bridge. Whistles shrilled as police in
shiny wet capes tried to disentangle the horse-drawn
traffic snarled up in the Place St Michel. 'I can't wait!'
Bertrand Laforge said.

At noon, the two men met Corinne Dubois at a seafood
brasserie near the Sorbonne, on the upper part of the
boulevard. They shared a huge bowl of *moules marinières*
and a one-litre carafe of dry white wine.

'You write about the doings of *Le Tout-Paris*, the
society set,' Crawford said when their plates were heaped
with the succulent stewed shellfish. 'Tell us about this
famous Poiret party. It's going to be something out of
the ordinary, even for him, if half what I've heard is
true.'

'And why is it so important that the rain should hold
off?' Laforge put in.

'Because all the set pieces are designed to take place

outdoors,' Corinne said. 'In the garden of his mansion. The place is on the Faubourg St Honoré, but the grounds stretch all the way back to the Champs Elysées.'

'Even so, it's just a fancy dress dance,' Laforge objected. 'What's so special about this one that it has to be in the open air?'

'The décor,' Corinne told him. 'The whisper is that the whole thing is contrived to promote his new "Persian Look" among the wealthy members of the upper crust. Poiret's been mad about everything Eastern and Near-Eastern ever since Diaghileff brought his Russian Ballet to Paris three years ago. Now he's commercializing his hobby with this Arabian Nights spectacle in the hope of coaxing even more fashion-conscious customers into his salon.'

'Explain,' said Tom Crawford.

'They'll see it all. Real camels bringing in panniers of exotic foodstuffs. Live monkeys in the shrubbery. Arab dancing girls, snake charmers and fortune tellers. Two hundred flamingoes, specially imported from Africa, on the ornamental pond. Probably a miniature *soukh*, with the merchants offering gifts to the guests. You can't do that kind of thing indoors!'

'Not in my house you can't!' Crawford agreed. 'Camels indeed!'

'But my God,' Bertrand Laforge said, 'it sounds absolutely stunning! You must do your damnedest, my friend, to see that we do get in.'

'I told you: I'll do my best.'

'Camille will help all she can,' Corinne promised. 'Specially if you remember, Tom, to stop trying to hustle her into your studio . . . and your bed.'

'It's a good bed,' Crawford said mildly. 'I have it on good authority.'

'On the authority of those two cheap little models? Of the midinettes you find in the Montmartre *bals-musettes*? Of the street girls you bring in? I won't believe it until I've tried it myself!'

'Yes, well, another time perhaps. Right now I think it's time we called for the bill,' Crawford said hastily. 'And don't let anyone tell you that professional models come cheap!'

'I want a coffee and a brandy,' said Corinne. 'Monsieur Laforge?'

'Excellent idea,' Bertrand concurred – and he had signalled the waiter and ordered three before the sculptor could intervene.

The rain had stopped, and dark clouds scudding across the lowering sky tore apart from time to time to reveal patches of blue when they left the brasserie. There had been a second round of *digestives* before Laforge finally asked for – and paid – the bill. Both men, mellowed by the wine, the brandy and the apéritifs they had drunk on the Quai Voltaire, were in an expansive mood. Corinne sized them up covertly as they piloted her across the busy street. 'Why don't you boys come back to my place for a siesta?' she asked, as if the thought had just occurred to her, when they reached the far side. 'You could stretch out and relax awhile. Camille won't be back from the *atelier* until six. And I have phonograph cylinders of the songs from the Max Reinhardt show at the Vaudeville – *Sumurum*, isn't it? – that might amuse you. They say that's where Poiret got half the ideas for his ball anyway.'

'I'd love to,' Laforge said. 'But I must get back to the factory. My Englishman's arriving at five, and I have to show him round the paint shop.'

Since Crawford lived – and worse, worked – in the same building as Corinne, no such avenue of escape was open to him. Thinking perhaps that it might be easier to evade her predatory grasp there, he suggested that they call in at his place first. At least he could stall with talk of his current group.

Error.

There was talk of the current group all right, but it wasn't a stall.

Imperial-size sheets of cartridge paper covered with charcoal sketches strewed the floor around the table on which Crawford's half completed *maquette* was posed. Corinne glanced at them and then at the huge wooden capital S on the model's dais. 'But you're much further ahead with the two top figures,' she exclaimed. 'You've only just blocked in a rough outline of the lowest one.'

'Yes, well . . .'

She studied the *maquette*. 'And the wire armature on this model's not even covered by the clay yet! On the bottom figure, I mean.'

'The girl I use for that one can't come as often as the others.'

'I'll take her place,' Corinne said swiftly, 'and then you can bring yourself up to date.'

'No, no!' – Crawford panicked suddenly – 'That would not do at all! She . . . that is, you are completely different . . . the morphology of the body . . . the balance of the composition, the relative weight of different masses, the line–'

'You can modify afterwards. This will at least give you a start on the basic forms. And if you're so worried about models' fees, this one won't cost you anything at all!' She had already thrown aside the raincape she wore. Now she tore open and stripped off a high-necked flowered blouse to reveal one of the new bust bodices that flattened the breasts and pushed out her stomach below the fashionably high waist of her long skirt.

'Corinne!' the sculptor cried angrily. 'Stop that at once! . . . I don't want to work this afternoon anyway. I'm not in the mood. We had a heavy lunch. And I told you, you are the wrong shape anyway.'

'You are tired? Relax then. Take a siesta. Lie down awhile, and you will work like a demon when you get up.' She had reached behind her to unfasten the bodice.

She wrenched the garment off, and her breasts sprang free. 'I can help you relax; I'm a specialist,' she breathed.

Crawford backed off nervously as she ran towards him, the breasts with their darkened nipples bouncing lewdly on the naked torso above that tight-fitting skirt. 'Keep away!' he called huskily. 'I tell you I don't want—'

But the half-dressed young woman, evading the hands outstretched to ward her off, was already dangerously close. One bare arm encircling his neck, she draped the whole lascivious length of her fleshy body firmly against his reluctant frame, trapping her other arm, which she held down at full length, between their hips. He was still mouthing an impassioned refusal when he felt a knee forced between his thighs, spreading his legs slightly apart. A hand crawled down his belly to cup his crotch.

Crawford gasped. Despite himself, he felt the pressure of that alien hand, sandwiched between their two bodies, stir a response from his loins.

The hand twisted. Knuckles rubbed his pelvic bone. Strong fingers touched the bulge of his genitals, probing, exploring, tweaking . . . and this time there could be no doubt: his masculinity was hardening, stiffening; even as he fought to deny it, to fight the physical reaction down, a painful tightening of his fly against the sensitive flesh of his male part proved the validity of his response.

'Corinne!'

She reached up and kissed him on the mouth. Her wet lips clung. Her tongue, furnace-hot, darted between his teeth. The fingers of the trapped hand, having outlined the lengthening shape of his manhood, clenched now on the muscled and sinewy staff thrusting out the stuff of his trousers.

The sculptor groaned. Involuntarily, his tongue surged forward to meet the intruder speared between his lips. The rigid shaft swelling under the manipulation of those massaging fingers was iron-hard now. His hands, which he had dropped to her shoulders with the intention of pushing her away, clenched on her naked flesh. Breath hissed through her nose and her breasts heaved, squashing themselves against his chest. Her tongue lashed wildly, scouring Crawford's teeth, forcing itself up between his gums and the inside of his cheek. Without any conscious intention, he allowed his hands to slide from her shoulders to her waist . . . and then around the sculpted hollow of her waist until he felt the warm weight of her breasts against his palms.

Corinne shivered. Deep in her throat, she choked out a wordless exclamation. Breaking free from him, she sprang away and leaped up onto the studio couch. Upright on the mattress, she reached down and hauled the narrow skirt up to her hips.

For the second time, the sculptor gasped aloud.

She was wearing no petticoats, no slip, no drawers. From the waist down, apart from her shoes and knee-length black stockings, she was nude.

Even in 1912, with the hastening emancipation of women, this was unheard of!

Crawford stood there, amazed. He shook his head like a dog coming out of the water. She couldn't understand his reluctance. She wasn't to know that this was the second time in a few days that he had been literally seduced – in exactly the same way – away from his work. Or that husky, six-foot Crawford, with his athlete's frame, blond hair and blue eyes, considered himself something of a Lothario; that any lovemaking not initiated by himself was a blow to his masculine pride. And as for it happening twice within a week . . . !

She dropped into a sitting position, bouncing on the bed with her legs stretched out in front of her. Then suddenly she flopped over onto her back, lying flat out with her thighs apart and her hands locked behind her head.

He stared, fascinated. Above the skirt bunched around

her waist, he saw the swelling mounds of her breasts and, beyond them, the point of her chin. Below the skirt there was just black and white – white nudity relieved only by the black stockings and the crisply curling raven hair that nestled in the fleshy triangle between her parted thighs.

Moving like a sleepwalking man, Crawford stumbled towards those columned thighs, that slope of alabaster belly, and the folds of wet flesh that gleamed palely amidst the hairy furrow between them.

'But I'll tell you one thing' – the sculptor confided to a crony in his favourite café-bar late that night – 'the woman's a bloody witch!'

The crony ordered another round of absinthe and looked expectant.

'Talk about octopus arms!' Crawford said. 'She was lying there with her legs apart and her quim gaping as wide as the Golden Gate. Her tits were quivering and her nipples were as thick as a baby's thumbs. By then I was as stiff as a plank myself, of course. But I was still fully dressed. She was lying with her hands behind her head.'

He paused to dribble water through the sugar held in a perforated spoon above his drink. He lifted the glass and sipped. 'I get to the edge of the bed,' he said, 'and I swear I never saw that arm move. But she had my fly open, my belt unbuckled, my trousers around my knees and my pego taking the air before you could say John Thomas! All one-handed if you please!'

'Well now!' said the crony.

'It's the type, of course,' Crawford said. 'She wears thick-lensed specs when she's working and she has buck teeth and a full lower lip. You can always tell. Randy as all getout that type is.'

'You shafted her PDQ, I imagine?'

'I did. I was in there like a rat up a drainpipe, with

John Thomas ploughing the deepest furrow since oats were invented . . . and *he* got his oats all right: she spent four times before I shot my load!'

'It's a good way to spend an afternoon,' the crony said. 'Louis! The same again, if you please.'

'I thought, of course, that that was that,' Crawford continued. 'But not a bit of it. I scarcely had time to get my breath back before Mademoiselle was at it again. We'd both parted with our clothes by then, you know. And I was hoping to take a rest. J.T. standing at ease after the battle, not expecting to be called to action until the buglers blew – when all of a sudden the hands were at work. I tell you, it was like four Japanese Geishas each trying to outdo the other!'

'Hard work for the unwary!' the crony chuckled.

'She took it in her mouth. We made an entry via the stage door, if you take my meaning. There was a session of mathematics, *soixante neuf* being the key number. Many hands made light work. And so on and so forth.'

'And after it,' the crony said, 'she sat to you, and you were able the better to serve the cause of Art?'

'Not on your life,' Crawford said. He quoted: '"Nature I loved, and after Nature, Art". Well, this Miss loves nature all right. But the only Art she approves of is Arthur Schopenhauer – and that's just because he was in favour of freedom for women!'

The crony drained his glass. 'An instructive afternoon,' he pronounced. 'And well spent.'

CHAPTER TEN

In 1912 there were 127 licensed brothels in Paris. Léo Taxil, a journalist who specialized in the 'exposure' of lesbianism in high society and pederasty among the literary establishment, wrote that the top echelon of these *maisons closes* was 'frequented by the magistrature, the army, the navy, high finance, officials of the Republic, important men of business, members of the exclusive Jockey Club, foreign princes and visiting millionaires.' The most famous and the most luxurious were No. 6, Rue des Moulins, once the home of the painter Toulouse Lautrec; No. 14, Rue de Monthyon, Mme Kelly's Chabanais; and 'The 222' – so named because of its street number. Les Marroniers, in the Bois de Boulogne, was a house exclusively reserved for couples who wished to change partners. None of its rooms were equipped with doors, and it was understood that a client, nakedly roaming its corridors, could – rather in the manner of a ballroom dancer 'cutting in' – walk in to any room and stake his claim on the beauty he could see hunched or spreadeagled on the bed.

The big brothels were sumptuously furnished. Taxil described one 'with a famous grotto, the prettiest torture chamber in Paris, and rooms richly decorated in the taste of various countries of the world – a Scotch room, a Russian room, an Italian room, a Spanish room, a Chinese room, an Indian room, a Persian room, a Negro room, etcetera.'

'Each of these *retiros*' – wrote Jules Macé, author of *La Police Parisienne* – 'has a comfortable luxury of which the particular and original character is a reminder to the foreigner of some intimate corner of his absent homeland. As you penetrate into their interiors you are dazzled by the glitter of cut glass, by the opulence of the hangings, the profusion of gilt and the brilliance of the illuminations.'

The 'darkened chamber' of a house not far from the Bourse and the Palais-Royal, he added, merited special attention. 'Lit by electricity, it contains a bed framed by black curtains with gold fringes and tassels. Rays of light with changing tones are directed onto a sky-blue ceiling in the centre of which may be seen soaring Eve in the costume of the Earthly Paradise.'

Heavenly approval of the pleasures of the flesh was similarly available in the Rue des Moulins, where No. 6 boasted a 'fantastically ornate wood-panelled room in a mixture of mock-Tudor and mock-Gothic styles, and a huge, richly carved mahogany bed in the shape of a shell with the headboard crowned by a life-size naked goddess smiling down at the happy occupants.'

It was however to the Chabanais that Bertrand Laforge and Tom Crawford had been persuaded to go, two days after the sculptor's encounter with Corinne Dubois. The persuader was the voluptuous Mademoiselle Dubois herself.

'They say you can go there just for a drink,' she explained to Crawford. 'But if I go alone it could be – well, open to misinterpretation. People might think I was one of the business girls there, and in my position as a society writer I cannot afford that.'

'Why do you want to go? Crawford asked.

'An article. The pleasures of the rich when they leave their wives at home. I can do it so much better if I've actually seen one of these places myself. From what I hear, the Chabanais makes Chez-Maxim look like a corner bistro – panelling inlaid with gold, eighteenth-century paintings, a Moorish room in imitation of the Alhambra at Granada with medallions by Boucher and Lautrec. There's even a marble hall modelled on the Roman baths at Pompeii!'

'Only for a drink then,' Crawford said cautiously. 'You'll come too, won't you Bertrand? There's safety in numbers after all.'

Laforge nodded. 'I was hoping to rope in my English friend, but it seems he has other plans for tonight. Business connections, I suppose. Tell you what, though: why don't I rope in his colleague, that extraordinary toff with the funny voice? Champney, isn't it? He would at least be good for a laugh.'

'The more the merrier,' said Corinne.

In fact it was raining again, there were no cabs to be had, the *Métropolitain* underground railway was inconvenient, and it was a walk of a mile and a half from the Brasserie Lipp on the Boulevard St Germain, where they met, to the Chabanais. When the thin drizzle turned into a downpour, they decided to change their plans.

'You've never been to Milady's, yet you live next door?' Crawford said to the girl in amazement. 'Dear friend, you have yet to live! It may not be the Chabanais or No. 6, but it's ornate enough and much of the clientele's the same. Also it's less than two hundred yards from here. I vote we go there and see what we can find for you behind her padded doors. You might even meet the Comtesse van den Bergh, and you'd never get that at the Chabanais.'

'I know the name,' said Corinne, 'but I'm not sure that I–'

'An habituée of the temple in the Rue Jacob; a leader of the Sapphic cult.'

'It takes all sorts,' the girl said. 'Not that it's my

particular cup of tea, but she might be worth a couple of lines. Danielle In The Lion's Den or The Darkest *Amazone* – A Male View.'

'Fine . . . except that her name is Dagmar and she happens to be a redhead.'

'My word! A girl who prefers other girls!' chortled Hector Champney. 'Still has to meet the right chap, what!'

They ran through the rain to the Rue St André-des-Arts and left their wet topcoats with the concierge. Corinne registered the chandeliers, the ebony Negro with the brass tray for visiting cards, the Impressionist landscape and the Greek figurines displayed on the way upstairs, scribbling hurriedly in a leather-covered notebook with a small gold pencil. 'I swear that painting's a Pissarro!' she whispered.

The first floor reception hall was lively. Boisterous laughter erupted from a table surrounded by army officers and over-painted girls wearing skirts short enough to expose their ankles. ('Dancers from the Moulin Rouge,' Crawford murmured.)

Nellie Lebérigot stood at the bar with a distinguished-looking American. Lily Leblanc sat with an elderly priest. Several couples conversed quietly over drinks among the Second Empire chairs at the far end of the room, and a tall woman wearing an enormous hat and a brocade gown encrusted with jewels was gazing earnestly at a fat man recounting an anecdote that evidently amused him. 'I recognize her,' Corinne said. 'She's one of the coquettes from Maxim's. But who is the old sport who doesn't trust the cloakroom girl?' She nodded her head towards the love seat, where a gentleman with a monocle and bushy white side-whiskers was ogling a busty girl who could not have been more than sixteen years old. Although it was pleasantly warm in the over-furnished room, he was wearing a domed hat with a curly brim and an Ulster buttoned up to the neck.

'That's the Arch-Duke,' Crawford told her, 'with his latest piece of fluff. He's in evening dress and he's covering up the decorations and orders splashed across his noble ministerial chest. He can't afford to be recognized by scandal-mongers like you!'

'I suppose he's afraid his wife might find out about that child,' Corinne said.

The sculptor shook his head. 'His wife knows. He's afraid his mistress might find out.'

Milady, full-rigged and with a favourable wind, was sailing towards them.

She was wearing the pink and grey striped satin again, only this time – perhaps in deference to the formal attire of the Arch-Duke – the elbow-length gloves were black.

'Bertrand!' she cooed, holding out a languid hand. 'How delightful to see you! And dear Hector! And even the Bohemian rascal from next door! You must introduce me to your lady friend.' Her appraising glance swept over Corinne, pricing her moss-green tussore dress, noting the bee-stung lower lip and the percentage of bosom revealed by the décolletage. No danger. An enthusiastic amateur. No money to be lost - though they would have to pay top price if they wanted a room and did one of her girls out of a trick. She turned to call the barman: 'Jules! A bottle of champagne. The Roederer '04, I think.'

Laforge made the introduction. Corinne shook hands. 'So nice, dear, to see someone here who has *de la classe,*' Milady said perfunctorily. 'One does so miss the company of one's equals.' She turned a roguish smile on Champney. 'And you, *cher ami*, I suppose you will be asking for one of my girls again? I shall see if I can organize two and a half minutes for you in between clients!'

'Haw!' The Englishman uttered his braying laugh. 'You know I'm getting old, m'dear. John Thomas is slowin' down and now the feller needs all of three!'

He paused to pluck a glass of champagne from a tray proffered by the barman, drained it at a single gulp, and laughed again. 'In any case – haw! – I'd much rather bed down with you, old thing. A man likes a bit of upholstery when he's workin', what! And these gels today are all too skinny for me!' He slapped Milady familiarly on the back and reached for another glass.

Milady choked, handed her empty glass to the barman, and dabbed champagne from her glove, her dress and the noble slopes of her bosom with a lace handkerchief. 'Dear boy, I'm sorry,' she said faintly, 'but I really cannot tonight. I – er – I have to do the books, you know. The tax inspectors are coming tomorrow, and . . . well, you know how it is. Maybe one of the girls . . . ?' She looked around. Nellie and her American were heading for the stairs. The big-breasted brunette waved at the three men and favoured Bertrand with a wink. Lily and the priest were deep in conversation.

'Perhaps, if you don't mind waiting,' Milady said, 'Lily could–'

'No, no. Another time,' the Englishman interrupted. 'I'm here for another week after all. It'd be a poor thing if old J.T. couldn't wait his turn once in a while, eh?'

Milady drifted away. Bertrand ordered another bottle of champagne. Several couples arrived, had a drink at the bar, then went upstairs. The army officers and their dancers were already installed in one of the upper rooms: laughter and the tinkle of the pianola punctuated the hum of conversation in the reception hall. Finally Lily, who was wearing a severely tailored black suit, a bow tie and laced knee boots, led her cleric to the floor above – presumably to undergo some penance for his non-spiritual desires.

It was soon after midnight when Corinne and her

escorts, hearing from newcomers that the rain had stopped, decided after all to go to the Chabanais. At this time there was a choice of cabs in the Place St Michel. A little tipsy now, all worries submerged in the flood of euphoria stimulated by the effects of the champagne, they took the first fiacre in the line.

The cabbie, pleased at the chance to return to the Right Bank and the better-off fares he might find there, took them across the river at a cracking pace – wheels rattling, springs bouncing, the horse's hoofs striking sparks from the cobbled roadway. Thrown about on the dusty, faded upholstery, the quartet were disposed to treat the turbulent journey as a private joke. Through lowered windows, they giggled at the dark swirl of the river, at the absurdity of the 16th-century Tour St Jacques – a spire without a church! – at the arcades of the Rue de Rivoli. The new electrical street lighting bathed the Avenue de l'Opéra in glaring brilliance, spilling long streamers of brightness into the black depths of the still-wet sidewalks, gleaming among the brasswork embellishing the harnesses of horses, winking from the polished coachwork of broughams, victorias and motor carriages transporting late revellers back to Neuilly and St Cloud. Beneath its gilded dome, the opera house was a blaze of colour.

But none of this matched the dazzle of the Chabanais's reception hall when they arrived.

Sombre amidst the glitter of crystal, the profusion of sumptuous furnishings and the warmth of rich brocades, a pale, thin woman dressed from head to foot in black greeted them. Her grey hair was drawn back into a tight chignon and the sole decoration she wore was a large solitaire diamond in the centre of a black velvet band encircling her neck.

She led them to a table in the crowded upstairs lobby, organized drinks, and told Corinne that a room could be available in less than thirty minutes if they wished.

Crawford and Laforge, already ensnared by the wiles of Bacchus, were in no mood to gainsay the initiative of their guest. But Hector Champney, uncharacteristically, withdrew.

'Beg pardon an' all that,' he said awkwardly, 'and certainly no reflection on the delights offered – Haw! – but I fancy I spy a soulmate on the far side of the room whose implicit invitation J.T. can in no way politely refuse.' He gestured towards a tall woman of forty with henna-ed hair, a thick waist and an immoderate amount of bosom jutting from the scooped-out neckline of her Empire-line dress.

Quick to recognize a positive signal, the woman moved slightly in the shadows at one side of the huge curving staircase, shifting the flesh of her slack body to emphasize breasts and belly and bottom. An eyebrow lifted a quarter of an inch; one corner of the painted mouth quirked into half a smile.

Message received and answered.

Too fuddled to waste more time on the niceties of good manners, Champney loped towards her remorselessly, inevitably as a fragment of iron filings drawn by a magnet.

A few minutes later they saw the woman gliding in a statuesque fashion up the shallow stairway with Champney lumbering in pursuit.

'Back to a trio then!' Bertrand said. 'I wonder if–?'

'There are times,' Corinne cut in slyly, 'when three really *isn't* a crowd.'

'Meaning?' Crawford enquired.

She smiled up into his face, the lower lip shining and prominent. ' "Let us praise while we can the vertical man" ', she misquoted, ' "though it could be more fun, were he the horizontal one"!'

'Corinne!' Bertrand exclaimed in mock outrage. 'I trust you are not suggesting activity of a depraved kind?'

Crawford was too inebriated to think clearly. The

word horizontal echoed in his mind, quivering with verbal harmonics on either side: horizontal . . . prone . . . stretched out . . . recumbent . . . flat . . . reclining . . .

Bed.

Forgotten the reservations, the affronted pride, the outrage at being seduced, twice, by women in his own studio. He felt good. He was sleepy. He wanted to lie down, beds were available, a female was within reach. He raised a finger to summon the madam in black with the diamond at her neck.

Ten minutes later, a maid ushered them into a large room on the fourth floor which resembled nothing so much as the foreigner's idea of a Turkish harem. The walls were hung with richly coloured oriental rugs. Beyond an arched window embrasure, stars in the night sky twinkled through the ornamental filigree of a wrought-iron grille. A log fire crackled beneath a hooded *cheminée* of beaten copper.

The furnishings were simple: three low divans; cushions covered in silk, satin, taffeta, silver brocade, strewn over the mosaic floor; a sunken bath behind a Persian screen.

On a wooden stand supporting a tray of Benares brass, tiny cups, eggshell thin, stood by a long-handled copper pan full of hot coffee. Beyond them was a flask of Arak and three liqueur glasses in diminutive silver frames. A subtle fragrance – sandalwood? myrrh? – rose from the warm water filling the marble bath.

All at once diffident, a little sobered, the two men stood awkwardly by the fire, avoiding each other's eyes. Corinne was prey to no such inhibitions. She had stripped off the green dress immediately the maid accepted her tip and left the room. Now she was unfastening her bust bodice and unravelling the tapes securing petticoat and drawers.

She was naked, the dancing firelight sculpting shadows from smooth flesh honeyed by the soft light of oil lamps burning in each corner of the room.

She sprawled back on a pile of cushions, arms out-flung, breasts tip-tilted as she languorously stretched, legs slightly spread to reveal the dark triangle between her thighs and the salmon lips pouting from its hairy furrow.

Through slitted eyes, she looked from one man to the other with a slow smile.

'I'm not often so lucky,' she murmured. 'But it is late. To avoid the time-wasting preliminaries and the risk of favouritism, of angering one friend or the other, why don't we forget the garment by garment undressing ritual? Take off all your clothes at once, now, and join me down here as quick as you can!'

This time Crawford and Bertrand Laforge did exchange glances. The industrialist's son was the first to react. With a smile and a shrug, he unbuttoned his jacket and allowed it slide from his arms. He loosened his necktie and removed it. A button flew from his starched shirt when he tore it open and pulled it over his head. Socks, shoes and underclothes followed in quick succession. Then he was down on his knees beside the nude girl, the erect proof of his interest spearing rigidly out from his loins.

Crawford, once the situation had registered, was not far behind. He was wearing less, and his artist's smock and floppy bow were easier to cast off than his friend's formal attire. He squatted down on the other side of Corinne.

She opened her eyes in admiration. Then, reaching out both arms, she wrapped a hand around each of the fleshy spikes angled her way and drew the two men towards her.

Bertrand extended himself by her side. With one hand he squeezed up the nearest breast, lowering his head to suck gently on the puckered skin of the nipple. His free hand reached down to fondle the pink folds showing through the tangle of hair sheathing Corinne's loins. Crawford, on the far side of her, acted as his mirror image.

Aware suddenly of two fingers ... three ... four ... parting the sensitive lips of her secret place, Corinne drew a sharp breath of excitement and anticipation. The fingers probed, circled, stroked. Her hips writhed among the cushions; her pelvis arched slightly to meet the intruding hands.

Beyond the outer lips, the inner now were eased apart as those fingers penetrated more deeply still, softly massaging the warm flesh.

A small, harsh noise deep in Corinne's throat translated itself into an explosive gasp. She felt a trembling surge in her loins and all at once she was wet, the raping fingers dabbling, gliding. A fingertip located the tender bud where all the quivering nerves of her sex were concentrated, the cushioned pad pressing, rotating, caressing the abruptly stiffened button of flesh.

She cried aloud. Her hands, still grasping the rigid staffs of her two companions, tightened and squeezed. Her hips convulsed and the centre of her body jerked higher off the silk and satin pillows.

The hands began to move, a slow dreamlike pumping of the throbbing shafts she held.

For minutes they remained locked in that triple embrace, a single, composite, naked element, immobile among the bright colours in the flickering firelight, whose individual components nevertheless subtly moved in sensuous writhing harmony. Then Corinne, tunnelled hands still wrapped around their prey, sat up, rose swiftly to her knees, and dragged the two men to the nearest divan.

Hector Champney was in a lofty, panelled room whose exposed oak beams, leaded windows and displayed horse brasses reminded him of a mediaeval Suffolk barn.

There was a wooden pitchfork and a stack of straw in one corner, and a striped horsehair mattress, unexpectedly comfortable, on which his lady lay.

Divested of the high-waisted Empire-line dress and the black lace underclothes that went with it, the lady revealed herself as a Junoesque nude of the kind imagined by painters of romantic classical scenes in the middle of the previous century.

The outsize breasts were neither flabby nor slack, but fullblown in the manner of the models favoured by Rembrandt and Rubens; the belly below that high waist was generous, the hips well padded and the thighs fleshy. The effect as a whole was that of a collapsible doll slightly over-inflated.

The lady's sexual equipment was concealed within a furry thicket that reached almost to her navel. Like many heavily-built women, she had slender ankles and small, exquisite feet.

Champney gazed at her approvingly as she waited, spreadeagled on the mattress.

His own clothes had been flung aside before she slid the drawers down over her hips. His figure was unexpectedly athletic and surprisingly well equipped. Now he advanced towards her, rested bony knees on the mattress and leaned over the blue-veined thighs spread open before him. 'Knew I'd be right,' he said. 'Got a stunning shape, m'dear. Plenty of bulk in all the right places, what!'

A Parisienne, after a brief romantic encounter some years before, had written to a friend: 'Monsieur C— is quite outstandingly virile! But there is no place within his lover's *schema* for that blissfully dawning awareness of emerging beauty, that titillating sense of imagination surpassed, as each fleshy treasure is rumoured, hinted at and finally explored with the removal of each successive layer of clothing designed to display what it conceals. The preliminaries of the supreme emotion do not, alas, exist for Monsieur C—.'

Champney lowered himself between the open legs of his choice. The muscular fingers spreading them still further and searching for the entrance to that citadel he proposed to storm were in fact gentler than she expected. What followed was beyond any expectations she might have harboured, good or bad. Champney slid one hand beneath her derrière, clamped the other over a breast, bunched his slim hips and thrust forward.

The woman on the mattress stifled a cry as he rammed the full length of his engine in, swiftly withdrew and then battered forward again. With the regularity of a steam hammer, he pumped energetically in and out of her receptive belly, bruising her hips with each successive stroke.

'It was indeed [wrote the Parisienne] reminiscent of an express train plunging into a tunnel. The penetrating shaft shared locomotive qualities with our Knights of the Iron Road, being steel-hard, fast-moving and possessed of relentless power. The engineer in charge too – despite a certain lack of subtlety – was clearly an expert of long experience, for his hands rotated the two halves of my bosom as if they were the control levers of a tramway car!'

For some seventy seconds, the Englishman maintained his pounding rhythm. Then suddenly he threw back his head with a curious yelping cry, his long stride as it were faltered, there was an abrupt, convulsive heave of his hips . . . and the hot spurt of his release spasmed within her.

For a moment he collapsed across her supine body. Then he pulled free to run for the shower cubicle on the far side of the room.

When he reappeared, the woman was sitting up, cradling one swollen breast in both hands as she inspected the reddened flesh where it had been manhandled.

'My word, that was good!' Champney enthused. 'Just

what the doctor ordered, what! Pretty good for you too, I shouldn't wonder. Don't get many like that in your line of country, I imagine?'

'No, darling,' the woman said truthfully. 'I don't think you'd get many to quarrel with you there.'

'Splendid. Don't know what we'd do without the occasional frolic, eh?' Champney squatted beside the mattress. 'But I do pride meself on a reasonable performance. I'm not saying, mind, that there may not be some coves even quicker. But at least I don't keep the gals hangin' around for half a bally hour like these bunglers who fumble around in the rough instead of taking out the No. 2 iron and driving straight for the hole.'

The woman's painted face cracked open in a disbelieving smile. 'You believe, then, that love should always be as swift as possible?'

'Good Lord, yes. Anything else is an insult to the lady. Selfish too, making her wait for the second shift.' For Champney, it was evident, the exercise was on a level with show-jumping, a squash match or the 220-yard hurdles. 'A fit man should be able to manage it in three to four minutes. Five at the most – haw! – if he's over forty. Anything longer shows lack of concentration. What I always say, if a thing's worth doing, it's worth doin' properly. No point wasting time after all. It simply delays the starter's pistol for the second heat!'

'You were . . . contemplating . . . further action?' His companion kept her two hands protectively over the swelling slopes of her breasts.

He stared at her. 'But of course. Two heats and the final, always. Used to get it down under three minutes on the last lap, but at my age you have to reckon on four plus.' He shook his head, leaning across to rummage among the clothes strewn on the floor by the straw stack. Finally he fished out a gold fob watch and sprang open the lid.

'Eleven and a half minutes already,' he said. He glanced down at his partly retumescent organ. 'Old J.T.'s almost ready to move out to the starting blocks. Be with you in a jiffy, old thing.'

'In that case,' the woman said carefully, 'perhaps you would allow me to lie face downwards, at least for the next time. There are moments, you see, when–'

'Spot on,' Champney interrupted. 'I like a filly with an eye for sport. Have it your way, by all means. Have it any way you like.'

He grinned, slapping her playfully on the rump. 'Just so long as you do have it!'

In the Oriental Room, Corinne was on her hands and knees on the divan. Tom Crawford knelt behind her, the upper part of his body leaning forward over her back, his thighs hard against the backs of her legs, both hands on her fleshy hips. The love tunnel at the base of her belly was impaled on the long, stiff spear of his desire, and he was pulling her back and then thrusting her away in a slow, rocking movement that had the tight globes of her backside quivering and all her abdominal muscles contracting with each forceful heave of his pelvis.

Immediately in front of her, Bertrand Laforge sat propped against the wall with his long legs stretched out and his thighs spread wide.

Supporting herself at the full length of her arms, Corinne had lowered her head until her lips closed over the throbbing head of the staff pricked up from the young man's loins. His hands, reaching around her shoulders and beneath her rib cage, fondled the breasts hanging there to jiggle lewdly each time Crawford thrust into her from behind.

Sporadic gasps of ecstasy escaped from the mouth sliding hungrily up and dawn Laforge's swollen member, for in this position the knobbed tip of the sculptor's cavalier rubbed hard against the hypersensitive bud at the entrance to Corinne's temple of love, and the delicate friction of two skins there sent waves of pleasure shuddering through her at every stroke.

Laforge's head was tipped back against the wall. His mouth was open and his breathing was hoarse. Each time that sucking mouth, and the hot tongue twirling within it, plunged to the root of his maleness, his hips arched up off the bed and the surge of excitement mounting inexorably within him climbed one step higher towards that excruciating summit from which the final release would explode him into the void.

Corinne's hips thrust fiercely back to meet Crawford's every drive. Lost in the multiple joys of sensation stimulated at each sensitive spot, she drifted in trance-like freedom on a plateau of sensual delight . . . lulled by the compulsive, continuous, reciprocal rhythm established with her partners into a dream state where her mind could wander while the body occupied itself with the pleasure principle.

Superinduced by the effects of alcohol, the images chasing through her memory succeeded one another with the rapidity of the flickering figures on a cinematograph screen. She saw the brothel in the Rue St Andrédes-Arts . . . the pretentious blonde who ran it . . . the hilarious cab ride . . . the strange, wiry Englishman with his air of contained force who had left them for a whore . . . an odd, equivocal look beamed her way by the thin, dark girl who had been dressed as a *dominatrice* with a priest in tow. But most of all her mind returned, again and again, to the unexpected sight of another Englishman – a colleague, Laforge had told her, of the first.

It had been while they were waiting to be shown up to this room.

In the shadows below the curving stairway, they had remained invisible to a couple returning from an upstairs room. A young, dark girl, all bottom and breasts, sheathed in some kind of revealing oriental gown. A young man in evening dress.

'Good God!' Laforge had whispered explosively to the sculptor. 'That's Paul Mackenzie – Hector's partner in the motor business!'

Crawford had nodded. 'I remember. You introduced us.'

'In St Michel. That's right.' Laforge chuckled. 'The old rascal! I wanted to ask him along tonight, but he told me he couldn't manage it. A business appointment, he said.' Another chuckle. A shake of the head. 'Business all right. Funny business! But I don't reckon the internal combustion he was concerned with tonight had much to do with motor cars!'

'Shall we surprise him? Tell him he's been rumbled?'

'No, no.' Laforge laid a hand on the sculptor's arm. 'Let him keep his little secret. Let the perfidy of Albion not be unmasked . . . you never know when it might be useful, springing it on the fellow!'

Soon afterwards, Mackenzie had left the Chabanais.

Corinne was disappointed. As soon as she saw him, she had fallen prey to the familiar feeling: a deep, barely perceptible shudder within her, a tingling, tiny whisper escaping from the seat of her sensibility, a message from the base of her belly telling her: *I want that! I like it! I must have it!*

Sexual attraction is hard to define, impossible to quantify. You only know about it when it's there. It cannot be planned, cannot be prophesied. It is, as the French say, *un coup de foudre!* A thunderclap. A lightning flash. A bolt from the blue.

Corinne was struck. The young man was tall, athletic, with bushy side-whiskers, a generous mouth and clear eyes. His skin was healthily tanned. She didn't give a fig for his business, his 'perfidy'; the only secret that interested her was the mystery of what lay beneath those formal clothes. And only the touch of his fingers, the feel of his mouth, could solve that. Mentally, she had filed Monsieur Mackenzie away for future attention.

Now, on the divan, she transferred him to the tray marked *Pending*.

The triple rhythm was accelerating.

Tom Crawford, thudding against the girl's hips with a sudden frantic eagerness, found himself almost on the crest of that wave that breaks about the ears with a thunder of delight. Pumping faster, ever faster up and down the quivering shaft engorging her mouth, Corinne felt all her muscles contract. Above her bobbing head, Laforge's panting translated itself into a groan.

Was it the thought of that other body she had yet to see, the tempting imagination of bone and sinew and flesh beneath the formal attire of Paul Mackenzie? Or was it the simple mechanical result of prolonged physical action, of the power curve on the squared graph paper reaching its predestined optimum? Corinne never knew. She was aware only that the tension constricting her belly broke abruptly to send her soaring into the long shuddering spasms of joyous relief.

The wave broke. Crawford jerked upright, threw back his head and shouted aloud. Laforge's groan climbed the scale to end in a yelp of delight.

When it was all over and they had separated themselves, exhausted, among the cushions, Corinne smiled lazily and said: 'Now we shall send for champagne. And after that I shall lie on my back and teach you both something else!'

Downstairs in the reception hall, Hector Champney sat with his raincape draped over his shoulders, staring moodily into a glass of whisky and soda. He had made love four times in seventy-two minutes. His bruised lady had retired hurt. Now he wanted to go home.

For the tenth time he sprang open his watch and glanced at the time. He gazed towards the staircase up which his companions had vanished. 'What on *earth* can they be doing?' he muttered.

CHAPTER ELEVEN

Paul Mackenzie's visit to the Chabanais had not been planned. He had in fact had no intention of spending a solitary evening 'on the town': he had pleaded a business engagement as an excuse for refusing Bertrand Laforge's invitation simply because he was beginning to find the hospitality pressed on him by the industrialist's son more than a little fatiguing. A quiet dinner and an early night, he thought, would bring him back down to earth . . . and perhaps allow him time to work out some strategy in respect of the manufacturing secret he was supposed to wheedle out of the Laforges.

Alas for good intentions! Drinking an apéritif in the American Bar of his hotel, Paul found his thoughts yet again centring on the cool blonde beauty who lived in an apartment above the sculptor Tom Crawford's studio. It was now the third day since he bungled the attempt to force a meeting after he had seen her crossing the Place St Michel with her groceries, and he was as far away from her as ever. It was when he was ruminating on his ill-fortune that he noticed the young woman seated near the bar's entrance doors.

She could never have been taken for a twin sister – the features were a little older, a little coarser, the figure a little fuller – but the general effect was nevertheless a startling reminder of the Parisienne whose presence or, more exactly, absence, haunted his waking hours. She was on her own at a small table nursing an untasted bock – a nubile blonde wearing a floor-length, plum-coloured velvet gown whose hourglass silhouette and sensuous texture conveyed without too much subtlety the qualities of the fleshy body within.

The likeness, strictly relative, was striking enough just the same to compel Paul's attention – and in the moment that he paused, with his gaze fixed on her, the young woman caught his eye. And smiled.

It was a practised-smile, the flesh at the corners of the eyes crinkling convincingly, one cheek dimpling. But it was effective. With his mind picturing the unattainable Camille, Mackenzie involuntarily returned it. Seconds later, obeying an imperious pat on the leather cushions of the banquette, he was sitting beside her and ordering a bottle of champagne.

The solitary hotel dinner turned into a tête-à-tête in the 'omnibus' at Maxim's. This, after an impromptu table-top performance by dancers from the Vienna Opera's *Armurier de Tolède* at the Scala theatre, was transformed somehow into a party of more than a dozen people. And the evening ended, for Paul, at the Chabanais – although by now the blonde had vanished and he was with a young dark girl wearing some kind of oriental robe.

The girl's name was Lin. She was half Chinese, and in the two hours Paul spent with her many secrets of the Yin and Yang with which he was unfamiliar were revealed to him, along with certain Eastern love techniques which left parts of his body scarred by teethmarks and pinpricks – all of which had vanished by breakfast time the next morning.

Breakfast, taken in bed, was restricted to a large bowl of black coffee. Together with the morning paper, the room service waiter delivered a letter from Bertrand Laforge.

From the newspaper, he learned that there was trouble brewing between Serbia and the Austro-Hungarian empire. Vienna's rule extended over Yugo-Slavs who lived in Bosnia, but the free Yugo-Slavs of Serbia wanted the empire broken up so that they and their fellow countrymen could be united under the same flag. At home, the Irish too were agitating for Home Rule and there were strikes in the North.

From Laforge's letter, Paul learned of the forthcoming costume ball at Poiret's mansion. A gilt-edged invitation with Mackenzie's name added in a flowing script was included in the envelope. 'I engineered invitations for all of us through a charming young friend who designs for the couturier,' Bertrand had written. 'I do hope you can find the time to come, for it promises to be a very jolly occasion as well as one of the highlights of the Paris Season.' He had added the name and address of a costumier where suitable *déguisements* could be hired.

Paul's pulses quickened, reading the message. For he knew of course who the 'charming young friend' must be. Just the thought of her, of knowing that her hands had touched the stiff gilt-edged card, chased all memories of Mademoiselle Lin, of the blonde, the Viennese dancers and even of Nellie out of his mind.

It also gave him an idea. Here at last was a departure point, a springboard from which he could launch an offensive to gain the acquaintance of the elusive ice-maiden so cavalierly dismissed by Laforge's sculptor friend.

He swallowed the rest of his coffee, bathed, shaved, and dressed quickly, and then seated himself at a bureau beneath his bedroom window. The sun had returned, and the leaves of the young plane trees lining the boulevard below fluttered green and silver in a gentle breeze. He drew a sheet of hotel notepaper towards him and began to write.

I understand from our mutual friend Bertrand

Laforge that it is through your good offices and generosity that I have been sent an invitation to Monsieur Poiret's costume ball later this week, a gesture for which I hasten to express my warmest appreciation.

He paused for a moment, tapping his teeth with the end of the penholder. Through the window he could see pigeons wheeling against the blue sky. A woman hanging washing from the dormer of a building across the street. Finally, Paul leaned forwards, dipped his nib into a silver inkwell, and drew the paper towards him again. He added:

It would give me great pleasure – and permit me to express my thanks in a more personal way – if you would allow me the honour of escorting you to the ball. Should you, however, have a prior engagement, perhaps at least we could meet sometime during the evening, when I could once more make known to you the extent of my indebtedness?
The favour of an early reply would immeasurably enhance the gratitude of–
Your obedient servant,

> *Paul Mackenzie*

He read the letter through. The courtly circumlocution and slightly pompous tone would, he hoped, give the impression of a formal, serious man, a gentleman who could be trusted neither to exploit not to take advantage of a young woman in an artistic profession.

He folded the paper, slipped it into an envelope, and sealed it. That was when he realized with a pang of dismay that he had no clear recollection of the girl's correct name. Two of them, he remembered, shared the apartment. He had not been paying too much attention when Crawford first mentioned them. There was a Camille and a Corinne – or was it Claudine? Or even Cécile or Clarice? The names were so similar; the family names, he recalled, even more so. Never mind. There were ways around it, and ways to ensure the right girl got the message.

The letter itself had been addressed simply, 'Mademoiselle'. On the envelope, he reckoned, it would be correct to remain equally discreet. He wrote: *To Mademoiselle C.D.,* and added: *No. 123 Rue St André-des-Arts. By hand.*

Somebody had said that she usually arrived back from Poiret's *atelier* at about 6 p.m. He waited until five, took a cab to the Left Bank, bought two dozen red roses in the Buci market, and rang the bell at No. 123 at a quarter to six.

He handed the flowers and the envelope to the concierge. 'These are for the fair-haired young lady,' he said. 'The one who works for Monsieur Poiret. Perhaps you would be kind enough to see that she gets them when she returns?' He dropped coins into the woman's hand.

'*Bien, M'sieu.*' The concierge curtseyed, stowing the money in the wide pocket of her apron. 'She should have them in fifteen minutes.'

Paul walked to the Place St Michel and took a cab back to his hotel.

As it happened, Camille was late home that day and it was Corinne who arrived first. The concierge emerged from her office as the girl closed the outer door. 'Oh, Mademoiselle,' she said. 'A foreign gentleman left some flowers and a note for Mademoiselle Camille. Beautiful red roses they are. The only thing is, I have to go out before the market closes, and I was wondering . . .?'

'Don't worry, Madame Garand,' Corinne said. 'I'll take them up with me now and give them to her when she arrives.' She collected the bouquet and the envelope and carried them upstairs.

CHAPTER TWELVE

For the second day running, Paul Mackenzie received a letter with his morning paper. It was enclosed in a stiff envelope lined with midnight-blue silk paper, and a faint scent of lavender rose when he tore open the gummed flap. The message had been delivered by hand.

The single sheet of expensive deckle-edge writing paper inside had been folded once. With trembling fingers, not daring to imagine what news it might bring, he smoothed it out on his bureau. The neat lines of handwritten script read:

Monsieur,
It was with pleasure that I read your courteous note, delivered last night with the flowers, for which I hasten to thank you. I was naturally gratified to know that any small service I was able to provide had been of use to yourself and Monsieur Laforge.

With reference to your kind invitation, I have to say that I already have an escort, but would be pleased nevertheless to make your acquaintance. Above the reception lobby of Monsieur Poiret's house, there is a gallery beneath a glass conservatory dome. In the centre of this gallery, between two curving staircase arms, there is a palm tree surrounded by a padded bench. I shall be sitting there with my escort at exactly midnight, when we should be able to meet. I shall be costumed as Cleopatra, Queen of Egypt.

                                        Yours – C.D.

Paul devoured the lines with mounting excitement. Here, at last, was the chance he had been waiting for! Now, even with the encumbrance of an escort to contend with, he had been presented with the possibility of realizing that fantasy he had been nurturing for so many days! He was actually going to meet the girl of his dreams – and if the presence of another man inhibited the true expression of his feelings for her, even if it reduced the meeting to a mere formality, no matter: the all-important initial contact would have been made, and he would be free to call upon her, to advance his cause as it were in his own right on future occasions.

He read the letter a second, and then a third time, searching for hidden meanings, for hints of intrigue, for expressions of unusual interest between the lines. Absurd! She didn't even know what he looked like! Even if she had contacted Bertrand to satisfy herself that he was an acceptable person and no ne'er-do-well, there was no reason on earth why she should at this stage betray more than a normal polite interest in the possibility of a new social acquaintance.

The midnight meeting, though, in a conservatory – didn't that smack somehow of secrecy, of illicit love and, yes, of intrigue? Not when there was a third party present and the meeting was immediately above a reception foyer probably crowded with hundreds of people! It was no more, doubtless, than a convenient place to describe to someone who didn't know the house. And so far as the time was concerned, it might well be that the girl herself was arriving at the ball late. No – if there was to be any intrigue, Paul himself would have to initiate it.

Relaxing in his bath, he chuckled aloud. He would have to ask young Laforge if he had been pumped on the subject of his English friend. Meanwhile, he would call a cab and pay a visit to the theatrical costumier Bertrand had recommended.

Like most rumours, the gossip concerning Paul Poiret's oriental costume ball had enlarged upon the truth. The guest list was nearer 750 than 2,000, for instance. It was however one of the highlights of the Paris season. And 200 flamingoes had indeed been specially imported from Africa. They were lodged in an aviary built over an outsize ornamental pond and illuminated with fifty Japanese lanterns of different colours.

If the party was intended, as the gossips said, to stimulate interest in orientalism and the exotic – and thus, indirectly, promote the host's new 'Persian Look' – it was certainly successful. Socialite Paris had seen nothing like it since the scandalous 'fêtes' given by Boni de Castellane and the Comte Robert de Montesquiou a decade earlier.

The whole of what the French call the park – and the English the grounds – of the mansion had been pressed into service. Monkeys and cockatoos chattered and shrieked in the shrubberies. Nearer the house, live parrots were chained to bushes ablaze with electric blossoms. An immense blue and gold canopy had been erected beneath the trees on the far side of the pond, and beneath this, black slaves served exotic food at tables seventy feet long and paler female slaves lay feigning sleep on a golden staircase. Another buffet was installed in the courtyard beneath an awning painted by Raoul Dufy. Opposite this, a recreated 'Persian Market' housed slave traders, fortune tellers, beggars, cobblers, the sellers of sweetmeats and marmoset merchants.

At the centre of the festivities, the couturier himself sat in splendour on an elaborately decorated throne, next to his 'Imperial Gold Cage of Beautiful Favourites' – a voluptuous collection of semi-nude lovelies whose breasts and buttocks were only partly veiled by swathes of muslin sequined with flowers.

Corinne Dubois, briefed by her editor to write up the ball for a special weekend supplement, retired behind a small bandstand on which the music of flutes and zithers was being played, to make hurried notes. 'Monsieur Poiret,' she wrote, 'was sumptuously dressed in a pale grey quilted caftan edged with fur and belted by green silk. He wore a pair of ruby-red velvet buskins which were decorated with gold filigree, on his head was a white, bejewelled silk turban, and he carried a short sabre and an ivory-handled whip as a symbol of his authority.'

Corinne chewed her pencil, gazing past a costumed butcher who presided over a table laden with dead lambs at the glittering crowd of guests, arriving at the mansion now in their dozens. She smoothed the page of her notebook and wrote: 'Sultan-fat and smiling through his dark beard, the host sent the actor, De Max, in a costume shimmering with a thousand pearls, to greet each group of masked revellers with a recital of specially-written poems.'

She closed the book, snapped an elastic band around it, and went to the buffet for a skewer of *shashlik* flamed in Arak and a small bowl of mint and cucumber salad.

Paul Mackenzie arrived with Bertrand Laforge and Crawford at ten-thirty. By then the ball was well under way. A dense crowd of sultans, caliphs, Indian maharajahs, witch-doctors, fellaheen, Siamese princesses, geishas, coolies, camel-masters, belly dancers and harem wives flooded the gardens, spread through the courtyard and packed the interior of the huge house. There was dancing by the pool. In the ballroom, the American stars Vernon and Irene Castle were demonstrating the new South American sensation, the tango – condemned and forbidden by the Archbishop of Paris as 'immodest and degrading'. On one of the lawns, guests sprawled on colourful cushions and oriental rugs to watch a Persian snake-charmer accompanied by a naked white slave pirouetting in a cloud of gauze.

Mackenzie had chosen the costume of an eighteenth-century Japanese *samurai*, which had the advantage that the armoured helmet ruled out the necessity of a separate mask. Laforge was dressed as a Chinese mandarin. The sculptor was a brawny Viking in a winged helmet, which suited his physique but was scarcely suitable for an oriental evening.

'Thirty thousand shrimps were consumed,' Corinne wrote after a word with the head chef, 'five hundred each of lobsters, melons, goose livers; and twelve hundred litres of champagne.' She saw Laforge approaching, adjusted her mask, and went to join a group of acolytes surrounding the dancer Nijinsky – whose graphic, near-nude interpretation of animal lust in *L'Aprés-midi d'un Faune* at the Châtelet theatre was the sensation of Paris. 'But that extraordinary, unbelievable leap with which you make your entrance, *maître*,' one of the dandified young men said. 'How do you explain such a triumph, an exploit no other dancer can equal?'

The Diaghileff star smiled. 'The technique is very simple,' he replied in his Russian-accented, slightly mincing voice. 'All you have to do is jump as high as you possibly can . . . and then remain immobile for a moment in mid-air before you descend!'

There was a burst of laughter. Corinne moved away behind a fortune-teller's tent and re-opened her notebook. On the far side of the group, Laforge's mandarin draped a wide sleeve around the plump shoulder of a nubile Scheherezade wearing a full-face cat mask. Tom Crawford's muscular arms were already clasped around the waist of a slave girl in the ballroom. Eyes glittered behind the holes in her black carnival mask. 'I do hope,' she giggled when the tango music stopped, 'that the horns on that helmet don't mean what I think they mean!'

In a rose garden behind the gold staircase, white peacocks screamed as Paul Mackenzie began threading his way back towards the house. He passed a flock of pink ibis, pecking and fluttering around a huge cornelian urn. It was almost midnight; nothing must hinder his arrival beneath the indoor palm tree for the rendezvous which had kept his pulses racing all day long.

At exactly midnight, there was a fanfare of trumpets below Poiret's sultan throne. Two Nubian slaves unlocked the golden cage, flung open the barred gate, and out stepped Madame Poiret in costume as the ruler's favourite. A shout of admiration and applause rippled through the exotic throng. Corinne – briefed by Camille, who had worked on the ensemble – already had the details of the costume noted. The entry in her book read: 'She wore her husband's latest creation: loosely cut harem "pantaloons" in ochre and white chiffon, fitting tightly at the waist and ankles, under a short, hooped tunic of gauzy gold lamé which swayed in the evening breeze like some exotic eastern flower. The bodice was of chiffon and gold lame held in by a wide cummerbund, and the wide sleeves were edged with fur. A silver lamé Persian turban supporting a tall egret feather fastened with a turquoise clip completed this exquisite outfit.'

[Later, Corinne was to add to her copy: 'More than fifty of Poiret's female guests besieged the couturier's showroom as a result of this spectacle, each determined to share the freedom – and of course the fashionable cachet – of this revolutionary "oriental" line. Half of these were queuing up before noon the very next day!']

Inside the mansion, a few entwined couples decorated the gilt ottomans and chaises-longues furnishing the reception foyer. Most of the guests had obeyed the summons of the trumpet fanfare and gone outside to witness Poiret's tour-de-force. A single Turk, his mask awry, an empty champagne glass upended beside him, lay snoring on the curving staircase.

Mackenzie stepped over the recumbent figure and ran swiftly up the remaining steps to the gallery.

He saw at once why the rendezvous had been timed for midnight. Oil lamps illuminating statues in marble niches cast wavering shadows around the semicircular walls, but the gallery was otherwise deserted.

His heart thumped in his chest. Deserted? Warily he approached the palm tree soaring up into the glass dome. A padded seat, as he had been told, encircled the wide bole. He walked out wide. A single figure, in deep shadow, was perched on the far side.

A single figure? He approached, treading softly, then halted as a husky voice quietly intoned: 'Monsieur Mackenzie?'

This time, Paul's heart leaped. Half hidden in the obscurity, it was Cleopatra all right. Avidly, his eyes took in the Pharaoh-style headdress surmounted by an ideogram in the form of a bird; the helmet-close black wig cut severely into a fringe over the forehead; a breast-plate fashioned from overlapping, concentric rows of shell *paillettes*, hanging from the shoulders; a long, slim gown ornately embroidered with mystic symbols. A gold velour mask covered the face from the eyebrows to the upper lip.

'Mademoiselle . . .?' Paul advanced hesitantly. 'May I be permitted to present myself? . . . Your servant, Paul M-m-m-mackenzie. From London.'

A soft laugh rippled from below the mask. He saw a gleam of teeth. One coarse, wide, embroidered sleeve fell away from a slender arm as the young woman extended a hand towards him. 'Advance, Paul M-m-m-mackenzie and be recognized,' she mocked.

He blushed, bowing stiffly, feet together, as he took the hand. His lips brushed ringless fingers.

'It is extremely kind of you, Mademoiselle, to consent to this meeting,' he said. 'I had not really hoped . . . that is, I had seen you at a distance while walking with our mutual friend, and I knew at once, so beautiful did you look, that I must make every conceivable effort to make your acquaintance.'

'Monsieur is charitable!'

'Far from it, I assure you. I had never seen . . . well, this perhaps gauche, so happily terminated stratagem is the result of that desire.' He swallowed, eyeing the vacant bench on either side of her. 'I was afraid, nevertheless . . . I mean I understood from your letter . . .?

'Oh,' she said. 'Yes of course. My . . . escort. He is . . . yes, he is concerned with the organization of Monsieur Poiret's fête. He apologises but he is obliged to consult with our host's major-domo.'

'What a shame. I am so sorry,' said Paul mendaciously. 'Will he . . . that is, shall he be able to join us later?'

'Not for some time.'

'I see.' Faced unexpectedly with a situation that was more than he dared hope for – the opportunity to monopolize his inamorata 'for some time' – the young Englishman was suddenly at a loss for words. He glanced over the gallery balustrade. Now that the big moment of the evening had come and gone, and the cheers and applause and ooh-aah's of the spectators were dying away, guests were crowding back, in twos and threes and groups, into the courtyard and from there to the main entrance hall below. Among them, waiters hurried with trays of champagne.

'Er . . . since your escort is unavoidably absent,' Paul said. 'The least I can do is take his place and fetch you something refreshing to drink. What can I get that would give you pleasure?'

'Thank you. Monsieur is very kind.' Beneath the golden mask, a smile appeared. A lower lip glistened enticingly in the shadows. Was there a glint of amusement in those hidden eyes. 'It may sound banal,' the girl said, 'but since I have been drinking it already, I fancy a glass of the champagne being so deftly dispensed below would be ideal.'

'At once,' said Paul, and he almost ran to the stairs. When he returned with two brimming glasses, she patted the deep-buttoned seat beside her – memories, quickly suppressed, of the blonde . . . the coarse and elderly and altogether detestable blonde! . . . in the hotel's American bar – and smiled invitingly again. 'Come, sit down,' she said, 'and tell me all about yourself. What are you doing in Paris?'

'Business originally. But I find . . .' He paused looking doubtfully at the stairhead. Several couples were heading for the gallery. A stout Queen of Sheba and her fat, perspiring escort lowered themselves to the seat on the far side of the palm. 'Isn't there somewhere,' he asked, 'perhaps a little more . . .?'

She rose swiftly to her feet, holding out one hand. 'Of course. I too detest private conversations before an audience.' She glanced angrily over her shoulder at the intruding heavyweights. 'But I know the house well. There are rooms . . . on the upper floors . . . where one can decently exchange confidences without fear of interruption.' She led him to an archway on the far side of the semicircular gallery. Beyond the arch was a thickly carpeted corridor and a double row of closed doors. At the end of this passageway, a second opening led to a small landing from which a back staircase rose to the mansion's third, fourth and fifth storeys.

Cleopatra, still holding a half-filled glass, climbed rapidly upwards. Paul, nursing what remained of his own champagne, hurried behind . . . and marvelled, seeing a foot in a gold slipper, a slender ankle, the elegantly tapered calf above and even – what scandalous license! – a flash of thigh, that the close-fitting

Egyptian robe was slit each side to a point well above the knee.

And what had she meant . . . what could she have meant . . . by an exchange of *confidences*? Was the word intended purely in a general sense? Or did this exquisite creature, Crawford's untouchable ice-maiden who wouldn't let any man come near her, really intend to confide in a perfect stranger, and a foreigner at that? Even the thought of it kept the young man's heart hammering against his ribs.

A broad hallway islanded with Louis XVI chairs was visible, passing the next floor. He saw costumed couples in earnest conversation. A Malay chieftain laid a plate piled high with sea-food on an escritoire inlaid with ivory and mother-of-pearl. A house-maid led a pug dog on a jewelled leash.

The girl kept climbing. On the third floor, Paul saw through an open door the shelved books and leather-covered easy chairs of a library. Beyond it, a row of tailor's dummies swathed in rich materials stood colourfully at attention. He heard subdued voices, an explosion of stifled laughter.

It was on the next flight of stairs that it happened.

There was a half-landing, and then a right-angle turn, after which the flight continued between two walls, closed in on either side. On the half-landing she turned to face him, drank what was left in her glass, then placed it on the sill of a small leaded window set in the outer wall. She smiled. 'Sometimes the last part is the hardest of all,' she said enigmatically.

He smiled back, drank his own drink, put the empty glass beside hers. No reply seemed necessary. She drew a deep breath, turned again, and started once more to climb.

It was on the third or fourth step that the thin leather sole of one of her gold pumps slipped on the edge, throwing her temporarily off balance. She fell backwards with a small cry, her arms flung wide.

A couple of paces behind, Paul naturally rushed to catch her, to break her fall, his hands shooting beneath those arms to clasp her around the waist.

She subsided against him, the headdress tipped back against his shoulder, her two hands dropped to cover his own. 'Thank you,' she said breathlessly. 'That was very silly of me. What a good thing you were there!'

He was about to make some would-be gallant rejoinder – what a splendid thing for him if he could always be there! – when she moved slightly . . . not away but closer. He couldn't believe it, but it was unquestionably, agonizingly true: her tight little bottom was thrusting, grinding against that part of his loins which had lusted after her in secret for so long! The whole voluptuous length of her was draped suggestively against him from shoulder to knee!

He sucked in his breath sharply, aware of the instant hardening of his flesh within the tight sheath of the costume's buckskin breeches. She took away her hands then – but in such a way that she shifted his own higher up her body.

Paul gasped again. The semicircular breastplate covered her from the neck down, falling over the swell of the bust to hang free above the waist. The robe hugged her from the hips to the diaphragm, fitting snugly skin-tight. But the breasts themselves, immediately above, were completely unclothed – nude beneath the cold caress of those rows of shell *paillettes*.

Paul barely had time to register this astonishing fact – his forefingers no more than brushing the full, taut lower curves of these fleshy mounds – before the girl had twisted around to face him and thrown her arms around his neck.

He staggered back, taken completely by surprise. Even the unmistakable pressure against his loins, in itself totally outside his wildest expectations, had not prepared him for this.

She kissed him then, standing on tiptoe to crush her mouth on his, kissed him fiercely, almost greedily, her hot tongue darting between his lips, across his teeth, along his gums. Her hands cradled the back of his head, drawing him down towards her; a knee thrust itself between his thighs; her belly swung hard against him.

Dazedly, he responded, hesitantly at first and then with increasing abandon as it was borne in on him that this was no fantasist's dream, that the nubile body plastered against him was shouting yes-yes-yes with everything except words. Their tongues met in a muscled, probing joust. His hands clenched on the soft flesh of her hips. The backs of her legs trembled.

Abruptly, she freed her mouth, leaning back against his embrace. Wet lips smiled. She was breathing hard, the rise and fall of her breasts provoking a faint rattle from the shells. Through the eyeholes in the gold mask he saw again that telltale gleam. 'Oh, you!' she murmured.

They kissed again. The velour of the mask scraped his cheek, displacing the fronds of artificial metal hanging from the peak of his helmet. The Pharaoh headdress fell to the floor. Breaking away, she stooped to pick it up and ran up the last flight of stairs.

Party noises, crowd sounds, the surge of music were all muted, here in the curtained luxury of the fourth floor. Heavy drapes covered the windows. Costly oriental rugs glowed in rich colours beneath crystal chandeliers whose electric lamps had been toned down to an amber radiance that blurred hard lines and suffused the wide corridor with warmth. Halfway along, a huge T'ang pot stood on a marble-topped Empire commode. 'Bedrooms, bathrooms, guest suites,' the girl whispered. 'Would you believe it, the house has *seven* bathrooms, counting one for the servants!' She took his hand. 'Come

– I know the most *stunning* room!'

Together, they ran down the passageway. The doors were ivory white, the panels picked out in gold. She stopped before one at the far end, twisted the decorated porcelain handle, and flung the door open ... to stiffen, stock still, with one hand flown to her mouth; to exclaim: '*Oh!* Oh, my goodness, I'm so sorry! I didn't know ...'

She backed out hastily, pulling the door shut after her – but not before Paul had glimpsed the tangle of limbs on the four-poster bed; pink, nippled flesh among a swirl of white lace; the sudden shock of black pubic hair – and a bearded face starting up angrily from the pillows.

Cleopatra giggled. She shook her head. 'I should have known,' she said. She tiptoed back down the corridor, listening outside each door. Murmurations, bawdy laughter, groans, small mewls of ecstasy, the smack of a hand on bare skin and the multiple creak of bedsprings ... Paul heard them all. Every single room was occupied.

The girl opened the double doors of a walk-in linen cupboard. Beyond the well-stocked slatted shelves, a wooden stairway led still further up. She pulled him towards it. 'We're beneath the dormers, here on the fifth,' she told him when they had climbed to the top floor. 'Where the servants used to be, only now they all sleep in the annexe. But there's a place I think you'd like along here.'

It was what had once been a housekeeper's sitting-room, but was now used as a kind of repository, an overflow depot, for pictures, ornaments, *objets* and items of furniture that no longer took their owner's fancy or – worse! – had gone out of style.

The original equipment – a rocking chair, a solid, plain oak dressing table, an enamel bidet on an iron stand, a brass bedstead with a chenille cover – was easily identifiable. Surrounding these pieces, flooding against them in a tide of Poiret bizarrerie, were cages of stuffed tropical birds, busts on plinths, cabinets of *chinoiserie*, a huge nineteenth-century clock displaying its innards beneath a glass dome, an *art-nouveau* settee whose curlicue wooden frame incorporated a small bookcase and a rack for bottles and glasses.

The windows were uncurtained. The only light, a changing pattern of reds and blues and greens, filtered up from the illuminations in the grounds to underline the Aladdin's-cave atmosphere of the room.

The girl stood by the bed, the ancient Egyptian costume less out of place here than it had been in the brightly lit rooms below. 'Come to me,' she said.

Paul's mind was reeling. He felt intoxicated with joy, a man walking on an invisible sheet of glass, a foot above the floor. 'I don't understand,' he stammered. 'This is the most fantastic, the most outstandingly marvellous . . .' His voice died away. He was speechless.

She laughed, a small melodious sound in the gloom. The gold mask rendered her face expressionless in the changing light. 'As your English poet has it, there are more things in heaven and earth than are dreamed of in your automobile manufactory!'

It was his turn to laugh. The spell was broken; he was in command of the situation. 'I don't know that Shakespeare's interest in the internal combustion engine ran very deep,' he said, 'but I accept unreservedly the proposition!'

She raised her arms, lifting the breastplate away from the bared perfection of her bosom. 'Come,' she said again. 'Do I have to ask a second time? Do I have to plead?'

He shook his head. Wordlessly, he moved towards her, his hands outstretched. 'Put them here,' she commanded. She took him by the wrists and planted his palms against her naked breasts.

The thrill that Paul experienced, feeling the cool weight of those swelling mounds fall into his hands like ripe fruit, shot through him from head to foot and then concentrated in his aching loins. 'Camille . . .' he said hoarsely. 'Mademoiselle . . . may I presume to address you by your first name?'

'We are not in a situation that encourages formality,' the girl said. She knocked away a bolt of luridly coloured satin that was leaning against the brass rail, brushed aside a stack of fashion magazines, and sat on the bed.

Giddy still from the sensation of those breasts within the clasp of his hands, the nipples hard and rubbery against his palms, he lowered himself to the mattress beside her. 'Now kiss me again, the way you did on the stairs,' she said.

He took her in his arms, pressing her back against the pillows.

It was then, while their questing tongues wrestled together in the hot caverns of their mouths, that he felt lean fingers tighten on the hard bulge thrusting out the crotch of his buckskin breeches.

He started, the heart thudding against his chest, as the fingers traced the vibrant outline of his manhood, circled the throbbing tip, and then grazed down the smooth material to cradle the sensitive pouch below. A second hand wedged itself between them now to close in on the rigid shaft.

Paul's whole body was shuddering with desire. He freed his mouth for long enough to gasp: 'Camille . . . my treasure, my beauty, my love . . . I want–'

She stopped him with a finger against his lips. Her breath was hot on his flushed face. 'I know exactly what you want,' she whispered. 'And fortunately for both of us, I want it too!'

She rolled suddenly out of his embrace. And then, mysteriously, almost magically, she turned away and re-turned, leaving the Egyptian robe, unwrapped and discarded, on the far side of the bed. Apart from the breastplate and a linen undershift, she was naked from neck to ankle!

While he watched, unbelieving, she reached behind her to unsnap a clasp and cast aside the shell breastplate. She kicked off the gold slippers and hauled the shift up to her waist.

In the diffuse light, the long pale length of her nudity glimmered mauve and ochre and tawny red as the illuminations changed in the gardens below. Fascinated by the reflections on her satined skin, Paul traced with his eyes the sensuous outline of hip and thigh and tapered leg. He exulted in the scooped subtlety of her waist and drowned in the fathomless depth between her breasts. In the shadows too where her belly dipped to the furred chalice between those thighs, his imagination wandered.

Only the black Cleopatra wig and the gold mask hid the totality of her nakedness from him now. He raised a hand to lift the mask . . . but she seized his wrist with both hands and pushed it forcefully away.

'Please,' he said, 'Camille . . .'

'No!' The voice was sharp. The black-fringed head shook from side to side. 'It's a *masked* costume ball. That's part of the rules. Faces must stay hidden until the sun rises.'

'Does that apply to me too?' He touched the *samurai* helmet. 'The peak is awkward and this fringe thing, this so-called metal curtain gets in the way when we kiss,' he objected.

'It applies to everyone; it's part of the rules,' the girl repeated.

Still holding his errant hand, she pressed it to the base of her belly. 'In any case, there are more interesting places for fingers to be! Here, for instance' – the pressure on his hand increased and he felt his forefinger glide suddenly into a warm damp crevice among the hairs – 'and of course *here!*' His breeches were ripped open and his drawers tweaked aside as an intruding hand seized the stiffened proof of his desire.

He leaned over her then with an inarticulate cry, lowering his mouth to the rosebud tip of one quivering breast. While he sucked and kissed, rotating with his tongue the erectile bud of flesh, his free hand crept up to fondle with loving care its twin. The fingers of the other hand, exploring, probing, dipping, invading the all-at-once sliding wetness of the girl's secret part, stroked small sighs of ecstasy from her parted lips.

She was massaging him now, forcefully, with determination, feeling the swollen tightness of his throbbing shaft pulse against her hand.

Her hips arched up off the bed to meet the quickening rhythm of his caress.

His loins ached with the intensity of his need, his every tingling nerve threatening to explode the spearhead of his lust as those cool fingers pumped his masculinity to fever pitch.

And then suddenly she pushed him away, both hands scrabbling at the quilted bulk of his false armour, wrenching down the waistband of his drawers.

'Take it off!' she panted. 'All of it, except the headdress. I want all of you . . . next to me . . . now!'

He leaped to the side of the bed, tearing off the different elements of the costume, casting away his own underclothes as fast as he could. His rigid member sprang free.

He turned back towards her . . . to find her lying shamelessly in the most obscene position. She had spread her thighs, drawn up her knees and grasped her ankles to expose the entire hairy furrow of her underparts to Paul's lascivious gaze.

Immediately, he scrambled back to kneel between those parted legs. At the same time, she let go of her ankles and grasped the fleshy staff spearing towards her with one urgent hand. With the other she grabbed the glandular sac hanging below. She pulled him fiercely down.

Paul shot forward, the upper half of his body hinged over her belly and breasts, his weight supported on outstretched arms. His hips sank between her raised thighs. Guided by demanding fingers, his genitals grazed the springy curls sheathing the girl's pubic mound.

A groan of suppressed excitement escaped him as she stirred the engorged tip of his magic wand into the warm clasp of her secret lips. Warmth, then wetness, then scalding heat surrounded the throbbing head. Hot flesh wrapped around the stiffened shaft.

Suddenly she straightened her legs, scissored them over his back, lowered her heels to press forcefully on his buttocks, driving him into her. The whole rigid length of him was swallowed within the burning, muscled grasp of her belly.

For a moment he remained there, buried to the hilt, staring down at the black wig, the mask, her quivering breasts. Then slowly he subsided, lying along her body, the breasts squashed against the hairs on his chest, his hands slipped beneath her bottom to press her hips ever more closely to his loins.

Beneath the mask, a full lower lip gleamed in the pulsing light. He sucked it into his mouth. Gently at first and then with increasing force, he started a rocking movement that drove him in and out of her in a compulsive rhythm matched perfectly by the arching of her loins off the bed. Her ankles crossed over the small of his back. Her arms tightened over his shoulders. Her nails raked the skin on either side of his spine as the heaving of her chest increased.

Hearts pounded, pulses hammered, breaths quickened. The reciprocal coupling of their two bodies accelerated, the rhythm faster, faster and more ferocious.

The slap and suck of flesh against flesh moved towards a manic crescendo, driving them ever closer to the summit of their shared lust with each pistoned thrust of his athletic hips.

And then suddenly – violently, passionately – every hypersensitive nerve end in Paul's pumping body seemed to gather itself into his loins. He cried aloud, and with the force of an oncoming, thundering waterfall spewed the proof of his devotion deep into the flesh of the girl beneath him.

Her response was instant. With a long shuddering groan that died away into a series of convulsive gasps, she spasmed her own release hard up against the muscular embrace of her lover.

Waking later, with the sounds of the revelry five floors below a little diminished, Paul found delicate fingers still wrapped around his quiescent male stem. She was sleeping with her back to him, the warm weight of one breast against a hand thrust beneath her recumbent form.

The realization that he lay nakedly entwined with the girl of his dreams, and the sudden delirious memory of the sexual rapport which had gone before, was enough to stir his manhood into immediate stiffened awareness.

He reached his free arm over to cup the still damp triangle of hair between her thighs in the moment that her fingers, aware in their turn of his reawakened desire, tightened on his staff.

The first idyllic encounter behind them, they were able this time to allow their imagination to order their actions. It started when she murmured against his searching mouth: 'There are other lips, you know, worthy of your kisses!' And continued, via successive adventures in lovemaking that dazzled him with their inventiveness, to a point where they both fell exhausted into a dreamless sleep.

Paul awoke for the second time with the memory of

the night's excesses still fresh in his excited mind. 'Camille . . .' he murmured drowsily. 'My God . . . Oh, my God, you're so wonderful . . .'

He was suddenly wide awake.

A clip-clop of horse's hooves was the only sound that came to his ears. A shaft of sunlight, slanting through the uncurtained window, lay across his face. Sunlight? Sunrise! At last he could see the features of the girl he loved! He rolled over on the mattress.

He was alone in the cluttered room. Of the girl with the golden mask there was no sign.

CHAPTER THIRTEEN

Dagmar van den Bergh was excited. A motor carriage she had ordered from an exclusive manufacturer had just arrived from England.

The car, designed by the Hon. C.S. Rolls and Mr. F.H. Royce and assembled in their Cook Street works, was immensely expensive, the engine and chassis alone costing nine hundred and fifty English pounds, and the coach-built body as much again.

This body, or *habitacle*, was huge. High and square, almost in the manner of a small stage-coach, it was equipped with two doors and four windows on each side, a panoramic, wrap-around rear window divided into three sections, and a vast plate-glass windscreen. Thin glass panels were also inset at each side of the windscreen and between the windows and roof. There were thus no less than 25 separate panes through which the occupants, cossetted by deep-button hide upholstery, could stare at the passing countryside and their less fortunate fellow citizens.

The seven-litre six-cylinder motor, with its elegant, silver-shuttered radiator, was stowed low down between flared front mudguards rather like a horse between its shafts.

A galleried roof on which the spare tyre was concealed, polished brass acetylene lamps, and a comprehensive hand-crafted mahogany toolbox screwed to one of the wide running-boards completed the equipment.

The silver bodywork was decorated with a deep maroon coach-line embodying the Van den Bergh crest and a VdB monogram on each door.

'They call it the "Silver Ghost",' the Comtesse told her German friend, Baroness Gisela von Zwickenheim, 'because the machinery that powers it is completely noiseless.'

'Fortunately there is a klaxon as well as a bulb horn,' said Gisela. 'Otherwise you would be massacring pedestrians who couldn't hear you coming!'

The Sunday after Paul Poiret's costume ball, Dagmar decided to celebrate the new acquisition with a country picnic. Her coachman was in England, attending a course in driving and maintenance, for the Rolls Royce company would only accept guarantee responsibility if a chauffeur had been trained by their own experts. It did not, it seemed, occur to them that anyone who could afford one of their machines would wish to conduct the vehicle themselves. Gertrude Margarete Zelle, however, was an efficient driver: she had learned on the big Minerva limousines manufactured in her country. It was agreed, therefore, that she should have the privilege of driving the Rolls on its first outing.

Apart from her and Dagmar, the party consisted of Gisela von Zwickenheim, Marie-Ange Foucault de la Roquette, Agathe Laforge and – surprisingly – Nellie Lebérigot. Six attractive women of whom only one (and she, paradoxically, the most sexually experienced) was ignorant of the Sapphic cult.

The drive, the Comtesse decided, would take them north through the suburb of Montmartre, past St Denis, and then to a stretch of country between the forest of Montmorency and the Parc de Courneuve, somewhere near the new aerodrome outside Le Bourget.

Dagmar, Gisela, Nellie and Mme Laforge occupied the salon-like rear compartment; Marie-Ange sat in front with Mademoiselle Zelle – or Mata Hari, as she preferred to be called.

It was a fine day, with high white clouds sailing in from the west, and frequent bright intervals, when the sun was very warm. 'Perfect for a picnic!' said Dagmar. 'I could not have wished for a better, had I ordered the weather myself!' (She had in fact ordered the picnic meal – from Fauchon, the exclusive food store in the Place de la Madeleine – which was packed into a fitted hamper twinned with the mahogany toolbox on the opposite running-board.)

The huge car sped silently up the hill to Montmartre, past the popular dance hall below the Moulin de la Galette, through narrow streets crowded with working folks in their Sunday best, east of the remaining farm and vineyard behind the baroque magnificence of the Sacré Coeur, and out along the flat country beyond.

They bypassed the town of Le Bourget and took a road that skirted the new aerodrome. Several monoplanes that looked like open parasols minus the handle were parked in front of the one-storey wooden clubhouse. Two 'flying birdcage' biplanes, with polished wood struts and doped fabric wings, stood nearby. A larger machine, manhandled across the grass towards a canvas hangar by a group of overalled mechanics, housed pilot and observer in a covered nacelle, with the engine and propeller behind them among a network of spars.

'That's an FE-2B,' Mata Hari said over her shoulder. 'F and E stand for Farman Experimental. Henri Farman hopes the French army may use the model as a mobile observation post, to correct the artillery's aim. The Nieuport company and the SPAD concern are also working on machines for the army, but those are concerned more with scouting activities.'

'You are very well informed, Margarete,' said Dagmar.

'I have a friend who works with the military,' the young woman replied.

Oak trees and lime and weeping willow shaded the secluded spot where they decided to lunch – a grassy dingle on the banks of the Croult river, not far from the hamlet of Les Maronniers.

Mata Hari ran the Rolls Royce fifty yards along a woodland ride, where it would be sheltered from the direct rays of the sun, while Dagmar and her German friend laid out the contents of the picnic hamper: fresh brioches and butter, gulls' eggs in aspic, a duck paté, shredded celery in a mustard sauce, cold salmon mayonnaise and a variety of salads and cheese. Bottles of Chablis had been kept cool in the four earthenware pockets incorporated – one at each inner corner – in the fitted hamper.

Seated around a white cloth spread on the grass, the six women – their wide straw hats loaded with fruit and flowers, their tight formal clothes discarded in favour of freer, looser garments in pale shades of mauve and pink and heliotrope – could have been posing for a conversation piece by Renoir or Vuillard.

There was a lot of laughter, a certain amount of badinage, every now and then a subtle undercurrent of ambiguity as one of Dagmar's guests or another lanced some conversational ball loaded with special meaning into the arena. Later, when the level in the wine bottles had appreciably sunk, the shafts became more pointed. At one moment, when the others were discussing the vulgarity of some *Amazone* in the Bois, the Comtesse drew Nellie aside and whispered: 'You know I'm very disappointed in you, my dear . . . No, don't say anything! You cannot deny it: you have not been once to our dear friend René Vivien's Temple of Friendship in the Rue Jacob! And I'll wager' – the Comtesse laughed her silvery laugh – 'I'll wager you never even saw another copy of our feminist magazine *La Fronde*!'

Smiling, Nellie had to admit that this was true.

'You don't know what you're missing,' Dagmar said. 'Especially . . . when . . .' She bit her lip and shook her head. 'Never mind.'

'Look, Madame, let us be frank,' said Nellie. 'You know very well the profession I follow; you yourself, after all, visit Milady's often enough. What you are suggesting is that, because I hire out my body to men, individuals with whom I have nothing in common but a commercial transaction, then I am unlikely to find genuine pleasure in the arms of yet another male. That the physical love of women, on the other hand, because it had no sordid overtones, could bring me delights that the profession otherwise denies me. Am I not right?'

'Something like that.'

'Well, permit me to tell you something, Madame. I *chose* my profession: I was not forced into it. Nothing else open to an uninformed girl from Brittany offered anything like the same rewards. Apart from which, I *like* having sex with men. Many of my clients – not all, of course – but many give me actual pleasure, and there are a few with whom I have established a caring relationship, not wholly based on the pleasures of the flesh.'

'Yes, my dear, but if only you realized–'

'I am of course,' Nellie continued, unwilling to be interrupted, 'fortunate in that I work at Milady's house. A street whore from Montmartre, a woman obliged to patrol the *promenoir* at the Folies Bergère, or one of the poor creatures working a *brasserie des filles* would doubtless view the matter differently. They, poor things, have no choice.'

Nellie wiped a fragment of brioche around her plate, recuperating the last of the salmon mayonnaise. She licked her lips. Watching the moist pink tip of that tongue brush the smooth skin, Dagmar saw that the wide brim of the young woman's hat, shading her face from the sun, had left her eyes too enigmatically shadowed. 'Let me pour you some wine,' she said. 'This is a particularly good vintage, don't you think? One can usually rely on Fauchon.'

'It is delicious,' Nellie said politely, accepting the glass and swallowing a mouthful. She dabbed her lips with a paper napkin.

'It's the same Sauvignon grape,' said Dagmar, 'but personally I find the dry quality of Chablis more agreeable than that full, fruity, rather *vulgar* flavour characterizing the other Loire whites – Sancerre, for instance.'

'Oh, yes,' said Nellie. She drank some more. 'I find your friends quite charming. All of them.' She stared across the wreckage of the meal. Beyond the white cloth, the used dishes, the *barquettes* still strewn with fragments of salad and the empty glasses, Marie-Ange Foucault de la Roquette and the Baroness lay on their backs, hands locked behind their heads, staring up into the leafy branches. Mata Hari and Agathe Laforge were sitting in the long grass, deep in conversation. The industrialist's wife, a blade of grass between her lips, was absently picking daisies and threading them into a chain.

'Charming,' Nellie repeated. 'And sympathetic. Beautiful too. But I have to tell you, Madame, much though I appreciate your invitation and your kindness, that my interest stops there. I have no wish to explore the . . . mysteries . . . of your cult. Or visit your meeting place in the Rue Jacob.'

The Comtesse laughed again. 'Your vehemence does you credit,' said she. 'Though I suspect it is due to the fact that something deep within you whispers that you would enjoy such an adventure . . . but are afraid to admit it! For the moment, however, there is only one small favour I would ask of you.'

'And that is?'

'That you would cease addressing me as Madame. My name is Dagmar.'

It was Nellie's turn to laugh. 'That is easily granted
. . . Dagmar!'

Agathe Laforge and Mata Hari had risen to their feet
and wandered away between the trees. In the dappled
sunlight, Nellie saw that they were holding hands. The
Dutch-Indonesian wore the daisy-chain around her
neck.

She brushed away a wasp that was hovering over the
depleted cheese board. 'Most interesting, your Dutch
friend. She told me, when we met at your house, that
she is a dancer.'

Dagmar nodded. 'A technique based on Javanese
temple rhythms. She was given a spot once in one of
the Moulin Rouge revues. She wears a most ornate
oriental costume. Poiret would love it. In fact he does –
she gave a private show to a few of his intimates during
the ball at his place a few nights ago. Were you there?'

Nellie shook her head. She was feeling sleepy. Her
glass was unaccountably full again. She sipped some
Chablis.

'It was quite fun,' the Comtesse said. 'Quite scandalous too! Private parties of course are where Margarete's talents can really be exploited.'

'What kind of talents?'

'Oh . . .' The Comtesse waved an airy hand. 'You
wouldn't approve, dear Nellie. But once she is unclothed,
she can suggest, most subtly, all manner of interesting
behaviour, involving all kinds of people and all kinds
of sex. On stage, unhappily, she is less free. She is
obliged, for one thing, to wear those extraordinary conical metal breastplates as part of her costume.' The
Comtesse giggled. 'You know what that dreadful Colette
said? She said: "So would I, if I had breasts like
hers!" . . . But that is unfair, really. Margarete's body is
soft, her waist is a little fleshy – but she can do the
most amazing things with that body when she feels like
it.'

'How nice for Madame Laforge,' Nellie said. She drained her glass.

The drowsy afternoon continued its inexorable progress. Flies buzzed. Water rippled. Around a bend in the stream, a train clanked across an iron bridge. In the woodland glade, the shadows lengthened. Dark, doll-like Marie-Ange was asleep with her head on Gisela von Zwickenheim's shoulder.

Nellie stretched and yawned. Her limbs felt heavy. The sun had reached her and she was suddenly too hot. 'Why don't we sit in the car until the others are ready to go?' Dagmar suggested. 'It will be cool there in the shade; you can drop off for a minute if you like; and we'll escape the ants I can see advancing towards us on the far side of our lunch remains!' She helped Nellie to her feet.

It *was* pleasantly cool in the spacious interior of the Rolls. A cloud of mosquitoes boiled in the fading sunshine beneath the trees, but they were on the far side of the limousine's closed windows. Inside, there was a comforting smell of rich leather and polished wood, of expensive carpeting and – a hint only – some subtle, exotic perfume. Nellie relaxed gratefully on the soft upholstery.

The Comtesse was perched on one of the folding occasional seats that hinged down from the partition separating the chauffeur from his passengers. Between the two seats, a shallow cabinet in figured walnut had been installed. The lid of this too folded down to reveal an interior lined with mirror glass, a rack of small goblets, and two flasks of liquor in silver cradles.

'A little cognac?' the Comtesse proposed. 'Unless you would prefer a calvados? No meal is complete without a *digestif*, I always think . . . and here, do try one of these madeleines. They're quite fresh: Gisela made them herself this morning.'

Obediently, Nellie bit into the small cake – it was

quite delicious – and swallowed a mouthful of the smooth, strong spirit. She was freed from all tension now, completely at her ease. The second brandy tasted even better than the first.

She awoke with her face pillowed on something soft and resilient.

The sun was much lower now. A shaft of light filtering through the branches struck gleams of gold from a brass clock set in the limousine's instrument panel. Over the clock's solemn tick, she could hear birdsong in the distance.

There was an arm around her shoulders. Gentle fingers cradled one cheek.

Dear God – she was sprawled shamelessly back on the seat with her head resting on the Comtesse's generous bosom! She struggled to sit up.

'Don't be alarmed: your virtue is quite safe!' said Dagmar van den Bergh.

'No, it's not that I was alarmed. But, really . . .' Nellie smiled. She found herself – quite unexpectedly – laughing. Why? What was so funny? Could she be laughing out of pure *pleasure*? What did it matter, after all? She felt good; she was relaxed; she had eaten a delicious lunch on a perfect day. Why should she worry just because, after a most satisfying little nap, her hostess had put an arm around her to stop her toppling over sideways on the seat?

It was ridiculous. Nellie stretched languorously. People paid far too much attention to the way things *looked*: it was the way one *felt* that counted.

Outside the car, the sunlight was a little hazy. A breeze rustled the trees; leaves tapped one of the limousine windows. Beckoning fingers. The song of birds, a whole chorus now, filling the dreamy woodland ride with melody, was suddenly very loud . . . and then faded away to a distant murmur.

Her head was still resting on Dagmar's breast!

Nellie opened her eyes (she didn't remember closing them: how odd). She was staring at the smoothest peach-bloom slope of skin . . . at a cleft separating that swelling mound from the exquisite curve of its twin. The Comtesse was wearing a silk blouse in sage green and gold stripes, with a scooped out neck and a wide collar set back to show her beautiful shoulders. The front of the blouse was closed with a crisscross of black silk cord, lacing the two sides together.

She shifted her position slightly on the wide seat, tightening the fingers that clasped Nellie's cheek, moving them higher to plunge in among the dark curls at her temple. Dagmar's own hair had become unpinned, its auburn profusion haloed by sunbeams slanting through the window. Her eyes were closed, her lips parted in a half smile.

The movement tipped Nellie's head forward, so that her face was now resting on the exposed flesh of the Comtesse's breast. How satin-smooth was that perfumed skin in comparison with the rich silk of the blouse!

Dagmar stretched her free hand over to steady her companion on the slippery leather of the seat, the narrow fingers resting lightly on the ruffled white *batiste* sheathing Nellie's hip. Sleepily, Nellie smiled again: one of her own hands lay on Dagmar's thigh. It was amazing, the woman must be almost forty, but the flesh of the limb she could feel through the closely woven stuff of her wide skirt was as firm and supple as a schoolgirl's!

The black cord lacing the bodice of Dagmar's ensemble seemed to have loosened itself somehow. As she moved again, drawing Nellie a fraction further back on the seat, the displacement of the arm around Nellie's shoulders lifted the flesh of her own pectoral muscles. Freed from the tight lacing, the breast nearest Nellie rose slightly, just enough for the dark areola and the nipple at its centre to slide into view above the scooped-out neckline of the blouse.

The hand teasing the dark hair at Nellie's temple fell away, to rest lightly on the warm, comfortable curve of her bosom. The fingers made no move, simply lay there, but their very quiescence served to confirm the timelessness of that particular moment, to preserve the special warmth of that hesitant intimacy that held the two women immured within the glass cage of the Rolls Royce like flies immortalised in amber, for no time at all – or forever.

Nellie's lips were less than an inch from the Comtesse's exposed nipple. Her hot breath played gently on the puckered skin. Imperceptibly, the pressure on her own breast increased, urging her minutely closer. It seemed the most natural thing in the world to stretch her lips forward and suck that bud of flesh into her mouth – so natural that it would scarcely have been possible *not* to do it.

A faint tremor shook Dagmar's hips. Her breathing was suddenly audible. The hand palming Nellie's breast pressed harder. The hand closed on her hip tightened its grasp, rolling her slightly to face the Comtesse's recumbent form.

Barely aware of what she was doing, Nellie nibbled the rosy tip of the breast on which her head was pillowed, grazing it with her teeth, rolling it from side to side with the pointed tip of her wet little tongue, sucking on it until the tiny shaft of flesh was taut and stiff with desire.

A hand – her own! – was squeezing the firm, resilient mound upward to meet the thrusting suction of those greedy lips. The hand that had been on Dagmar's thigh was now resting on the junction between thighs and belly. Beneath it, the hips squirmed lazily in slow gyrations, and from the loins themselves, especially the padded cushion of the Comtesse's sexual mound, a remarkable heat was diffused.

The hand supporting Nellie's breast was moving too – kneading the flesh, balancing its weight, sweeping over the contours and caressing the nipple through layers of white lawn.

She heard a low moan – of pain? of pleasure? of bewilderment? – escape her lips. At the same time she realized the hold on her hip had been relinquished. It had been transferred to . . . heavens, to the inside of her thigh! Hot fingers on her cool skin! Why didn't she protest? Why didn't she cry *Stop!*

The fingers smoothed, caressed, swept upwards to tease the curls of her pubic hair. The hand cupped her secret place. A probing forefinger delicately traced the outline of . . . sank suddenly between the . . .

Horrors! Abruptly Nellie was aware that she was wet! What could she . . .?

Her skirt and petticoats were up around her waist. Her drawers had been plundered. The alien fingers were inside her. Somewhere deep in the centre of her being a trembling sensation was gathering force, sweeping her onwards relentlessly as the notes of an organ crescendo so low they can scarcely be heard.

Encountering the young woman's secret flesh, Dagmar's breath quickened, the heaving of her chest thrusting that bared breast ever closer into Nellie's mouth . . .

And abruptly the auburn-haired beauty twisted around, sat up, and took Nellie in her arms.

They kissed mouth to mouth then, lips clasped, tongues enlaced, the urgent breaths accelerating still. Nellie's legs were spread, her clothes bunched around her quaking hips, the buttons of her bodice torn open. A hot hand cupped one of her breasts. Below, the heel of a hand pressing hard against her mons, the invading fingers teasing, sliding, spreading apart then plunging, her loins responded involuntarily to Dagmar's expert touch. The familiar pre-release surge of excitement was tremoring through her. But this time, somehow, there was a caring quality, a delicacy and a gentleness about her lover that she had never known before.

Paradoxically, this stimulated in her a sudden force. She wound one leg around the Comtesse's slender calf, thrusting her pelvis fiercely up against the body bearing her down on the seat. She ripped away the black cord lacing, spilling out both Dagmar's breasts to crush against her own now naked bosom, exulting in the swift dark current of heartbeats thudding against her own flesh. A groan – it was almost a growl – of ecstasy bubbled deep in her throat.

Then all at once everything was music, and she was lost in a tumult of shared joy . . . until the late sunshine dried the moisture on her bare skin and the drowsy buzz of an imprisoned fly awoke her to reality.

To reality – and the awareness that the Rolls was rocking on its springs and the Baroness was with Marie-Ange on the front seat! How long had they been there? To Nellie Lebérigot, it mattered not at all.

'Amazing,' said Dagmar van den Bergh to the Baroness when they were alone, later that evening, in the house on the Avenue Kléber. 'Just what was it that you put in those madeleines, my dearest?' She smiled her secret smile.

Gisela von Zwickenheim smiled back – an expression of infinite complicity. 'It is astonishing, *Liebchen*, what a few grains of Moroccan hashish can accomplish,' she said. 'Our friend Agathe, for example, persuaded by Margarete to sample a little extra refreshment, has decided to ask almost everyone we know – everyone, at all events, in whom we are interested – to a weekend party at her country house in Normandy.'

'In many ways,' said Dagmar, 'that could be the most revealing gathering of the year!'

CHAPTER FOURTEEN

My dear old Charlie,

Hot from that hotbed of vice and vigour, gossip from Gay Paree comes winging your way, as promised, from your humble s., Champney, H. Wish it could literally have been flying, clutched in my clammy hand, in the old balloon. But now I'm a stalwart of the motor carriage business that cannot be: dispatches from those on active service must be entrusted to the Iron Horse and a uniformed functionary of His Majesty riding a red bicycle!

Active service, you ask? Well, yes, indeed. The former word is the key. I'm here, as you know, with the guv'nor's son, Paul, scion of the noble house of Mackenzie. Squiring the lad around is my principal assignment, and there's certainly action there. But so far as servicing goes, young Paul is in a class of his own! More of which later.

Our brief – did I tell you this? – is to wrest a manufacturing secret from a family called Laforge, who fabricate large, rather dull motor cars. The son, a nice enough young fellow, spends more time squiring Paul around than I do, extolling the delights of the French Way of Life and generally showing him, as the Yankees say, a good time. Champney has a suspicion, no more, that they, the Laforges, are trying in their turn to worm some mechanical secret out of Paul!! Ho, hum.

Ho-ho! We shall see.

And that brings me, sooner perhaps than expected, to later. The squiring, you see – Laforge model – has to date included a very special stag party with naked dancers as dessert; visits (naturally) to the Folies Bergère and the Moulin Rouge; a tryst with a Chinese lady at the city's most luxurious bawdy-house; a whole night with a mysterious masked female met at a costume ball; and another with a buxom beldam he believes to be a socialite smitten by his manly charms (but who is in truth a harlot paid by the Laforges to give that impression).

Some of this I know from His Nibs himself, some from my activities as a spy, and most of it from the last-named lady – for who should she turn out to be but my old, old playmate Nellie! (You remember little – or rather big – Nell? Filly I imported from France in the old Montgolfier a dozen years ago. We spent a couple of weeks at the Metropole in Brighton before we moved to that bungalow near Henley).

Happy days, Charlie. Happy days. Naturally I paid, and I do mean paid, a courtesy visit to the dear old thing myself. As much of a sport as ever, but the trouble is . . . well, dash it, she keeps a chap at it for so long!

Keeping an eye on the young squire, I too found myself at this posh bordel one night. Place called the Chabanais. Run by an Irishwoman, can you imagine. Anyone here seen Kelly, what! As it happened I fell in with quite a nice little dark thing there – no! I tell a lie: she was a redhead. Irish too, perhaps. At any rate we went aloft and I dipped my wick four times in a little over an hour. Longer than it would have been, old pal, in the good old summertime, but time's winged chariot, don't you know. We who are sere and gray and all that.

But talking of young Mac, a deuced rum thing happened when he and I took our constitutional this a.m. We were in St Michael's Place or somesuch, heading for a bar where we were to quaff a stoup of ale with an artist – one of those chaps who make statues out of clay – when suddenly Paul sees this absolute stunner crossing the street. I mean a real beauty, fresh-picked, dew still on the petals. She was the princess kind – you know, straight nose, blue eyes, pale hair and a shape out of a Greek museum. More of a goddess perhaps.

Anyway, the son and heir takes off like a bally greyhound out of a trap. Without so much as a by-your-leave or a see-you-for-lunch-then? he whizzes across the street between the cabs and drays and omnibuses and reins in before the lady with his hat sweeping dust from the pavement! I admit she was a peach, a pipparoo, but I confess I was a mite surprised. I mean, not the lad's style really.

I was halfway through the traffic myself before I realised Paul actually knew this houri, and there was no need for me to read him my how-not-to-behave-with-strangers-in-a foreign-country lecture. By then it was too late to turn back, so I completed the voyage and discreetly studied the items on display in a hatter's window. I was in time to hear him say: 'That absolutely stupendous night we spent together, and I've been dying to see you again ever since.'

Well, of course that pricked up the old Champney flappers. Agog to hear more is what I was. I said Paul knew the lady. He certainly seemed to think so, but this particular Chloe clearly thought *otherwise. She said, in one of those disdainful ice-maiden voices you and I know so well from Cheltenham tennis parties: 'Why, how dare you! I never set eyes on you before in my life!'*

That, plus the curl of lip on that luscious mouth, would have been enough for me, but the young are made of sterner stuff. Paul shook his head. He smiled – the innocent schoolboy grin, redolent of honesty and inviting the shared confidence – and he moved towards her. He said something I couldn't hear, and he reached for her. There was nothing of the brutal and licentious soldiery about the gesture, but there's no denying there was a touch of the proprietorial there.

And that's when she sloshed him.

I saw it all reflected in the window, framed by two toppers, a rather flashy panama and a selection of tweed caps for Le Sport. *She took a step back and biffed him on the boko! Forehand and backhand, with all the strength in that slender frame! The backhand was a beauty – wristy, the palm turned outwards, with a practised follow-through.*

To say the boy's jaw dropped would be an understatement. It was out of sight. He stammered: 'B-but your letter . . . the costume ball . . . I was the s-s-samurai . . . ?' By this time, however, the lady, her damask cheeks pink with vexation, had turned on her heel, as they say, and stalked away.

Paul's cheeks were pink too: the marks of four fingers and a girlish thumb were etched clearly on each. I hurried across to proffer a hankie, for a touch of claret – as the pugilistic fraternity have it – had also been tapped from the old noggin.

When the bleeding had stopped, we continued on our way. Naturally, I was agog again . . . this time for some kind of explanation. What had happened? Who was the angry bird? Was it a case of mistaken identity? Here in the street? Earlier at that party? But the lad refused point blank to talk about it, and I could hardly pry in the circs. Brought down as he undeniably was, all he could mutter sounded like: 'And she didn't even thank me for the flowers . . .'

In the bar, I confided a bit in the artist fellow while Paul whisked off to take a leak and wipe the blood from his chin. But all he would say, with a shake of the head and a knowing leer, was: 'Never try to understand a woman. They play a game with different rules!'

Perfectly true of course, but I think you'll agree this particular gossip item warrants a follow-up. I'll keep you in touch.

For the moment, those of us interested in the pleasures of the flesh await what promises to be an 'interesting' country-house weekend hosted by the wife of the Laforge boss. Rumour hath it that the cove is something of an old goat . . . and that the Lady W, deprived of hubby's amorous attentions, seeks solace in the arms of the lezzie brigade who seem so numerous around here! (I simply can't understand that, Charlie, can you? I mean, you'd think there were enough chaps to go round, wouldn't you, even in France?)

Anyway, yours truly will surely be part of the queue waiting to buy tweed caps from the hatter, because Le Sport threatens to be fast and furious at the party, seeing as how there will be a bisexual countess, a baroness from Bavaria, a couple of dancing girls, a female gossip writer and several much-fancied fillies from well-connected stables among the guests. I shall keep you abreast (haha!) of the ensuing entanglements.

The best to you and yours meanwhile, with deep salaams to the memsahib, from your old chum and Number Two oar –

Hector

Part Two

Country Life

Normandy –
April, 1912

CHAPTER FIFTEEN

The Auberge du Cheval Blanc – the White Horse Inn – was not in the strict sense an inn at all, since it boasted no sleeping accommodation and it was not possible to obtain a proper meal there. Nor were there any horses, white or otherwise, to be found among the cows grazing in the willow-shaded water meadows surrounding the place.

The auberge was in fact a *guinguette*, a riverside café with iron tables and parasols set out on a grassy terrace. The stream, meandering through a wooded land-scape to join the Seine near Mantes-la-Jolie, ran beside a canal bordered by poplar trees here, and there was a lock-keeper's cottage behind the wooden, chalet-style building. On the towpath beside the weir, an old man with a barrow sold hot, spiced sausages, whelks and roasted chestnuts.

'No sleeping accommodation – as such,' Bertrand told Tom Crawford and Paul Mackenzie as he braked the yellow Laforge tourer to a halt in a cloud of dust. 'But there are certainly private rooms for hire . . . occupied already, I'll wager, by those who prefer a more *discreet* atmosphere for their champagne!' He jerked his thumb at an open space on the far side of the narrow, gravelled road. A huge silver Rolls Royce limousine, a stateroom on wheels, towered over the dogcarts, traps and bicycles standing there. 'The Comtesse and her court,' said Bertrand drily.

Dagmar van den Bergh had certainly reserved one of the two rooms available so that the fellow guests she was ferrying to Agathe Laforge's weekend house party in Normandy could break their journey in the most agreeable surroundings possible. Apart from Gisela, the Dutch-Indonesian who called herself Mata Hari and the Comtesse herself, the Rolls Royce had accommodated Gabrielle Dorziat, Mme Foucault de la Roquette and a muscular young woman with short, dark hair and thick, straight eyebrows whose name was Dawn Broad.

Miss Broad was an equestrienne, a leading member of the English team due to compete in a show-jumping and *dressage* championship at Maisons-Laffitte, the race-horse training centre northwest of Paris, the following week. Wearing a severely cut habit with riding boots and a hard hat, she provided a startling contrast to the other ladies, most of whom were dressed in frothy spring pastels with headgear that was feathered or flowered.

The luncheon hamper from the limousine was in use again, and four bottles of 1904 Veuve Clicquot champagne stood in earthenware coolers beneath the wide first-floor window that looked over the garden, the weir and the canal.

For the moment, though, no more than a murmur of conversation spiced from time to time with a burst of ladylike laughter was audible below the open casement. The rowdy merriment and snatches of song occasionally drowning the rush of water from the weir came from a crowd of straw-hatted young men and their female companions who had cycled out from Paris and now occupied three of the tables nearest the river. Among them, Tom Crawford was astonished to see his two models, Sophie and Sylvie, apparently escorted by a couple of apaches in striped jerseys, berets and red neckerchiefs.

Laforge and his guests seated themselves nearer two family groups who were clearly locals. 'A jug of dry white wine,' Bertrand called to a waiter in a long white apron who stood near the entrance to the *guinguette*. 'And see that it is well cooled, if you please.'

'*Bien, m'sieu*. Will the local Muscadet be satisfactory?'

Bertrand glanced at his friends, then nodded. 'Perfect.'

The wine in the jug was a little below the halfway mark when Crawford turned around in his chair to glance at the three tables of young Parisians. Sophie and Sylvie, a little flushed now, sitting on the knees of their male companions, giggled and waved. The sculptor raised his glass in their direction . . . and then stiffened. 'I say,' he murmured to Bertrand, 'isn't that one of yours? Over there under the trees, beyond those tables?'

Bertrand looked across. Half hidden by low, sweeping branches, a closed car stood at the edge of the wood. It was a bulbous maroon saloon, with black mudguards and a black roof in the middle of which a small glass skylight was propped open. 'It's one of ours all right,' Bertrand agreed. 'But not only is it a Laforge: it's my old man's personal transport!'

He turned, sweeping the whole garden with a single searching glance – the noisy Parisians, the families, the waiter leaning against a wrought-iron arch supporting a rose pergola, two more local couples who were choosing a table. There was no sign of Laforge Senior.

'The old goat!' Bertrand said, bursting out into a bawdy laugh. 'I'll bet he's gone to earth in the other private room. I'd give a lot to know who he's got stabled in there. It won't be *Maman*, and that's for sure!'

In fact the second private room at the auberge was occupied by Bertrand's father and Nellie Lebérigot.

Agathe Laforge, who had talked to the young woman at Dagmar's tea party and liked her, had invited her for the weekend through the Comtesse. And the industrialist, thinking that this would strengthen the fiction of

Nellie the 'socialite' and thus further impress Paul Mackenzie, had readily agreed to drive her down himself.

She would of course, he assured her, be well paid if she could contrive to sustain the lady-of-leisure rôle she had already created and tempt the young Englishman into her bed again. For this was the time, Laforge was convinced, to *jouer le tout pour le tout* – to risk everything for everything and strike while the iron was hot - and if the boy wasn't seduced into a state of complaisance by the heat of this particular iron . . . well, he'd have to plunge others into the Mackenzie fire and beat out the secret another way.

Meanwhile, since he was paying her anyway, what more pleasant than a little dalliance at a riverside inn? A bottle of champagne, after all, never harmed anyone.

'A magnum of the Clicquot '04, Monsieur, perhaps?' the *patron* offered.

'Certainly not,' Laforge said brusquely. 'That's a woman's drink. Bring me a special blend Pol Roger. The '06, I think: it's still young, but there's an authentic bite to it, mature in the finish and long on the tongue. Be sure, though, not to over-chill it and ruin the taste.'

'As you wish, Monsieur.' The innkeeper bowed and withdrew.

'So far as you and I are concerned,' Laforge said to Nellie, 'I was simply asked to bring you down to the manor house. You are a guest of my wife's; I don't even know you. Apart from my son Bertrand, nobody knows, nobody shall know, that we have had any kind of . . . business dealings. I have in any case to go back to Paris to bring down a guest of my own, so there won't be much chance of any gossip linking one of us to the other.'

'You can rely on me to act with the utmost discretion,' Nellie said.

'Splendid, splendid,' Laforge enthused when the wine

178

had been served. 'And I must say, I approve whole-heartedly of my son's taste: you are a very fine-looking woman, my dear.' He coughed. 'Tell me – in these days of female freedom, how do you preserve such a stimulating shape? You do not by any chance wear a . . . an old-fashioned corset or stays, do you?'

Nellie smiled, sipping her champagne. 'You are one of those who . . . deplore . . . the emancipated females' rejection of the corset?' she asked.

The industrialist coughed again. He cleared his throat. 'I have always thought,' he said, 'that the *constriction* of that garment, the tightness, the very rigidity of whale-bone and satin and laced leather, offer a most charming contrast to the softness and freedom of flesh above and – ah – below.' He reddened, looking past her and out of the window. The two artist's models and their apaches were running along the towpath towards a barge that was manoeuvring into the lock. 'A woman's bosom,' Laforge said, 'is always a haven of warmth and deli-cacy, a tender variation from the firmness of shoulders and chest. Just as the . . . parts below . . . gain so much allure in comparison with the muscles of hips and thighs.' He sighed. 'But how much more appealing, more excit-ing, those contrasts are when the comparison is made between the soft flesh itself and the imprisoning clasp of tight-laced leather!'

Nellie's lips twitched into a wider smile. She laid her empty glass on a table, put up her hands, and pulled pins from her hair. 'Monsieur, I suspect, is something of an enthusiast?' she murmured.

'Yes, yes. I freely admit it. There is nothing to be ashamed of. But tell me, please . . . tell me . . .' He rose to his feet and reached for her waist, but she twisted away. 'Do you . . . are you . . . wearing one?'

'Perhaps.'

Another smile, more provocative, almost explicit. Laforge fell to his knees, his clasped hands in her lap.

'I must know. I want to see. I'll give you anything you want, if only–'

'You know very well what I want,' Nellie interrupted roughly. 'And it's money.'

He wrenched open his jacket, and felt for a wallet in the inside pocket.

'Put that away,' she said. 'I'd rather have you owe it to me. That way I have a closer hold . . . but pay sometime you must, or you'll never appreciate what you have!'

'Then you will? You'll allow me to . . .?'

Nellie shook her head, releasing the unpinned hair in a dark cloud around her shoulders. She raised a hand to unfasten the top button of her dress (she had chosen it carefully: it was maroon silk, the same colour as Laforge's limousine). 'Maybe. If you behave yourself.'

'Oh, I will, I will. I promise you. I'll do anything you say if only you'll permit me–'

'Sit down in your chair again.' She rose to her feet, poured more champagne, drank, and then stood in front of him. Her slender finger twisted the second button, and then the third, out of their buttonholes. Slowly, she drew apart the edges of her dress to reveal the creamy slopes of her bust. Laforge's eyes were staring; he was breathing fast.

Paul Mackenzie would have recognized the black braid and crisscross lacing of the red corset that was exposed immediately below the swell of her naked breasts when the fourth and fifth buttons were undone. Laforge uttered a hoarse cry.

There was a loud burst of female laughter from the other side of the wall. 'Don't worry,' Nellie said. 'It's only the lezzies having fun next door.' She settled herself in his lap and draped an arm around his neck. 'Now tell me: how quick are those itchy fingers of yours, loosening laces?'

* * *

A fresh supply of champagne had been brought to the room next door, although the bottles consumed already appeared to have gone down only too well. The Comtesse was laughing as she splashed froth into the empty glasses. Marie-Ange Foucault de la Roquette had entwined herself with the Baroness von Zwickenheim on a sofa. They stared languorously into one another's eyes, with pouting lips searching, sucking. Behind them, Mata Hari stood on a table, swaying her hips while the actress Dorziat clapped her hands and Miss Broad, the English horsewoman, beat time on the polished wood with a riding crop. Outside, in the garden below, someone was playing an accordion and the young folks from Paris danced on the river bank.

Mata Hari quickened the tempo of her movements. She was wearing a ruffled lawn top and a skirt that swathed her in diagonal flounces from the waist down. The flounces jumped and quivered as she gyrated those fleshy hips; the ruffles trembled with the shaking of her small breasts. Dawn Broad and Dorziat were singing now, the Englishwoman's deep voice melding with the braying of the accordion below. The crop thwacked the table. Dagmar van den Bergh clapped in counterpoint with Gabrielle Dorziat.

The dancer whirled, stamped. Champagne glasses jingled and shook. Mata's expressive arms and hands snaked in front of her, behind, and then curled up and over her head. The three women standing around the table huzza-ed in appreciation as she snatched off a belt, unwrapped the skirt, and flung it to the floor.

Now an olive-skinned swell of belly was visible between the lower edge of her bust bodice and the waistband, slightly sagging, of her drawers. Stiff-fingered, she plunged both hands between the waistband and her flesh . . . and suddenly the rhythm of the dance slowed and changed.

In an expert, decelerating *rallentendo*, the body appeared to gain weight, to shift itself more heavily, in a lazy motion that was almost dreamlike. The pelvis heaved sporadically as wavelets rolling over on a summer shore. Beneath the linen stuff of her drawers, the outline of Mata Hari's fingers began kneading the soft slope of her abdomen. She was caressing herself under cover of the light-weight garment.

There was no more clapping, the singing had stopped, the riding crop was stilled. Mata Hari tilted her head back. A low crooning issued from her open mouth. The watchers stared in fascination as the give-away shapes of those hidden hands swept across the dancer's loins, eased together, and then clawed lower. The knuckles peaked, thrusting out the crotch of the drawers, when they reached the junction of the thighs . . . and then subsided as the fingers sank into flesh.

A slow rotating movement, gradually quickening, became apparent. The white linen darkened with moisture. Hips jerked and pelvis shuddered. And then, as Dawn Broad picked up the crop and beat a light tattoo on the dancer's shivering posterior, the whole arched body shook in a series of diminishing spasms and an explosion of breath too long held-in groaned from Mata Hari's gasping mouth.

On the sofa, Gisela von Zwickenheim's scalding tongue speared between Marie-Ange's lips, and the dark, doll-like beauty clamped herself fiercely to the older woman in ecstatic surrender.

In the riverside garden, there was a burst of male laughter and Bertrand Laforge, together with his two companions, sprang to his feet, pointing at the entrance to the *guinguette*. A two-horse Victoria with the soft top folded down had pulled up outside the gates. Late afternoon sunbeams slanting through the trees picked out the four familiar people climbing down from the carriage: Camille Dufour, Corinne Dubois, Hector Champney, and Corinne's music-critic colleague, Patrice Delgano.

'Bravo!' young Laforge shouted to the Englishman. 'I knew you'd make it somehow – but I didn't realise you'd have the sense to team up with the other guests. You must all come and join us at once.'

'What-ho!' Champney approved, eyeing the jug of wine as the newcomers seated themselves around Laforge's table. 'Sorry I couldn't make the conducted tour in your own bus' – he nodded towards the yellow tourer on the far side of the road – 'but the guv'nor in the old sceptred isle was baying for a progress report, and I had to get something in the post. Needs must, don't you know, when the bally employer drives!'

'That's all right,' Bertrand said. 'Just so long as you're here. You can pay off the cabbie and we'll all go down to the manor house in my car.' He noticed a number of uneasy glances around the table, and added hastily: 'Forgive me. You don't all know each other. Let me introduce . . .'

Smiles, nods, handshakes, murmurs of acknowledgement . . . until it came, at the far end of the table, to Paul Mackenzie and Camille Dufour.

'I am desolated,' the girl said, 'but I have no wish whatever to meet this . . . gentleman . . . who has indeed already seen fit to importune me in the street as if I was some common–'

'Who? Paul?' Laforge was incredulous. 'Surely not! There must be some–'

'There is no mistake, I assure you. I do not easily forget the faces of persons who dare to affront me.'

'B-but, Mademoiselle,' the luckless Englishman stammered, 'there was absolutely no intention to insult you, I promise. I mean, I'm sorry if I . . . that is, I sent flowers, I wrote to you, I received a reply. And, after that, the costume–'

'What nonsense!' She turned angrily to Laforge. 'Until he forced himself upon me in the street, I had never set eyes on this man. Nor do I wish to do so now.' The voice was icy with disdain, the classic features set in an expression of supreme contempt. 'If he is to be a guest of your mother's, I pray you, keep us as far apart as possible. And advise her to put the silver under lock and key!'

'Now look here,' Mackenzie cried, finally stung into a spirited rejoinder. 'Just what is all this about? You know perfectly well you agreed to meet me at the Poiret ball. Even if you wished to forget what happened after we met – which in my turn I would consider extremely ill-mannered – I cannot see why–'

'Be quiet!' the girl stormed. 'What are you talking about? Have you gone mad? I was not at the Poiret ball. I helped design some of the costumes, I arranged some invitations for Bertrand here, but I did not go to the party myself.'

'You . . . *w-w-what?* You didn't go?' Paul's face was a mask of stupefaction. 'But my l-l-letter? The flowers? The reply that you–?'

'What letter? I have never received a letter from you. I told you, the first time I knew of your existence was when–'

'*Bertrand!*' Corinne exclaimed suddenly. 'The wine is finished! We're all thirsty. Come – the waiter is busy with those young people. Let us go inside and fetch a couple of jugs ourselves. I'll come with you and help.'

Grabbing the empty pitcher, she seized him by the arm and propelled him hurriedly towards the *guinguette*.

All of which, Hector Champney wrote to his friend Charlie that evening, *seemed very rum indeed to me. Especially since I distinctly heard the filly say to our host as they trotted away: 'Bertrand, I have a kind of confession to make!' What do you think of that?*

*I know what the young squire made of it all.
The poor lad was flabbergasted. I didn't know
what the devil was going on, at the time. He'd
stayed mum about the whole story. But when I
pressed him, he poured it all out and Hector C
was suddenly a Dutch uncle! It seems, to put it in
the proverbial nutshell, that he'd had a yen for
this bird, showered her with roses, thanked her
for wangling him an invite, and offered to escort
her to the ball. By letter of course. And he'd had
a reply, apparently agreeing, that suggested a jolly
old midnight tryst, as in all the best froggie farces
. . . in disguise, don't forget, as in all the same.*

*Remember, too, that Paul had never actually
met the girl, never seen her close to, never even
heard her voice. So when the package duly turned
up, wrapped as advertised, he naturally assumed
it was the article ordered. Only it wasn't.*

*That seems clear now. But at the time, since
the masks never came off, he never twigged. He
had the whale of a time, pleasuring old JT nightlong
. . . and was understandably a mite flummoxed
when, chancing to meet the girl he thought he'd
shafted, she denied all knowledge and hit him for
six (as described in my last) into the bargain! The
question now is: will A continue to pursue his
original fancy, despite the lady being at the moment seriously miffed; or will he instead try to
identify the partner he really did spend the night
with; object, a return engagement? Your guess is
as good as mine, Charlie. But I suspect the heart
of the mystery lies in the fact that the missive that
caused all the trouble was signed simply with two
initials . . . and there's more than one lady in the
Laforge-Mackenzie entourage sharing the same
capital letters!*

That said and explained, there remains the ac-

count of my own peregrinations during the afternoon we spent at this agreeable riverside haunt.

I wandered off, you see, after the little drama
over the introductions and what-not. I mean it
was becoming a bit too family. Embarrassing. A
chap didn't know where to look or what to do. So
there I was, drifting along the towpath, mouth
open and nostrils flared, ready to breathe in all
the delights provided by Mother N, when I happen across this barge. Just floated out of the lock
and now tied up by the bank. The bargee and his
missus are legging it to the auberge, clearly determined on one for the canal, and the deck is
occupied by as saucy a pair of demoiselles as you
could imagine. They weren't part of the crew, but
I reckon they were friends, because I'd seen them
nattering with said bargee when the craft was
tying up. I'd also seen a couple of roughs with
them, ugly-looking characters with striped footer
shirts, but by the time I hove-to alongside these
coves had vanished.

Well, Charlie, what would you have done? So
did I. I engaged the ladies in light conversation.
Artist's models, they said they were, from the Latin
Quarter in Paris. I guess it's as good a descrip-
tion as any. One was called Sylvie and the other
Sophie (same initials again, ho-ho!). Anyway, to
cut a short story even shorter, like Mr Dickens'
Barkis, the fillies were willing. Able too.

They seemed to have the run of the barge, and
they were certainly familiar — if you'll excuse the
word — with the wide bunk in the saloon! In a
trice it was Oh-this-heat! and Do-remove-your-
jacket and Mind-if-I-slip-out-of-this? Pretty little
tits, Charlie, ripe little bums, and as for the rest —
well, believe it or not, one was shaved bald as a
monk, and the other sported a pussy whose old

man must definitely have been a Persian! Don't ask me which was which. I'm not sure they knew themselves.

What fun, what fun! It cost me, of course (something, I seem to remember, about the cab fare back to Paris). But what better way to spend a spring afternoon! Did I say spend? It was Sylvie, then Sophie; then Sophie before Sylvie – and, for an encore, something extremely instructive involving the three of us on said divan. You've heard the term arse-about-face? Well, never mind: verb. sap. *and 'nuff said.*

Point is, I was back with the young squire, bright-eyed and bushy-tailed, before the second cargo of wine had been fully unloaded. Fifty minutes? An hour? I don't think they even noticed I'd gone. You'd have noticed, Charlie Boy – but then we're birds of a feather, ain't we?

Watch this space for more news from your old chum –

Hector

CHAPTER SIXTEEN

The Laforges' country house, dignified now with the title Manor, had started life in the seventeenth century as a fortified farm. Robert Laforge's grandfather, a blacksmith in the town of Evreux, had acquired it as a dilapidated ruin, the surrounding land neglected, and used the extensive outhouses to enlarge the scope of his ironwork. Starting with the hooped wheels of carts and carriages, he had progressed to leaf springs and chassis members; by the time his son, Robert's father, was old enough to share the work, he was making entire dogcarts and pony traps for the gentry who even then had inaugurated the fashion for weekend '*fermettes*' in Normandy to escape the rigours of life in the capital.

A small workforce of local experts was added later, and the business had expanded to embrace the manufacture of hand-crafted landaus, cabriolets and berlines for the dignitaries of Rouen, Dreux and Chartres by the turn of the century. It was Robert, who had studied engineering in Lille and St Quentin, who decided the company's future lay with carriages that were horseless rather than animal-powered. The château that served as the family's town house was bought in 1903 and the Behrens-designed factory at Le Bourget built two years later. Since then the Normandy property had been transformed. Electricity, running water and steam heating had lent the long, low, ivy-covered building with its projecting gable-ends a deceptively modern air once the heavy, iron-studded doors were opened. The out-houses had been turned into guest wings. One of the barns was arranged as a miniature museum displaying early models of the Laforge motor car. The abandoned farmlands had been landscaped, planted with trees, and metamorphosed into a spacious park through which a white driveway curled lazily up to the house.

There were already a dozen cars parked in the stable yard when Mata Hari eased the silver Rolls through the entrance archway – a Delage, an Austro-Daimler, a Delaunay-Belleville limousine, even a rakish Brescia Bugatti among the more mundane marques. Bertrand's yellow tourer stood at the entrance to a flagged rose garden, beside a small ornamental lake.

Servants supervised by a major-domo swarmed into the yard to remove the hat boxes and valises stowed on the rack topping the Rolls Royce's roof. The guests were shown to their rooms and informed that their hostess would greet them over an apéritif in the Chinese drawing room at six o'clock.

There were twenty house guests. Apart from Bertrand's friends and the Dagmar van den Bergh *coterie*, they included the Comte de la Ferrière, Patrice Delgado, Camille and Corinne, Dr Gaston Despierre, the two bankers who had been at the latter's stag party and several couples who lived in the neighbourhood.

The Chinese drawing room was perhaps fifty feet long, with French windows overlooking the lake. It was a colourful crowd that eddied between the modernistic bamboo chairs, lacquered cabinets and painted silk screens as a team of white-coated waiters carrying trays of cock-tails surged into the room on the stroke of six.

Agathe Laforge received her guests by the french windows, her black velvet dress, garlanded with pearls, dramatic against a saffron sunset which suffused the western sky above the park outside. The local ladies – ahead, as provincials often are, of their city sisters –

displayed the very latest of uncluttered 'freedom' fashions: Poiret turbans above loose, shapeless tubes of cinnamon and sage and oyster silk over-wrapped with exotic oriental gauzes. Gisela von Zwickenheim blazed in bronze grosgrain. Nellie had played safe with the ivory brocade she wore at her first meeting with Paul Mackenzie. Dorziat wore crimson and Marie-Ange jade green. But Dagmar was the most vivid of all: she was dressed in a startling Doucet creation of brilliant turquoise dupion, admirably designed to set off her creamy shoulders and lustrous auburn hair. The style of the ensemble was Japanese, a separate top, cuffed and collared with ermine, echoing a kimono shape with multi-layered shoulders overloading the torso and cascading down to a narrow hemline that enforced a delicate, mincing walk. The sole exception to this bird-of-paradise exhibition was the English huntress Dawn Broad, attired as soberly as the men in a two-piece black barathea *tailleur*, relieved only at the neck by a white silk foulard.

There was one absentee from the party: Robert Laforge, the host himself.

'My goodness, Uncle Gaston,' Bertrand murmured, manoeuvring Despierre into a corner as he surveyed the glittering throng, 'what a party it would be if we could have all the women *here* naked on a table after dinner!'

'You should be ashamed of yourself, even to think it,' Despierre replied with mock severity. 'But, take my word for it, my boy, more than half of these butterflies are going to be naked where they've no right to be before the night is over!'

'Well I hope at least one will be sufficiently attracted by the flame of love to land on my wick!' said the young man. He glanced covertly at Corinne, who was looking unusually seductive in a softly draped robe printed with autumn leaves. The hemline of the dress was gathered at the front and raised to show her ankles – a daring innovation anticipating the shorter skirts which the fashion prophets swore were due to arrive any season now. Had he in fact surprised a look – of amusement? of understanding? of complicity even? – when he stole a look himself at those slender feet some minutes before?

'It might be a good idea,' Despierre was saying, 'if your mother were to adopt the English country house system whereby a bell is discreetly rung about six-thirty so that guests can dress themselves and get back to their own rooms before early-morning tea is served!'

'Bertrand! Where on earth is your father?' Agathe Laforge herself stalked up and demanded before the young man could reply. She turned to Nellie, who was sipping a cocktail nearby. 'I believe he brought you from Paris, my dear. Did he give you any indication of what he planned to do next?'

Nellie shook her head. 'We arrived quite early. But I think he left again almost at once. He said he had someone else to fetch.'

'Indeed? I should be most interested to know who.'

But the hostess had to wait until halfway through dinner before her curiosity was satisfied. And then it was a shock rather than a revelation. For Robert Laforge's surprise guest was none other than Milady!

The major-domo was sharpening his knives prior to carving a baron of beef, and the footmen were standing by with silver entrée dishes of vegetables, when the double doors to the oak-beamed dining room were flung open and the couple made their entrance.

It was certainly an effective introduction, dramatic even, if the impact of Milady's appearance was taken into account.

Her pale hair was swept up in a Pompadour, garnished with fruit and feathers, and plaited with three strings of pearls. A diamond collar graced her neck and there were diamond rings on all her fingers. The dress she wore was gold satin – an absurd confection with enormous leg-of-mutton sleeves, a wide stand-up collar and a skin-tight waist that could have left her escort in no doubt as to whether or not a corset formed part of the ensemble. Below the waist, the dress hugged Milady's hips and thighs and then flared out theatrically below the knees. The small amount of her generous breasts not bared by the wide, scooped neckline was hidden by a huge bow with long trailing ends.

'Greetings!' roared Laforge, red-faced and clearly a little tipsy. 'I bring you a bright star to embellish the f-f-firmament of your evening!' Milady smiled winningly and sketched as much of a curtsey as the tightness of the skirt at her knees would allow.

The diners at the long refectory table had all fallen silent at the first manifestation of this apparition. Now, suddenly, a babble of conversation broke out as Agathe Laforge said faintly: 'Straight from the Folies! I don't believe it!'

Laforge made a grand performance out of the introduction, presenting Milady by her real name, then took the vacant chair at the foot of the table and seated her on his right. She found herself next to Despierre, whom she had met more than once professionally. The surgeon repressed a smile as she began explaining, in a loud voice, what a relief it was to find oneself, at last, among those 'of one's own class, dear'. He wondered why his friend had chosen to arrive late at his own dinner party, with a whore who was dressed – or so it seemed – deliberately to accent her whorishness. At the very least, Despierre thought, the action would be construed as a public insult to his wife.

This, in fact, was precisely Laforge's intention. Reserving to himself the inalienable right to sleep where and with whom he chose, the industrialist – like many men – regarded his neglected wife's consequent interest in her own sex as a personal affront, a slight on his masculinity. His arrival with Milady was a gesture of defiance, the equivalent of a child putting out his tongue.

Most of the guests were embarrassed by the overt lack of consideration implied by the act, and covered their confusion by talking animatedly about something else. Those more gossip-minded lowered their voices and exchanged questions and answers with sidelong glances and an occasional raised eyebrow. Dagmar van den Bergh, who felt perhaps more sympathy for Agathe Laforge than anyone, conducted a spirited conversation with her hostess – across one of the bankers, who separated them – on the subject of gardens and the correct pruning of roses. Milady, enjoying herself, ate and drank.

As soon as was decently possible, when the canapés had been served and the *petits-fours* circulated, Agathe rose to her feet and announced: 'Well, I think it is time, now, for the . . . ladies' – with a swift look at her husband and his guest – 'to withdraw, leaving the gentlemen to follow their, shall I say, pursuits? There will be dancing in the ballroom from ten o'clock for those who care to indulge.' With Dagmar and Gisela in tow, she swept from the room.

Milady, about to deliver the critical line of a risqué story, stuffed a final spoonful of *Soufflé au Grand Marnier* into her mouth and hurried out on the resulting burst of laughter. In the drawing room she attached herself to Nellie and stayed as far away from Agathe Laforge as possible. The hostess, however, did not trouble to hide her feelings when they were rejoined by the male guests. 'Robert!' she stormed. 'How dare you bring that . . . that person . . . into my house in front of all our friends?'

Laforge grinned. Alcohol and the thrill of a successful dare had made him bold. 'A remark,' he said silkily, 'that might more properly be made by myself. My choice at least' – with a nod towards Dagmar, the severely dressed Miss Broad and the German Baroness – 'at least falls normally, dare I say healthily, upon the *opposite* sex!'

His wife flushed a dark red, turned on her heel, and left him.

Theirs was not the only undercurrent of unease running through the colourful gathering. A certain coldness had developed between Marie-Ange Foucault de la Roquette, Mata Hari and Dawn Broad - due, it seemed, to what was considered to be the Englishwoman's slightly proprietorial tapping of the dancer's buttocks with her riding crop during the performance at the *guinguette*. Tom Crawford, too, was in an awkward position, the apparent object of Corinne's amorous intentions, whereas his own desires were firmly fixed on a buxom country girl employed by his hostess as a chambermaid. 'A snip, my friend,' Bertrand had told him. 'She initiated me in the delights of love during a school holiday when I was sixteen.'

As for Paul Mackenzie, bewilderment was the emotion uppermost in his mind. Still dazed by Camille's rejection – as he saw it – of their shared and splendid intimacy, he found himself, placed next to Nellie at dinner, in an analogous position vis-à-vis the young woman he still believed to be a socialite who had taken a fancy to him. Guilty because he had never followed up the titanic night they spent together, he was nevertheless determined to fend off the advances Nellie was still being paid to make: any weakening on his part would inevitably support Camille's view of him as a pushy libertine. And despite everything, Paul still had hopes that he might in some way get under the beautiful young woman's guard and make himself accepted as an ordinary human being.

For the moment he thrust as far away as he could the inexplicable behaviour of the girl who had, he had every reason to believe, only a few days ago shared with him a mutual tenderness and passion.

Meanwhile there was Nellie, generous, attractive Nellie, whom he had no wish in the world to hurt or offend, but . . .

And there was this unaccountable hostility between their hostess and the woman he knew only as the owner of a 'club' – the very place indeed where Agathe's son had introduced him to Nellie!

Really, what had promised to be a vivacious and amusing weekend was turning out to be quite tiresome.

When the dancing began – in a ballroom that had once been the shop where Laforge *grandpère* shrank iron hoops onto cartwheels – he was again buttonholed by Nellie. 'I was so hoping you would be here,' she confided, draping her voluptuous body against him with a white-gloved hand resting on the nape of his neck. 'After that first rather splendid meeting at the . . . club . . . I was sure that somehow, somewhere, Fate would draw us together again.'

'It was most ungallant of me,' Paul said politely, clearing his throat, 'not to have insisted before I left that you favoured me with your private address. Unfortunately, what with business and everything, I have not even had time to pass by that club again. And as for–'

She laid a finger on his lips. 'What will be, will be. The exact time and place are of no importance. We are together again. So . . . let us dance!'

The band, a trio of violin, accordion and piano from nearby Evreux, played a lively selection of waltzes, mazurkas and polkas, enlivened every now and then with one of the new foxtrots or a daring tango – the South American speciality categorized by the Church as 'sinful and promiscuous'.

'Don't you yourself feel sinful and promiscuous . . . from time to time?' Nellie asked as they tried to fit their feet to the jumpy rhythm.

'Of course. Whenever I find myself near someone

like you,' said Paul, supplying the expected answer. He fingered his collar away from his neck. 'You must forgive me . . . after this dance . . . I see that she is disengaged, and in my country it is considered unforgivable if one does not beg one's hostess for at least one dance.'

The young Englishman's request was exactly what Agathe Laforge had been waiting for. Although by birth and upbringing she was the kind of woman for whom a public display of emotion was unthinkable, she was nevertheless as prone to anger, outrage and the desire for revenge as anyone. And tonight she was prepared to indulge all seven of the deadly sins and break most of the ten commandments if that would help repay the insult and avenge the humiliation she had suffered at her husband's hands.

When she reproached him, he had sneeringly made reference to her involvement with Dagmar and the other *Amazones* – and thus, by implication, inferred that this was the reason for his cavalier treatment of her. Whereas the exact opposite was the case: it was *because* of that treatment, because of his neglect that she had first resorted to sympathetic members of her own sex.

Her first impulse had been to flaunt her interest in her lesbian guests: openly to flirt, to dance suggestively with Gisela, with Marie-Ange, with the Englishwoman. To insult Robert in turn with her total lack of interest in him. But she had realised in fact that this would simply have been playing his game, the equivalent again of the child putting out its tongue. To the guests, it would go some way to explain – perhaps even to excuse? – his own conduct, bringing that woman here.

How much more satisfying, how much more stinging the slap in the face, if she were to lavish affection openly on another man! Especially a man who was younger, better looking, and certainly more virile than Robert himself. That would really fit the boot of rejection upon the other foot!

'Thank you, I should adore to dance,' she said to Paul Mackenzie.

The young man was a little surprised – the band had swung into a foxtrot – to find that his hostess clung to him even more tightly than Nellie had. Perhaps the French style of dancing was more . . . well, intimate, than the English? Which would be odd, just the same, since in everything else socially the style was more formal. But there was no doubt about it: the pressure of the palm in the small of his back was insistent; he could feel the warmth of Agathe's bosom through the stiff piquet of his shirtfront; on some of the turns, her cheek rested momentarily against his own.

The dance was over. Together with the other guests, Paul clapped perfunctorily. His partner did not: one of her gloved hands rested on his upper arm. 'That was good,' she said. 'You dance very well. Listen . . . they are going to play a waltz. Unless your programme is full, do stay with me. I so love to waltz.'

Paul stayed. Nellie had been whisked away by Tom Crawford. Corinne was with Bertrand. Camille – from whom his gaze was seldom absent – laughed at some pleasantry advanced by one of the bankers. He danced. The black velvet gown under his hand was vibrant with life . . . and there could be no mistaking the knee wedged softly between his thighs each time he reversed!

A little breathless at the beginning of the intermission, Mme Laforge looked up at him. Her cheeks were flushed and her dark eyes shining. 'If you are interested,' she said – Paul had been mouthing inanities about the house – 'there's quite a story to tell. It was a farm once, then a sort of factory.'

She glanced around the room. On the far side of the dance floor Robert had been cavorting with Milady. Now he was looking their way. She smiled brightly. 'All the guests ever see,' she said, 'is a bedroom and a selection of public places – the dining and drawing rooms, the gunroom, the library. Come – I'll show you a priest hole, the museum, what we call the services.' Taking his hand, she led him away.

Twenty-five minutes later they stood at the edge of the ornamental lake. The air was fresh but not too cold; a faint breeze carried the scent of roses from the formal garden behind them. In front, a three-quarter moon silvered the surface of the water and threw the leafless branches of elms into stark silhouette against the western sky. Paul was reminded of the outline of his hostess at the start of the evening, black against the sunset. Was the life of this strange, unhappy woman as barren as the boughs of those trees?

In the distance, from the sombre bulk of the manor that was blotting out the stars, the energetic strains of a polka suddenly spilled over the hubbub of conversation and laughter. Agathe Laforge sighed. She leaned forward to stare into the water. Their twin reflections shivered and spun away as the wind ruffled the surface. 'A lot of money was spent on it,' she said. 'It was drained and dredged and paved and stocked with fish, but basically it's still the duckpond it always was.' She straightened and for an instant laid her head on his shoulder.

Paul was totally confused. He had drunk enough at the *guinguette* and, later, during dinner, to blunt his normal reactions. He was still numbed by Camille's hostility yet yearning to be with her; he was guiltily embarrassed by his own treatment of Nellie . . . and here was this woman – she must be at least forty – making a play for him! He couldn't be making a mistake, could he? Imagining things? Fuddled with drink, subconsciously influenced by the flattering attentions of Nellie? Absolutely not. There was nothing imagined about the fingers laid just a little too long on his sleeve, about the arm encircling his waist, the tendril of hair against his cheek.

So what was he supposed to do about it? What did he *want* to do?

He did nothing.

When she reckoned they had been away long enough to cause the gossip tongues to wag, Agathe steered him back to the ballroom.

The crowd had thinned a little. Some of the locals had gone home; a few of the guests had retired to bed. Corinne was with Bertrand and Crawford. Camille was nowhere to be seen. Milady was holding court with Despierre, the bankers, Delgado and of course Robert in attendance. Agathe instructed the band to play something dreamy and shepherded the Englishman out onto the dance floor.

They played *Goodbye, Dolly Gray* and *It's Time to Sail Away*.

At the end of the second dance, Agathe levered herself away from Paul and said: 'I enjoyed that. But you must be exhausted, dragging me around all that time! Let's sit the next one out – or, better still, allow me to finish our conducted tour. You've seen the guest wings, but you haven't penetrated upstairs in this part of the house. Come on: I'll show you the Egyptian bathroom and the Mies van de Rohe study where Laforge invents his automobiles.' Again she led him from the room. Her husband missed the point of a Milady anecdote: he was staring furiously after the couple when the others laughed.

Paul didn't remember the Egyptian bathroom. He was in a large suite overlooking the park and the entrance drive. The furniture was luxurious, antique rather than novelty art-nouveau. It was dwarfed by a huge four-poster on a dais, spread with a white fur rug, draped in midnight-blue damask. A coal fire burned in the wide grate.

Agathe moved to a small table inlaid with mother-of-pearl that stood by an armchair near the dais. Bottles, glasses and an ice bucket were arranged on the table. 'You must be thirsty after all that dancing,' she said. 'No, no – I insist! A brandy, I think. Champagne has become tedious at this hour.' She poured, then handed him a well-filled balloon. And if you will excuse me, I must leave you for a few seconds. This tight velvet dress is perfectly suitable if one is receiving guests, but as the evening wears on, one does like to change into something more comfortable.' She smiled and vanished through a doorway that led to a dressing room.

When she came back – there was still some brandy in the glass – Paul gasped. She was wearing a filmy *peignoir* – a gossamer négligée of dusky organza, fastened only at the waist – and nothing else!

She walked up to him, standing very close, and picked something – a hair, a thread, a speck of dust? – from his lapel. A faint, obscurely oriental scent rose from her warm, perfumed body. 'Well?' she said huskily.

He didn't know what to say. The woman's mouth was generous. She had what a friend of his called bedroom eyes. The ripe body, lacking the trimness of a girl his own age, was nevertheless voluptuous enough in the manner of a Rubens or a Renoir. And Paul was sufficiently inexperienced to be stirred by the mere fact of near-nakedness . . . even of someone almost twice his age. At last he blurted out: 'You're seducing me!' - the words escaping before he knew they were coming.

'That's right. Successfully, I hope!'

She smiled up at him. Her warm, winey breath played on his face. He realised she had probably drunk as much as he had. 'A more . . . intimate atmosphere might help,' she murmured as if to herself. She stepped away and tugged a tasselled cord that hung from a rose in the ceiling, where two moulded plaster cornices made a right-angle. At once the three crimson-shaded standard lamps illuminating the room were extinguished. Moonbeams slanting through the undraped windows provided the only light.

It took Paul seconds only to accustom himself to the changed conditions. Agathe Laforge looked almost ethereal in the wan radiance, still half turned away from him with one hand on the cord. But there was no mistaking the sexuality of her statuesque figure. One profiled breast, rounded, heavy, perhaps dropped but only slightly, thrust out the diaphanous material of her négligée, the darkened areola showing through the flimsy material like an exclamation point. And below the cushioned swell of her hips, a triangle that was darker still shadowed the overlapping layers of gauzy stuff.

Stirred by near-nakedness! He smiled inwardly. He might be besotted with Camille, bowled over by Nellie, but something was stirring all right down below the waistband of his trousers: the proximity of this older woman with her luscious body and beguiling smell was hardening him to the point of discomfort!

'You're a very good-looking young man,' Agathe said throatily, allowing her gaze to wander from his face to his crotch, where it stayed. 'And I see something exciting between your legs that I very much want to have between mine.'

Paul swallowed. Good manners dictated, at home, that one must ask one's hostess for at least one dance; in France, it seemed, the well-bred guest was expected go one step further!

'And that, I am sure, is not the only exciting thing about you,' Agathe Laforge whispered.

He strode forward and kissed her then. The flesh of her upper arms was cool through the sleeves of her négligée as he laid his hands on her. Her mouth trembled as his lips closed over it. Her arms circled his shoulders and cool fingers laced over the nape of his neck.

There was nothing cool about the breasts clamped to his chest or the pelvis swung hard against his hardness: he could feel the heat of her loins through the thick stuff of his trousers.

It seemed a long time before they drew apart. Agathe leaned back in his embrace and looked up at him. He could see that she was smiling, but the expression in her eyes was fathomless in the pale moonlight filtering through the windows. She put up a finger and touched his mouth. 'Such tender lips . . . and such a hard, muscular body!'

'Your own lips, Madame, are – what do they say? – the stuff that dreams are made of,' Paul said awkwardly.

She laughed, a small silvery sound. 'Oh Paul, Paul! My name is Agathe. Or anything else you want to call me. Anything except Madame! I feel quite old enough without that.'

'But you're beautiful!' he cried. 'What has age to do with it?'

'Monsieur is gallant . . . again!'

He grinned, nipping the finger against his mouth between his teeth. 'Oh Agathe, Agathe! My name is Paul. Anything except Monsieur!'

She tapped him playfully on the cheek. 'Since we are agreed on that then . . . and since we seem to agree about lips . . . and since, thirdly, there are so many fascinating things two pairs of lips can do, why don't we' – a slight grind of the hips against his loins – 'move over to the bed where we shall be much more comfortable?'

She sat on the four-poster while he stood before her and, still smiling, began to undress him. She unbuttoned the jacket, untied his tie and prised the starched shirt front away from its gold studs. She pushed shirt and jacket back over his shoulders, and then down his arms to drop on the floor. Bare to the waist, he gazed down at her.

Agathe touched the hair on his chest, his two nipples, the flat, taut plane of his abdomen, mouthing small, humming, appreciative murmurs each time her fingers brushed his skin. 'You sound like a gourmet savouring the chef's special,' Paul said, amused.

'That's exactly how I feel,' said Agathe. She unfastened the belt at his waist and tore open the buttons below. 'Oh, my! Special indeed! Shall we say . . . *Coq au Vin*?'

Paul's breath hissed in sharply as the supple fingers closed around his hardness, cradling the sensitive, hairy pouch beneath. He bent forward and slid the négligée off her shoulders, exposing the rich mounds of her heavy breasts. The dark buds at their tips swung against his thighs as she moved.

'Come to me!' Agathe cried. 'I want to feel you next to me all the way!' She untied her waist belt and stripped off the garment.

Paul kicked away trousers, drawers, shoes and socks and leaped to join her on the wide bed, his whole body quivering with eagerness.

Naked, Agathe Laforge was extraordinary. Everything about her was soft – the breasts, the belly, her waist, the flesh of her thighs, the generous cushions of her lips. Yet all of it at the same time was resilient and firm, none of it slack or flabby.

Paul caressed her with delight, his roving hands exploring each swell and curve and hollow as their mouths rejoined and the delicious dialogue of tongues continued. Between them, her expert hands coaxed thrills of ecstasy from the throbbing proof of his desire.

For a long time, while their breaths quickened and the thudding of their two hearts grew more rapid, they lay wrapped together. And then – he never quite knew how it happened: a slight shifting of her hips, the spreading of a thigh? - he was sunk between her legs and the whole hard shaking length of him was swallowed, engulfed in the hot, wet clasp of her belly . . .

CHAPTER SEVENTEEN

The Laforge's major-domo was a voyeur. His name was Giacomo Serafini, and he took a great deal of pleasure in his very private vice. He was a thickset man with thin, dark hair and a permanently blue chin.

Serafini's greatest *coup*, the one that gave him the most pleasure in every sense of the word, derived from the fact that he had once – deliberately, although nobody knew that – cracked an antique mirror in Agathe Laforge's bedroom, through careless manipulation of a heavy brass lamp-stand. He had of course insisted that he replace the glass at his own expense.

The major-domo in fact had a cousin who was a *maquereau*, a ponce, in Paris. And, this gentleman being concerned with the refurbishing of a small-time brothel in the XVIIIth Arrondissement, there happened to be an area of two-way mirror glass available that could be cut to fit the empty frame on Agathe's wall. Add that there was a walk-in linen cupboard on the far side of the wall, which could be entered from a convenient corridor, and Serafini's joy was complete.

Thereafter, many of his late evenings and most of his free afternoons were profitably spent spying on his employers.

There had been a hiatus, of course, after Robert Laforge stopped sleeping with his wife, but this had been amply made up for once Agathe had started suggesting to her female luncheon guests that they should share a siesta in her apartment. Nor indeed was the linen cupboard Serafini's only source of visual satisfaction. Several of the guest rooms were equipped with spyholes whose inner ends were concealed among plasterwork scrolls or in the beading of wooden panels. An offcut from the famous mirror had been incorporated into the art-nouveau décor of a bathroom, and the occupants of a suite in a converted barn would have been astonished to learn that a person prone among the rafters of the old hayloft could look down upon their bed through a cunning adaptation of the chandelier rose.

In slack seasons when the family was away, Serafini had been known to insist that housemaids desirous of maintaining their position should masturbate in front of him. A minor triumph that he treasured concerned the elderly, ill-tempered cook whom he had once – while perched with field glasses in an oak tree – seen pleasure herself in a summerhouse on the far side of the lake with the aid of a feathered clockwork device known as a St Louis Tickler.

From a distance, on the first night of the house party, he had kept a discreet watch on his mistress. That eruption of the old man and the tart in the middle of dinner would, he was sure, produce something special in the nature of reactions. The rest of them – as lewd a crowd of libertines as he had ever seen! – could wait until later. Once he had eavesdropped on the scene by the lake, he knew that action could not be far away: it was time to make for the linen cupboard.

Now, crouched between shelves stacked with sheets and blankets and pillowcases, he slid aside the false panel hiding the mirror and stared through the two-way glass at the blue-draped four-poster.

The scene that he witnessed was, as the guidebooks say, worth the detour.

Agathe Laforge, naked, was lying on her back on the bed with her knees raised and her ankles locked around the back of the young Englishman. Mackenzie was working hard. Between the woman's spread thighs the flexed hemispheres of his bottom rose and fell with machine-like precision. Her breasts were squashed beneath the weight of his chest. He had entwined his fingers with hers and spread her plump arms wide on the silk sheets.

Serafini licked his lips. That was the way to treat the bitch: give it to her hard and strong! So far as he could see when the splatting hips drew far enough apart, the foreign stud was unusually well endowed. Well hung too, the major-domo observed, shifting his position so that his cheek lay against the glass and he could see the couple from a different angle. He hoped the boy would shaft her to a standstill.

Agathe's head moved from side to side on the pillow. Her mouth opened and closed spasmodically. One of the disadvantages of the linen cupboard mirror was that no sounds could penetrate the thick wall from the bedroom, but he assumed she was crooning and slobbering the way they did when a release was near.

Leaping light from the coal fire, flickering redly on the heaving torsos and writhing limbs, complemented the pallid illumination from the moon, but it would have been a great improvement – Serafini thought – if at least one of the lamps had been left alight.

Ah! The end of Act One was in sight. Agathe had suddenly stiffened, her heels drumming on the young man's spine. Her belly quaked. Her lips parted . . . and even through the wall the ghost of choked cry of ecstasy was audible. Mackenzie's buttocks clenched, his hips ground her down into the mattress, his head jerked up and his mouth too opened wide as he spasmed his liquid tribute into her receptive frame.

Maybe now, in a very short time – the young man had rolled off her and lay panting by her side – there would be more light?

Yes – the second time was always slower, and usually they wanted to see. Mackenzie was sitting on the bed, with one hand resting on her thigh. She was saying something, smiling, with one forearm laid across her forehead. He rose and walked across to the light cord, tugging at the tassel. *Formidable!* All three of the lamps blazed to life.

Serafini nodded. Now that he could see properly . . . well, this Mackenzie fellow certainly had the lean, spare figure of an athlete. And as for his equipment – there could be no doubt about the use for which that slack but heavy staff, and the bullish sac beneath it, had been designed!

Agathe was lying with her legs apart, the dark lips of her secret place gaping in eloquent testimony to the forced entry so recently made. Now she sat up, swinging those legs over the edge of the bed. She spoke again, pointing to the inlaid table. Mackenzie picked up his glass, splashed more brandy into the liquor already there, poured some for the woman, and carried the two balloons over to the four-poster. They smiled into each other's eyes and drank.

Five minutes later – her glass was almost empty – Agathe reached for him. She fondled the massive tube of flesh, rolling it between forefinger and thumb, cupping the head in her palm, milking the fleshy shaft.

Mackenzie laid down his glass. He stretched out to cradle her two breasts, weighing the soft mounds in his own palms, tweaking the rosy nipples. And now, as Serafini watched, he was hardening, lengthening visibly under her touch. Webbed veins throbbed along each side of his rigid cock.

Abruptly there was a flurry of action. Mackenzie was kneeling on the bed, his masculine pride jutting out like the bowsprit of a grain clipper. He turned her onto her face, spread her thighs and moved in between them. He snatched away one of the pillows and stuffed it beneath her hips. Then, lowering himself carefully, he seized those hips, dragging her pelvis towards him, and rammed into her from behind.

As he moved in and out with long, steady strokes, Agathe's hands, bunched into fists, pummelled the remaining pillows in delight.

Behind the mirror, Serafini nodded again. Dogs and bitches, that was the way! He rubbed his hands together with satisfaction.

But he couldn't afford to spend the whole night with this one couple, enjoyable though it might be. Other couples, other scenes claimed his attention. Never a man to shirk a self-imposed duty, the major-domo recovered the secret mirror and stole away.

No mirror and no spyhole permitted the curious to gaze into Robert Laforge's room. The risk was too great, the Master was too shrewd. But a man with a good ear could listen outside the door to his dressing-room. And tonight, Serafini knew, there would be something to listen to.

There were two reasons for this – or, more properly, a single reason with two separate aspects. The reason was the present hostility between the Master and the Mistress.

No sound from Agathe Laforge's room penetrated the linen cupboard, but the same could not be said of the dressing-room which separated that apartment from Robert Laforge's. There was a connecting door, locked on Agathe's side certainly, but the major-domo knew from his own experiments that anything and everything she did was clearly audible on the far side of that door. And presumably the reverse was also true.

Given that the Mistress had seduced the young Englishman precisely because of this fact, knowing that her husband would be infuriated when he heard the evidence of her infidelity, it was a reasonable assumption that he would play tit-for-tat and make sure that his own behaviour with the tart he had brought to the house was equally audible.

And audible to anyone in the corridor listening by the dressing-room's outer door.

The assumption was correct.

The voices of Robert Laforge and Milady could clearly be heard from that position.

The two apartments were situated in a private wing of the manor; no guests would be using the corridor, and Bertrand's rooms were on the far side of the house. Serafini settled himself with his ear pressed to the crack between the door and the jamb.

' . . . so pleased to see that you still wear that very fetching corset, my dear,' Robert Laforge's voice was saying.

And then the woman's reply: 'Well, if I didn't know what you liked by now, you naughty man, I certainly ought to!'

'No, don't take it off yet. I like the way these padded – busks, are they called? – I like the way they push your bosom out. I'll unlace it for you later.'

'If you insist on having your pleasure your way, you'll have to pay for it, sirrah!'

'Don't I always?'

'I'm not talking about money, silly. You know very well what I mean. Now get down there and do your duty like a gentleman.'

For a moment there was silence, broken by the sounds of movement, and then a small, stifled noise that could have been a gasp of female pleasure. Serafini heard something like the smacking of lips.

'Ooh, that tickles! . . . *Ah!*' Milady's voice was suddenly husky. 'I'm happy to see, Robert, that you have not lost your touch.'

A flurry, again, of movement; rustle of silk and scrape of heavier material over muscled flesh. A quick, brief, breathless exchange: 'I have to have . . .' (laforge).

'Mind – don't tear it!' (Milady). 'No, let me: I want to see' (the man). 'Up here, then' (the woman). 'So soft; such creamy lips!' 'Oh, my! What a dutiful soldier we have here: always at attention!'

'Oh, my God, that's so *good*!' Robert Laforge said hoarsely. 'Why are you so kind to me?'

Milady giggled. 'You know very well why,' she said.

Outside the door, Serafini tensed, waiting during the ensuing pause for the tell-tale signs that he knew from experience would signal the final phase – at least for the next hour or so – of the encounter.

He heard them on schedule.

A lowering of weight. An indrawn breath and then a groan from the man. A rhythmic creak of bedsprings, steady and slow, then gradually accelerating towards a crescendo . . .

The major-domo glanced at his fob watch. He switched off the lights in the passage and tiptoed away.

Corinne Dubois, the excesses she had shared with Bertrand and Tom Crawford at the Chabanais still fresh in her mind, had hoped to repeat the threesome during Agathe Laforge's house party. Failing that, her preference would have been for the sculptor, the tougher, the more muscular of the two men. Unfortunately, Crawford had proved impossible to pin down. He had been evasive, a little distant even, and finally he had vanished altogether. Having at one point seen him deep in conversation with that wretched butler fellow, Corinne suspected that he had gone off with a pert, busty little housemaid over whom Serafini seemed to wield something of a proprietorial air.

She had wondered if it might be worthwhile tracking them down and insinuating herself to make a threesome of a different kind, but thought better of it, realising that the girl came from the local village. However 'accessible' they might be, country servants were less sophisticated than Parisiennes . . . and the last thing Corinne wanted was a scandal that could lose her her job.

Eventually she settled after all for the son of the house. He was at least enthusiastic – which was more than could be said for her newspaper colleague, Patrice Delgado – and it would save her from the less than welcome attentions of Agathe's brother, Uncle Gaston Despierre, or the odious Comte de la Ferrière.

Less adventurous than some, young Bertrand Laforge customarily confined such amorous exploits as he indulged in at home to the wide bed which was centred between shelves of technical books and engineering journals in his private attic apartment. Such lack of sexual variety suited Serafini very well, and the spyhole he had bored through the beading of the room's oak panelling was focused, together with its miniature magnifying lens, directly on the mattress.

The major-domo's vantage point, as in the case of Bertrand's mother, was in a store-room – a loft this time crammed with steamer trunks, hampers of old clothes and discarded bedding, and furniture in need of repair. An easy chair with a broken arm had been dragged across to the dividing wall, and from this he could comfortably survey everything that went on in and around Bertrand's bed.

It was late when Serafini at last installed himself. The strains of the final waltz selection drifted up from the ground floor, and he could near voices, laughter and the splutter of a motor car engine from the stable yard. Clearly, however, young Laforge and his girl had only just arrived in the apartment. They were standing, one on either side of the bed, undressing as unconcernedly as an old married couple. Squinting through his eyepiece, Serafini shook his head.

What a waste! All the titillating indelicacies of disrobing – the spilling of breasts out of the bust bodice, the rise into view of the hairy pubic triangle as drawers were lowered, the sudden, spearing appearance of an excited male's equipment – all thrown away through an unpardonable lack of imagination!

The loss of course was the couple's: it was they who missed out on the fascinated appreciation of each separate layer of nudity as it was exposed. Serafini could at least – he hastily switching his attention from one to the other – gather together the tattered remnants of what might have been. But he missed the communication of shared excitement inseparable from mutual undressing.

Never mind. The girl at least seemed to be in a hurry. Perhaps the force of their coupling would in some way make up for the loss. She was certainly as choice a morsel as the young master had ever brought up here!

Very good breasts. Serafini smiled to himself, thinking of the French slang phrase, *il y a du monde au balcon* – the balcony is crowded – to describe a woman with a full bust. He couldn't think of an equivalent term for billowing hips, a taut, rounded little belly, and springy hair that cried out for fingers to be run through it. If there was no such expression, he would have to invent one!

Suddenly there was action on the bed. Both of them were naked. Bertrand sat on the edge of the mattress. He pulled her across and sat her on his lap with her back to him. Corinne smiled a slow, mischievous and infinitely seductive smile. Her full lower lip gleamed in the light from the room's one bedside lamp. Very deliberately, she parted her fleshy thighs. Between them, a demon king in a sexual pantomime, his erect organ sprang into view.

Bertrand reached around her, lowered his hands, and drew aside the creased outer lips that sheltered the entrance to her secret place.

She leaned back against him, her features set in a

blank, perhaps even faintly bemused expression, but relieved still by that enigmatic smile. With her own hands she grasped the blood-engorged proof of his desire and pressed the satin-smooth tip against the dark inner lips.

Squirming on the shelf of his thighs, she advanced her pelvis, fingertips pressing harder at the same time so that the head of Bertrand's shaft sank between those sensitive pads of flesh, forcing them apart until the outer end of his treasure – and then, inch by inch, the whole pulsing length of him – was sucked in.

Supporting himself now on his two hands, the young man flexed his hips, arching them up and down while she rose and lowered herself to meet his thrusts, her feet pressing the floor.

Serafini watched in fascination as they settled into a studied, dreamlike rhythm as matched and inexorable as the opposing poles in a beam engine or a piston in a cylinder. From the position he was in, the setting of the spyglass afforded him a perfect frontal view of the couple, looking slightly up . . . at Bertrand's bony knees overlapped by the young woman's fleshier thighs, at the rise and fall of belly and hips, the slow bounce of rose-nippled breasts and the wrinkled, tight pouch of scrotum between her spread legs. And above all at the reciprocating genitals themselves: the ridged shaft, glistening now with moisture, plunging and then re-emerging from those darkly sucking lips opening among the wet hairs furring her loins.

Serafini frowned. The rhythm was quickening, becoming sporadic, almost convulsive. Bertrand's mouth opened and his head tilted back. Surely they weren't going to spoil so well-conceived a tableau with a premature . . . But no! The major-domo nodded his appreciation. The girl was no novice; she knew what she was about.

With a single lithe movement, she separated herself,

swung over one leg, and stood facing him. She scrambled up onto the bed. With her mouth close to his ear she whispered something Serafini was unable to hear. She laughed, and the knowing, intimate chuckle was clearly audible in the loft where the voyeur sat.

Corinne was on her hands and knees, looking over her shoulder with an inviting smile.

Bertrand, still wet and gleaming, knelt rapidly behind her. He shuffled as near as he could, then softly drawing apart the twin globes of her bottom, he thrust savagely forward with his hips.

Corinne jerked, uttering a stifled cry as the young man's hardened staff slammed into her. He leaned forward across her back, cupping the breasts swinging beneath her rib-cage in both hands. She heaved back her pelvis, meeting each of the strokes impaling her belly with a forceful push of her own.

For Serafini, the picture was less enticing than the previous scene: the copulating pair were in profile now, and apart from an occasional glance at Bertrand's stiffened rod when he drew unusually far back before some extra-ferocious thrust, their sexual equipment was invisible. He took what pleasure he could from an exact scrutiny of each abandoned face as they ground together with the even precision of a clockwork toy. But again, as the tempo increased, it was Corinne who staved off a climax. Collapsing flat on her face, she twisted away from him, rolled over onto her back and raised her knees. Bertrand was left half upright, his rigid prow accusingly pointed at his erstwhile partner. Corinne giggled. She raised herself up on one elbow, reaching out her free hand to clasp the nape of his neck and draw his head down to her loins. His face sank between her thighs.

Serafini watched the centre part of the girl's body arch up to meet his questing mouth. She lay back with her arms outflung and a beatific expression illuminating her features. She drew her knees up further still, compressing her own breasts, so that the whole of her sex was on offer and his sucking lips could make way for the tongue probing her lewdly displayed underparts. Then, when Bertrand shifted his position, stretching up long arms to fondle the breasts, she straightened her legs and insinuated her feet beneath him to massage his manhood with her toes.

Later he stood beside the bed and she lay with her buttocks on the edge of the mattress, her legs draped over his shoulders while he penetrated more deeply still the gaping wound of her desire.

When they were both back on the bed and he ma-noeuvred himself on top of her splayed body, the ma-jor-domo hung a framed biblical text over his spyhole and crept away.

The scene in the bedroom suite allotted to the Comtesse van den Bergh and her German friend was far more discreet – though not without its tantalizing possibilities, for the two *Amazones* were playing secret host to the music-hall critic, Patrice Delgado.

Tantalizing might be the operative word, however – for this was the least successful of Serafini's viewpoints, being a simple hole bored through the scrollwork of a door panel, which offered only a very limited angle on the room beyond.

There was the additional risk here of discovery: the passageway led to one of the bathrooms, and there was always a chance that a guest might appear at the stairhead or emerge from another corridor running at right-angles to the first.

Perhaps the element of danger added spice to the major-domo's solitary pleasures. He crouched down unconcernedly with his eye to the spyhole, well aware that a barefoot nocturnal prowler, silently manifesting himself or herself, could surprise him long before he could leap to his feet and play the rôle of the dutiful servant on his rounds.

The segment of Dagmar's room that was visible included a wide, heavily upholstered armchair, a padded stool in front of a grate banked up with glowing embers, and the upper corner of a bed, together with its night-table and electric lamp.

The Comtesse was reclining in the chair, still wearing her turquoise Doucet robe. Gisela von Zwickenheim, dressed only in a thick, oyster silk négligée, perched on one of the padded arms, a sturdy hand teasing the auburn tendrils curling on Dagmar's neck. Delgado squatted on the stool. Astonishingly, he was completely naked.

Giacomo Serafini cursed under his breath. He had stayed too long with Bertrand and his girl! He would have given a lot to see just how those two lezzies had got the critic out of his clothes . . .

No matter: Scene Two could prove to be just as fascinating – so long as the actors remained in view. He shifted his position, moving his eye up and down, from side to side. No good: the difference in the area visible was minimal.

The pulsing firelight glowed on Delgado's skin. Like many spare, wiry men, he was streaked with a lot of body hair, matted on his chest and growing thickly on forearms and thighs. Yet, seated on the low stool with his knees canted up – and a dark rod of flesh spearing at the same angle from the black thatch covering his loins – he looked curiously vulnerable before the two large, well-formed women.

' . . . should have thought,' the Baroness was saying, 'that your music-hall experiences would have brought you more into contact with ladies of our . . . shall we say persuasion?'

The critic cleared his throat. 'Well, of course . . . I mean, I was at the Moulin Rouge when Colette played that sketch with the Marquise of Belbeuf pretending to be her husband, and the audience threw cushions at them. Bernhardt took me to the place in the Rue Jacob. The Duchess of . . .'

'No, no,' Dagmar interrupted. 'Privately. Not making a point of daring the scandalmongers. In more intimate situations.' The soft lips curled mischievously. 'Like tonight, for instance.'

Delgado swallowed. Serafini wondered again exactly what had led to his nudity. Whose suggestion had it been? On what grounds? The man was clearly excited sexually, but it was beyond belief that two such *Amazones* would sit calmly by and permit him to strip in front of them unless there had been some kind of mutual accord. And equally abnormal for them to want him to.

He sighed. All Madame Laforge's guests seemed to be abnormal these days!

'And you really think, little man' – it was the German speaking – 'that with what you have down there you can offer a woman as much pleasure as a sister spirit with what *she* has?'

'I didn't state it as a fact,' Delgado said defensively. 'I said I didn't see why not. Not necessarily, anyway.'

The Baroness's fingers had relinquished Dagmar's hair; now they swept across the creamy skin of her shoulders, around the scooped neckline of the dress, and plunged into the hollow separating her breasts. 'We shall see,' she said.

She leaned suddenly forward. Both her hands slid beneath the heavy, sleek blue material. Her knuckles showed against the bust line as she cupped the Comtesse's breasts, displacing them gently while the reclining beauty sighed and squirmed her hips against the brocaded cushion. 'All right then, Delgado,' Dagmar said throatily. 'Come this way and . . . prove your point!'

The young man rose swiftly to his feet. His eyes were gleaming.

Dagmar reached down, seized the tight hem of her skirt, and dragged it forcefully up until it was bunched around her hips. She was wearing nothing underneath it.

Delgado licked his lips, gazing lustfully at the soft mound of belly exposed, the curls of auburn hair between those alabaster thighs. Seizing the jutting proof of his virility in one hand he strode manfully forward. 'Not like that!' Gisela said sharply. 'Get down there, down on your knees! Now kiss her . . . No! There, *there*!'

She bent right over, the pink tip of her tongue brushing the Comtesse's parted lips.

Dagmar spread her legs. She raised her knees. Serafini could no longer see Delgado's face. One of the *Amazone's* hands had vanished among the folds of silk sheathing Gisela's thighs.

The watching man drew in his breath . . . and it was at that moment that he realized he wasn't the only voyeur on the scene. In the firelit room, a fourth figure walked suddenly into view. It was the actress, Gabrielle Dorziat. She had changed into a jacket and skirt of sombre material, and she was smoking a cigarette in a long black holder. 'Come, come,' she said, speaking for the first time. 'A little more elegance! A sense of drama, of *mise en scène,* my friends.' She took the holder from her mouth and made an expansive gesture. 'Pray what do you think that bed is for?'

In the corridor, Serafini gritted his teeth in frustration. The trio which had looked so promising had scrambled out of his sight. All he could see now were the heels of Delgado's feet. Dorziat was sitting in the armchair, turned towards the bed, her eyebrows raised and her lips twisted into a quizzical smile around the ebony mouthpiece.

Startled, the major-domo jerked upright. Heavy footsteps sounded on the stairs. Still fully dressed, Gaston

Despierre strode into view on his way to the bathroom. 'Ah, Serafini,' he said genially. 'A successful evening, wouldn't you say?'

The servant was halfway to the stairhead. 'Undoubtedly, Doctor. Most – ah – interesting,' he murmured.

A simple old-fashioned keyhole was the sole viewpoint available to Serafini on his next port of call. The room, at the far end of the guest wing, was seldom used and he had never found time to equip it with one of his more sophisticated viewing devices.

It was occupied tonight by the Dutch-Indonesian woman, Mademoiselle Zelle – or, as it seemed her preference, Mata Hari. A performer of some kind, one of the kitchen-maids had reported, but not in the same class as Dorziat, who had been trained at the Comédie Française.

Mlle Zelle was performing all right tonight. On one of his surreptitious reconnaissance forays, Serafini had seen the odd, loud-voiced Englishman, Champney, haring up the back stairs soon after the dancer had retired. And according to Agathe Laforge's housekeeper, very unladylike noises, accompanied by energetic male snorts, had been audible – indeed were impossible to shut out – soon afterwards.

An odd pairing, the major-domo considered, especially as the female member had seemed on arrival more than closely connected with the lezzies. Oh, well . . . it took all sorts. He put his eye to the keyhole.

Anything energetic was clearly over, at least for the moment. Champney and the woman were sitting on the floor at each side of the fire, with a half-empty bottle of champagne between them. She was wearing a towelling bath-robe; he was naked, the light from the flames gilding his sandy hair.

'Very rum,' Champney was saying, 'you bein' up in

all this engineering stuff, metallurgy and suchlike. Never have thought it.'

'I have a friend with an interest in the Fokker concern,' she said. 'A Baron von Richthofen, in the German army. You know him?'

'Haven't had the pleasure, old thing.' Champney shook his head. 'Tell you the truth, we're not too close to our Teutonic cousins these days. Something to do with politics, I shouldn't wonder . . . Here! What say we swig the rest of this bottle of fizz and leg it back to ye olde divan, hey?'

'You wish to . . . make love . . . for a third time?' Mata Hari sounded incredulous.

So was Serafini. He grinned. If this lanky, explosive *type anglais* had already done it twice and was now ready for a third try – and ready he was: he jutted, he quivered, he glistened – then he was certainly a runner to watch!

The trouble was (Serafini banged a fist on his thigh in exasperation), he *couldn't* be watched. Or not all of him. He had picked up the heavily built Mlle Zelle, carried her to the bed, and laid her on it in a single athletic movement . . . and from the keyhole the bed could not be seen! The major-domo was left with a fleeting memory of female legs flung wide, of hairy male thighs, of a sudden sharp exhalation of breath from the woman. And then there was nothing to watch but two pairs of feet: her heels on the floor, jerking up spasmodically and then relaxing; his toes between them, shoving up rhythmically. Clearly she was half on and half off the bed. Maybe the man simply couldn't wait!

What was certain, partly from the frantic evidence of the feet, more from the suck and slap of flesh, the measured gasps and grunts, was the demonic intensity, the sheer force of Champney's copulation. He performed with the mechanical regularity of one of those clockwork frogs set hopping on the pavements of Paris by the vendors of novelties at Christmas time.

Serafini stared at the fire, watched the feet, listened to the sounds of love. It must, he thought, be something like bulling a cow. Soon afterwards – three minutes? four? – he heard a strangled shout of triumph. Then even the feet disappeared.

He wasn't left alone for long. The Englishman was back from the bidet with a towel around his waist, pouring the last drain from the champagne bottle; Mata Hari sat on the floor by the brass fender. She had a slightly dazed air. Beyond the open edges of the bathrobe, red fingermarks striped her sallow skin.

'By George, that was good!' Champney enthused. 'What I like about you, old thing, you're a good sport. No messing about. No waste of time with the bally prelims. I'm all for that.'

He stared at her, yellow teeth bared in a grin beneath the fierce moustache. 'And I thought you were one of the she-she, girls-are-for-girls, merchants!'

'It is possible to enjoy both kinds of . . . love,' Mata Hari said carefully. 'For different reasons. With men, it is true, I do prefer the more – what shall I say? – the more direct approach. Women are for the slower, easier, perhaps more tender intimacies.'

'Well, I don't know about that. I mean, well . . . I suppose, after all, there are some people . . .' Champney paused. Evidently, the concept of tenderness, as related to intimacy, was beyond him.

'To come back to things that really interest you' – Mata Hari hurried to his rescue – 'I believe you are having an enviable success in your country with the Mackenzie sporting car?'

'Oh, my goodness, yes! Specially in hillclimbs an' that kind of thing. Trouble is, with the rain and all that mud, we're kind of vulnerable, don't you know, to the old devil rust.'

'To rust?'

Champney nodded. 'Very sparse bodywork, mud-guards practically non-existent, half the works exposed. Floorboards and panels like bloody lace in no time; put your foot straight through onto the road! Our host has some secret process he uses on *his* cars. Tell you a secret.' The Englishman laid a finger against his nose. 'One of the reasons young Paul is here is to try and coax the old man into letting us know just how he does the trick. Goodbye rust, I mean.'

'He's got his troubles too, so I hear,' Mata Hari said. 'Bertrand tells they want to cut down weight, use a lighter, faster engine, but none of the experimental mod-els they have produced are reliable enough. Broken con-rods, cracked heads, metal fatigue and sheering stress because the faster motor runs hotter. Even the big cars have some of the same problems.' She smiled. 'But that, I gather, is one of the crosses Mackenzie doesn't have to bear?'

'Not on your life. We've got a little four-cylinder fifteen-hundred that'll hit five thou before the needle goes into the red. Even our seventeen-fifty can make four-fifty. Stay there all day, too!'

'Remarkable! How splendid!' One of her hands lay carelessly in Champney's lap, the fingers brushing a towelling bulge thrust out at the top of his thighs. 'Tell me: how do you explain this success?'

'Alloys, old dear. Tougher, much lighter, higher melt-ing point, less risk of seizing. Give the engine a longer life anyway.'

The hand moved, turned palm downwards, stroked. 'You know the French saying, *Jamais deux sans trois*,' Mata Hari said. 'Never two without a third. We already proved that, didn't we? But I never met a man who was magician enough to turn three into four!'

Champney was on his feet almost before the words were out of her mouth. 'What ho!' he crowed, reaching down to pull her upright. 'Meet Mister Four, the man of your life!'

She wound her arms around his neck as he carried her to the divan. 'And exactly what kind of alloy would that be, *chéri*?' she cooed.

'What? Oh, that. Frankly, I'm supposed to keep mum about that. Mustn't tell a soul. But I don't s'pose it counts with a girl, what!'

'You can tell me; we're friends, aren't we?'

'Absolutely.' The couple passed out of Serafini's view. He heard the creak of springs. 'You know about manganese, of course. Element number twenty-five, atomic weight fifty-four point nine three, melts at twelve sixty degrees Centigrade, used in the purification of iron. Well, have you heard of vanadium and titanium…?'

The major-domo was already on his way.

Nellie Lebérigot was probably the happiest person in the manor house that night. Freed from the responsibility of seducing Paul Mackenzie – Bertrand had merely shrugged helplessly when he saw the young man carried off by his mother – Nellie had retired early. Now, warmed and downed and quilted, curled up like a kitten in her silken sheets, she slept soundly, without dreams . . . and alone.

There had been a last-minute mix-up over the guests' sleeping arrangements, and it was the housekeeper – not Giacomo Serafini – who finally decided upon the occupants of the room in the converted barn.

The viewpoint was difficult to reach, and the rafters uncomfortable to lie on. There was a risk, too, that a thump or scrape could alert the occupants, or an unguarded move put a foot through the ceiling. Once installed, however, the watcher was afforded a panoramic spectacle, only fifteen feet away and immediately above the bed.

Serafini considered it worth the risk . . . provided

there was anything to watch.

Or worth watching.

Tonight, the vantage point in the converted barn was to prove his big disappointment. The guests lodged in the suite were the petite, flower-like Mme Foucault de la Roquette and Miss Dawn Broad, the English horse-woman.

That in itself would not necessarily have discouraged the major-domo. He was perfectly content to spy on women. When it came to sexual activity, he found it more stimulating when both men *and* women were involved, individually or severally. But the amorous exertions of the *Amazones* made a perfectly acceptable second best. What interested him, though, in either case, was the fleshy manipulation – not the maltreatment – of the bodies involved. And it appeared to be a scene of the latter variety that he was secretly observing through the concealed spyhole in the chandelier rose.

Marie-Ange Foucault de la Roquette was lying face-down on the bed. She was naked, her small fists clenched on the pillow into which her tear-stained face was pressed.

The Englishwoman stood by the night-table, wearing nothing but her riding boots. She was almost flat-chested, with a trim waist that was oddly at variance with muscular haunches and the calves of an athlete. She was holding a leather-covered quirt in her left hand.

Marie-Ange was speaking when Serafini took up his position. 'Oh, please Miss Broad,' she gasped. 'I'm sorry . . . I didn't mean . . . Please don't beat me again.'

'I've told you before,' Dawn Broad's deep voice said evenly, 'I will not tolerate this kind of possessiveness. Your behaviour at the *guinguette*, your childish sulks this evening, were quite insupportable.'

'It's only because I love you,' Marie-Ange wailed. 'When you pay attention to someone –'

'Silence! The fact that I happened to tap Mata Hari with this' – she raised the riding crop – 'as she reached

225

the climax of her performance was a part of *her* act, and in no sense an emotional involvement of mine. It had no more significance than Gabrielle Dorziat or you yourself clapping your own hands. To make it the cause for a jealous scene is ridiculous!'

'I already said I'm sorry.'

The horsewoman moved across to the bed. The thick, dark brows were knitted into a straight, frowning line. Serafini noticed that her upper lip was shadowed with a faint down of hairs. 'It's high time you learned your lesson,' she said, raising the crop again.

Marie-Ange was broad-shouldered, with small, pointed breasts. Her hips and bottom, however, wcrc generous – and the skin of the buttocks was already reddened and striped with parallel marks where blows had fallen before. 'I hope I don't have to tell you again,' the Englishwoman said, punctuating her remarks with lashes from the riding crop. 'I will not . . . *Thwack!* . . .tolerate . . . *Thwack!* . . . any more of this absurd . . . *Thwack! Thwack!* . . . jealousy. I do what I want . . . *Thwack!* . . . when I want to. And the sooner you realise it . . . *Thwack!* . . . the better for you.'

After a final blow, she tossed the crop aside.

Marie-Ange had squealed, kicking her slender legs ineffectually as each stroke fell. Now Miss Broad sat beside her and took the naked, sobbing young woman in her arms.

Moving with infinite care, Serafini levered himself away from the spyhole and inched back towards the safety of the old hayloft. He had never heard of Sigmund Freud and he was unfamiliar with the works of the Herr Doktor Krafft-Ebing. He had better things to do than waste his time watching this kind of thing.

There was a full-length mirror in the door of a wardrobe in his own room. Twenty minutes later he stood in front of it, contemplating with approval his own reflection as he slowly removed his clothes.

CHAPTER EIGHTEEN

Paul Mackenzie was awakened by a sound so mournful that it appeared to him in his half-sleeping state like the cries of a defeated hero denied entrance to Valhalla or Oscar Wilde's great tritons 'who far out upon the sea blew hoarsely on their horns'.

He struggled out of bed. It seemed to him that very little time had passed since he left the arms of his hostess, and it was in fact still ten minutes short of seven o'clock. He went to the window of his room.

The sound was indeed produced by a horn: a flat, bell-mouthed instrument with brass tubes arranged in concentric circles. It was canted up one-handed and blown by a horseman.

He repeated the call, and Paul – suddenly aware of the yelping of hounds – remembered that the local stag hunt meet was due that morning at the manor.

Paul's window overlooked the stable yard. He watched the hunt assemble. Robert Laforge had offered to mount any of the guests who wished to follow, and the Comte de la Ferrière, Uncle Gaston, one of the bankers and Hector Champney had accepted the invitation. They were soon to be joined by Gisela, Dagmar, Gabrielle Dorziat and – not unexpectedly – the English rider, Miss Dawn Broad.

Mackenzie was unfamiliar with the French equivalent of hunting pink, but the crowd forming up behind the Master were colourful enough – the side-saddled

227

females with their tall hats, long skirts and shiny boots; most of the men wearing stark white breeches with dark coats and peaked, black velvet hunting caps.

The Huntsman blew his melancholy dirge a final time, and the cavalcade, awash with a tide of hounds, clattered out of the yard and rode away towards the forest where their quarry was to be found.

From an attic dormer above Paul Mackenzie's window, Yvette Tambay, one of Laforge's maidservants, had also watched the hunt assemble. She had observed, with a smile of quiet amusement, Giacomo Serafini's supervision of the footmen distributing the traditional stirrup cups to the riders. The major-domo, obsequious as usual, had nevertheless seemed a trifle preoccupied, his face haggard and his chin disfigured by a small cut where he had gashed himself shaving.

Yvette of course knew why. The old fox had been up half the night eavesdropping and spying on Madam's guests. Probably on Madam herself, too. Maybe even on the Master and his fancy woman, if he had the nerve. And wasn't *that* a spicy subject for discussion in the servants' hall!

Serafini, in any case, would by now know more about the guests' personal idiosyncrasies than any one of them knew about all the others. Yvette's smile broadened. There were things she knew, too – things the blue-chinned voyeur, for all his cleverness, would be ignorant of. One of them was the fact that Tom Crawford had spent the entire night with her in the deep-mattress feather bed beneath the sloping ceiling of this attic room.

Another was the fact that the sculptor was still with her. The smile grew wider still. Yvette was leaning out of the window, her elbows on the sill, her heavy breasts supported between them. She was standing with her feet spread wide apart.

A third thing that Serafini wouldn't know was that

Crawford had pulled up her skirt and draped it over her hips to expose her naked buttocks and the hairy furrow separating them. Nude from the waist down, she had been open to his sexual advance since the first blast on the Huntsman's horn!

Different sort of hunter, different kind of horn, Yvette thought to herself coarsely. She squirmed her hips back to meet the sculptor's thrusts.

Hunched behind her, invisible from the yard below, Crawford crouched with his splayed artist's fingers clenched over her meaty haunches, shafting in and out of her as regularly as a metronome.

Yvette smiled at the mounted guests, she nodded to the footmen, to the unsuspecting Serafini. She was breathing fast, the breasts swelling against the tiles of the windowsill. 'Monsieur,' she whispered, 'you must stop . . . or at least slow down. I am very close to the . . . I am very near–'

'Nonsense!' Crawford said behind her. 'I want you to come in front of all those people, and none of them knowing a thing about it!'

He was enjoying himself. The big, busty, hot-blooded country girl was exactly his cup of tea – no messing about, no false modesty, no please-sir-we-really-shouldn't, no coyness or clinging; just a hearty, healthy, lustful appreciation, a mutual enjoyment of the pleasures of the flesh. And what flesh! In the soft clasp of the feather bed, Crawford had wallowed all night long among buttocks and thighs and billowing hips, his skin afire with the hot contact of belly and breasts, his lips and tongue scorched with the flames of desire. The girl was willing to learn, too: one of the ablest and most inventive pupils he had ever had. A night, in short, that he would long remember.

The members of the hunt had ridden out of the yard. The yelping of dogs was dying away. Serafini and the footmen were clearing up – horse droppings, glasses, empty champagne and brandy bottles. Serafini looked up and saw the girl leaning out of the window.

'Have you nothing better to do than stare?' he demanded.

Crawford was lunging into her with redoubled force. 'I'm not,' she replied breathlessly, 'not on . . . duty today . . . I'm not on duty until . . . Oh! *Aah!* . . . until nine o'clock.'

'*What* was that you said?'

'I said it looks like a fine day!' Yvette laughed.

It was a fine day. Early morning mists shrouding the trees in the park had vanished soon after dawn, and there were sunbeams slanting through the leaded panes of the breakfast room windows when Paul sat down with a plate of grilled kidneys, coddled eggs and a huge cup of black coffee. The remaining banker was joking with Nellie and Milady at the far end of the long refectory table. Patrice Delgado stood at the serve-yourself buffet, lifting the domed lids of silver entrée dishes and sniffing the hot contents.

Bertrand Laforge walked into the room, nodded to the Englishman, poured coffee, and sat down beside him.

'Old fellow,' he said, 'there is something I have to tell you.'

Paul's eyebrows raised. 'Really?'

'Something – ah – a little delicate. Something that wouldn't have been necessary had you not been guilty of indelicacy yourself, keeping your friends in the dark.'

The young man gulped. My God! Bertrand must have found out about the passionate, the inexplicable night with his mother! He felt himself flushing a dark red. What was he going to say?

'It's . . . well, it's about the costume ball at Poiret's,' Bertrand went on, seeming a trifle ill-at-ease himself.

Paul heaved a sigh of relief. He swallowed a mouth-

ful of coffee. Bertrand continued: 'It seems you had an
. . . assignation . . . . there with a young lady who shall
be nameless. It seems further' – he coughed – 'that the
meeting was more than satisfactory. Not to put too fine
a point on it, I gather you had the time of your life!'

'Well?' Emboldened by the knowledge that the previous night's excess remained a secret, Paul allowed a
haughty note to tinge his voice.

'Well, the fact is, owing to the masks and disguises
and suchlike, the fact is that the person you spent the
night with was not the person you believed you had the
assignation with. Although you were unaware of it, there
had been a . . . substitution.'

'My God!' Mackenzie jerked upright, a forkful of
kidney poised halfway to his mouth. 'Who the devil
was it then?'

'Honour, my friend, forbids me to reveal the name:
it would be breaking the strictest of confidences.'

'But . . .? I fail to understand. How could such a
substitution be effected? There was an exchange of letters, arrangements were made – and kept to the last
detail. How–?'

'Letters can he intercepted. The reply you received
may not actually have been written by the person to
whom your own message was addressed.'

'I see.' Paul was frowning. 'That would certainly
explain why the arrangements suggested in the false
letter were followed so exactly! It would also explain
why Mademoiselle–'

'We shall quote no names, if you please. But, yes, it
would explain why a certain lady – whom you took to
be your erstwhile partner, but who was in fact totally
ignorant of the entire affair – has to date been . . .'

'. . . shall we say *ill-disposed* to my efforts to follow
it up?'

'Exactly.' Bertrand drained his coffee and put down
the cup. 'It all comes, you see, from a mistaken kind of

prudishness and a refusal to confide in one's friends. Had you mentioned this project to Tom or myself, we would surely have warned you against it. Considering, that is, the characters likely to be involved. There is, however, one thing I can tell you now: any confusion there is would probably have been due to the use of initials rather than names.'

Paul pushed back his chair and went to the buffet, forking a slice of mountain ham onto his plate. Initials! Of course! He remembered now: he had heard Camille's family name when Bertrand and the sculptor had first spoken about her, but by the time he wrote his note, he had forgotten it . . . so he had simply addressed the letter to 'Mademoiselle C.D.' The flowers, too.

And of course – why in Heaven's name hadn't it occurred to him before! – there was another Mlle C.D. living in the same house, in the same apartment.

Corinne Dubois.

The letter he received in return had been signed with the same initials. No more; no less. No wonder his night-time companion had steadfastly refused to remove her mask! No wonder Camille had been outraged!

But how could he have been so innocent, so naive as to imagine that a girl repeatedly described as cold and frigid could all at once have been turned into an abandoned seductress, just because of his manly charms?

Paul carried his plate back to the table. 'I feel such a fool!' he confessed.

'You behaved like a fool,' Bertrand said unsympathetically. And then, remembering that the young foreigner was supposed to be buttered up, he added hastily: 'But given those circumstances, anyone could have made the same mistake.'

'Perhaps. What I'd like to know is: was the deception deliberate, or was it a genuine mistake on account of the similarity in initials? I left the flowers and the letter with the concierge, you see, and asked her to deliver them to the young lady upstairs with fair hair. Do you suppose she simply left them in the hallway and the . . . wrong person . . . happened to come in first and assumed they were for her?'

Bertrand glanced down the long table. Nellie, Milady and the banker had opened the French windows and strolled out into the garden. Delgado was munching his breakfast, hidden behind a newspaper. 'Frankly,' Bertrand said, 'I don't. Knowing the persons involved, that is. Theoretically, it could have happened that way, of course. But not with this particular cast.' He shook his head. 'Take my word for it, old boy: the lady knew what she was doing. You have been – as our Yankee friends would say – taken for a ride!'

'You could say that!' Paul smiled reminiscently. 'It was a stunning night! The thing is – do I go back to the lady who really was with me at the party, say I Know All, and hope for a repeat performance? Or would it be better to forget the whole thing and keep trying for the girl who originally attracted me?'

'Forget it,' Bertrand advised. He glanced again at Delgado and lowered his voice. 'The lady with the mask is good fun. She's nice. She's an enthusiast, a sport. But she's a scalp-hunter, what Doctor Freud would call a nymphomaniac. So far as you are concerned, she's had you; you are no longer a counter on the board. What interests her is who comes next.'

Paul laughed aloud. 'Are you telling me, sir, that the lady is . . . promiscuous?'

Young Laforge clapped him on the shoulder. 'You could say that!' he said.

It was not often that Giacomo Serafini was surprised, less frequently still that he could be said to be astonished. There were, after all, very few things, especially those of an intimate nature, with which he was not familiar. But this time it would not be an exaggeration to say that the major-domo was flabbergasted.

And at ten-forty-five in the morning, too!

He had not even intended to hold one of what he called his watching briefs. Breakfast was over; the arrangements for luncheon were completed, a dinner menu had been decided upon, and the necessary instructions issued to the housekeeping and cleaning staff. In the free time that remained to him before any guest was likely to require an apéritif, Serafini determined that, for once, he would pay attention to his health. He did not take enough exercise. He knew it. The exigencies of his employment – and of his private interests – forbade such trivial pursuits as tennis or horseriding or even croquet. But the spring sunshine today was tempting, it was warm for the time of the year, and there was an indefinable air of promise in the atmosphere. He would, he decided, take a walk in the park.

The promise was fulfilled before he was three hundred yards from the manor.

What he saw there sent him hurrying back to the house for a powerful pair of Zeiss field-glasses that he kept hidden in his room.

Climbing the oak tree was not difficult; he had done it often enough before. In bright sunshine, with a score of guests distributed around the estate, it demanded a certain amount of discretion. And speed and even courage if the ascent was to be swift and the purpose of the binoculars disguised.

But those he wished to observe were not short of these very qualities – excepting perhaps discretion. And if they could dare, so could he. He lay along his favourite branch and focused on the summerhouse, which was built out over the water on the far side of an arm of thee irregularly shaped ornamental lake.

It was a wooden structure, no larger than a medium-sized living room, with a shingled roof and a wide verandah sheltered by a painted wood canopy with scalloped edges that reminded him of a country railway station. A flight of steps led to the verandah from a small landing stage. Beneath its roof the summerhouse wall was pierced by a large picture window and a door whose upper panels were also glass.

Serafini's hands shook. Yes – he had not been mistaken. The summerhouse was most definitely the site of 'goings-on'!

The field-glasses showed him, about seventy feet away, the single pane of the window . . . and, on the far side of it, a pair of hairy buttocks, undeniably male. Beyond those masculine hips, in the sharpest detail, was a face, unmistakably female, the lips of its painted mouth opened wide.

The buttocks moved – Serafini was seeing them from directly behind – and the face disappeared. The buttocks were oscillating now, and a pair of slender, beringed hands were visible on the hips above them, pressing the owner forward.

Very slightly, Serafini adjusted the focus wheel. He could see further into the room. The summerhouse was sparsely furnished – half a dozen rattan armchairs, a bamboo table with a glass top, two striped canvas recliners folded up and propped against a wall. On the wooden floorboards between these items, a woman knelt with her bobbing head sporadically appearing beyond the hirsute hips and posterior the major-domo had first seen.

. The man was not entirely naked, he saw as the couple swayed this way and that: a shirt, undervest and waistcoat were bunched around his waist. The woman, he knew from that first telltale glimpse when he was starting his constitutional, was that new friend of the Mistress's, Mademoiselle Lebérigot. He was not surprised: at her age and still unmarried! Clearly no better than she ought to be!

He swung the Zeiss binoculars to one side: there was

movement behind the glass panels of the door. Another notch of the wheel.

Serafini caught his breath. A stout woman in a flowered dress was standing there, one hand resting on the table, watching the labouring couple.

It was, of course, the one they called Milady. Milady indeed! – the eavesdropping servant snorted – As common a tart as he had ever seen! He was astonished that the Master had dared to bring her. But the Master was away with the Hunt today. And when the cat's away . . .

Bunched, clenched, the buttocks contracted and relaxed in a sudden spasm. The legs below them quaked.

Nellie Lebérigot, fully dressed in a blue and white striped ensemble, rose to her feet and moved out of sight to the rear of the summerhouse. As the man bent down to pick up his trousers and drawers, Serafini saw that it was the banker with whom the two women had been joking at breakfast time. That was not surprising, given the type of women they were. What *was* surprising – he saw it clearly through the glass panels of the door – was that money changed hands just before the banker left a few minutes later.

The brazen hussies were operating an impromptu brothel right here on the Master's property!

The banker hurried down the steps and disappeared into the woods behind the summerhouse. A few minutes later he reappeared on a path two hundred yards away, whistling and swinging a bunch of keys on a chain as he strolled towards the Manor.

Serafini remained in his oak tree. He transferred his attention back to the summerhouse. Faintly, from across the water, he fancied he heard the sound of female laughter. A gust of wind rustled the new spring leaves around him. On the lake, a fish surfaced, leaving a widening circle of ripples. Someone was approaching from the other direction.

Another house guest: Dr Hamid Azad, a bearded

surgeon, a colleague of Gaston Despierre's. He was treading carelessly around the water's edge, as if wondering where to go next.

When he drew level with the summerhouse, he glanced hastily left and right, then scrambled up the steps. The door opened and closed.

No time was wasted on preliminaries. A couple of minutes later, the Lebérigot woman hoisted her skirt and petticoats up around her waist and climbed onto the table. She was wearing nothing beneath, the shameless jezebel, but knee-length stockings and black patent leather shoes with silver buckles.

Milady was standing very close to the surgeon. She was smiling up into his face, smoothing a lapel with one hand, adjusting his tie. Her free hand, at the full stretch of the arm, was tracing arabesques on the rapidly growing protuberance thrusting out the crotch of his striped trousers.

Azad was looking over her shoulder. Nellie was flat on her back on the glass table top, her knees drawn up and her heels resting on the bamboo framework.

Between the parted thighs, pink lips opened darkly among the dense black hairs furring her loins. Azad licked his lips. He snatched off his pince-nez and shoved them into his breast pocket. Absently, his other hand squeezed one of Milady's breasts.

Both her hands were busy now about his own loins. The fly of his trousers gaped. White drawers were thrust aside, and she dragged out the tumescent proof of his lust.

If this was the signal of the old fellow's manhood, Serafini thought, then the signal was definitely up – and showing red!

Milady seized the engorged member and used it to drag the owner towards the young woman splayed on the table. Standing at the edge, Azad gazed lewdly down at the treasure so wantonly offered.

Milady leaned over Nellie's hips and, with two fingers delicately poised, spread apart the lips guarding her secret place. She looked up and smiled again at the surgeon in a conspiratorial way.

Azad shook his head, opened his mouth in a gasp of desire, and lurched forward.

The purplish head, and then the entire rigid length, of his shaft was swallowed up between those inviting lips. Milady pushed with both hands on the small of his back; the silver-buckled shoes locked over his waist, and the surgeon sank into a dreamlike to-and-fro rhythm – met perfectly by the upthrust of the prone young woman's hips – that accelerated enticingly towards the climax that seemed as inevitable as the dusk that follows the dawn.

Seconds later, Milady had moved to the head of the table, her plump thighs wide on either side of Nellie's head. The head was obscured beneath the flounces or the older woman's skirts. Milady's tightly corseted body quivered.

The branch on which Serafini lay was shaking with his excitement. Holding on with one hand, he was obliged to let the binoculars drop to the length of their strap so that he could attend to his private needs with the other.

No sound penetrated the walls of the summerhouse, but the graphic drama of the mime within was enough to stir him unbearably once more when he resumed his watch and witnessed the scene reach its climactic conclusion.

Once again money changed hands before the surgeon left.

The music-hall critic, Patrice Delgado, was the next client. An unsatisfactory one for the major-domo: Delgado appeared anxious that his amorous adventures might be overlooked, and his appetites were satisfied on the floor, out of sight below the level of the windowsill.

The last visitor before lunch was a soldier, a general

of artillery who had been at school with Robert Laforge before he went to St Cyr. As a weekend house guest, the General had renounced his splendid uniform and settled for a high white collar and military stock with a frock coat and striped trousers. But his intimate behaviour retained nevertheless something of a parade-ground flavour.

At the command Three, retire to the wall. About turn. Place the hands, palm outwards, against the wall, equidistant from the body and at shoulder height. Retire the rump and spread the legs. Upon the advance of the partner, thrust the hips to the rear to meet his reconnaissance in depth . . . and so on.

When he had gone, Serafini shinned down his tree, skirted the lake, and approached the summerhouse. At the top of the steps, he rapped on the door. Milady, standing guard as always, opened it warily. 'What do you want?' she inquired.

'A moment's conversation,' replied the major-domo. He edged past her into the interior. Nellie took one look at him and turned her back.

'What have you to say?' Milady asked.

'Just this. That I have been watching you all morning. That I very much doubt that Monsieur Laforge would appreciate the fact that a guest was presuming to mount an affair of commercial fornication on his premises. That Madame Laforge' – with a glance at Nellie – 'would be equally distressed to learn of the questionable behaviour of her latest . . . friend. But that, in a world of rational people, there is no problem incapable of an amicable solution.'

Milady was a professional. She knew when she was dealing with a hustler. 'How much?' she said.

'Insofar as we are, in a sense, collaborators, shall we say . . . fifty percent of the take?'

'This is blackmail, pure and simple,' Milady said tightly.

Serafini smiled. 'I prefer the euphemism, where there is one available. Shall we call it . . . a service charge?'

'There is very little, I am afraid, that one can do here on a weekend afternoon,' Agathe Laforge said to Paul Mackenzie at lunch. As a guest from abroad, he was seated in the place of honour at her right. 'Unless, that is,' she added, 'you are keen on hunting and that kind of thing.'

'Rather the reverse, *I* am afraid,' said Paul. 'I feel, perhaps priggishly, that wild animals have the right to lead a natural life, instead of being reared with a sole purpose: to be slaughtered for the amusement – if that be the word – of man.'

Further down the table, Camille Dufour looked up suddenly from her plate. She bent her head and said something in a low voice to her room-mate. Corinne glanced towards the head of the table and nodded.

The young Englishman was too concerned with his cold salmon and Chablis – and with his hostess – to register the fact.

Agathe herself, in appearance coolly in command, was in fact confused. A very recent convert to the Sapphic expression of love, she had originally tempted Mackenzie into her room purely as a slight to her husband. But after the transports of delight shared the previous night, and the evidence of what a young and virile man could stimulate within her . . . She stole a glance at her companion. Really, he was *so* good-looking! The way those immature sideburns curled over his pink, boyish cheeks reminded her . . . well, never mind. Perhaps as the day wore on, before Robert and his hearties returned . . .?

Wind suddenly stammered the windows in their frames. The branch of a tree tapped, and tapped again, against the glass. 'Sky's clouding over,' Tom Crawford observed from the far end of the table. 'Wouldn't surprise me if it rained before tea-time. Oh, well' – he squinted over his shoulder at Yvette, who was leaning forward to proffer a dish of cucumber salad – 'it's an ill wind, what!'

'A ramble in the woods would have been nice,' Agathe said, looking Paul straight in the eye, 'but if it proved impossible, what could one offer as an alternative stimulus to the imagination? I tell you what!' She laid persuasive fingers on his arm. 'You're in the automotive profession. One presumes you are an enthusiast. In my husband's dressing room, which is also his study, there is a collection of photographs of motor carriages dating back fifteen years, from dear Gottfried Daimler's first horseless carriage to the present day. One asks oneself whether such an assemblage could interest a professional such as yourself?'

'One would, of course, be delighted to see such a collection,' Paul said politely.

Twenty minutes later – rain was already beating against the windowpanes and gurgling in the gutters – he sat in a swivel chair in Robert Laforge's room, turning the pages of a heavy album. He was looking not at the machine represented in the photographs on his knees but at the row of wooden filing cabinets ranged against one wall. 'Is this the holy of holies,' he said, 'where your husband squirrels away all his factory secrets?'

She glanced at the cabinets. 'Yes, copies of all the registered patents – and some minor inventions where the patent has been applied for but not even granted yet – he keeps them all in there. Among other things he keeps,' she added bitterly, thinking of Milady.

'Let me tell *you* a secret,' said Paul sensing her antagonism. 'Your husband has a process that seems to be applied to the underneath of his cars to protect them from rust in wet weather. I gather it's most efficient.'

'Oh, yes – what we call the whirly-bird. The stuff is sprayed on as liquid when the chassis passes over something like a miniature garden sprinkler; it has a diluted bitumen base, but it dries hard.'

'That's it. Well, my father would give anything, absolutely anything, to learn the formula of that liquid.'

For the briefest of moments Agathe Laforge was silent. And then, 'He doesn't have to give anything,' she said abruptly. 'But you do.'

Paul stared at her.

She was wearing a tight-waisted green dress with a round neck and buttons down the front. She clutched the garment at the neck, hooking her fingers beneath the material. Then, quite deliberately, she wrenched her hands apart, ripping open the dress and the bust bodice beneath so that her breasts spilled out.

His eyes opened wide, fixed in amazement on the soft swells of flesh, the puckered brown areolas and the stiffening buds at their centre. One of the buttons had hit him on the cheek when the linen of the dress split.

'I will be totally frank with you,' Agathe said hoarsely. 'I find – indeed I found – you an extremely attractive young man. If you will accompany me to the adjoining room, my bedroom, for, say, the next hour . . . then you shall have the whole anti-rust file. You may copy it as you will, just so long as it is back in place when the . . . when my husband returns with the hunt.'

Paul was a very normal young man. The sudden lewd display of female flesh amongst torn clothing, the nakedly exposed breasts rising and falling as the woman's breath quickened in anticipation, put all thoughts of Camille and Corinne out of his mind. Already he could feel the stirring of his own lust tightening the material sheathing his loins. 'Madame Laforge,' he said, 'it would be a pleasure indeed.'

'My friend,' Mata Hari said to Robert Laforge, 'I think I may have the information you need.' They had reined in on the edge of a copse. The quarry was halfway up the wooded slope on the far side of the valley below them, but the yelping of hounds was closing in. An occasional horseman could be seen among the trees.

'Excellent,' Laforge said. 'It is some kind of alloy, of course?'

'Naturally. But the components are unusual. And the proportions of one to the other less common still. I have the details all written down and will confide them to you on our return.'

'Better still. Come to my dressing room before dinner. You will be well paid, as I promised. Perhaps even' – Laforge coughed – 'we could discuss business of . . . another kind?'

The dancer smiled her inscrutable smile. 'Perhaps,' she said.

CHAPTER NINETEEN

My Dear Old Boy,
  Charlie, you wouldn't believe it: you – would – not – believe – it: I mean, we all know those funny stories about Gay Paree and those naughty, naughty, Ooh-la-la! demoiselles, don't we? But the thing is, old son, the stories are true! At least they certainly are in the circs I've been chucked into. Listen and you shall hear.
  I told you about the goings-on in this riverside pub place, didn't I? Well, you can shout going, going, gone! when you compare that quaint little foretaste with what actually happened at the old ancestral home. To start with, the hostess is surrounded on all sides by the bally she-she crowd, ogling and licking (if you will pardon the expression) their lips. Yet, come the witching hour, and she whizzes aloft with none other than the young squire, heir to the Mackenzie millions, himself! Mine jovial host, meanwhile, has waltzed in with an actual Madam, a tart (whom I happen to know) operating a bawdy house in the Latin Quarter. You guessed it: Milady again.
  A situation which had his ever-loving more than a trifle miffed, if you get my meaning. In addition to that, I gather from spies in the household, there was a most intriguing threesome – no, by George, a quartet! – in one of the rooms which involved

245

the Baroness, the Comtesse, a writer fellow from one of the newspapers, and an actress.

I might have found out more, if it wasn't that a fairly rum thing happened to yours truly: an assignation, no less; discreet but fervid. And not initiated by YT either!

You might think, knowing the lineaments and outward appearance of H. Champney, Esquire, that this in itself warranted a mention in the Old Thunderer. But the really odd thing was that the filly in question is generally thought to be securely clamped to the lezzie ladder. A lady from the Low Countries – with a touch of the old tarbrush too, I fancy – she really laid it on thick, with the result that jolly old JT dove in at the deep end more than once. Or twice, if the truth be known.

Apparently, this Dutch Auntie earns her living as some kind of a dancer, but as it happens she's a jolly intelligent girl, too. Knows all about motor cars and aeroplanes and even artillery. We were able to have a most interesting talk when the action was over. So you never can tell.

But all this nightlife turned out to be no more than an appetizer for the treats in store on the morrow. It all started, you see, on a stag hunt in the forest. And do you remember, Charlie, that naughty little jingle we sang when Nannie was out of the nursery:

Down in the woods when the nuts are brown,
Petticoats up and knickers down.
You like bottom and I like top:
See if my key will fit your lock!

Well, that infant ditty could have been the theme song for our stag hunt! Childish giggles apart, it was Midsummer Night's Dream *without the wall to hide behind. And the Bottom who was everyone's fool . . . well, let me tell you.*

It was a nice day – good, crisp spring air, with a spot of sunshine to warm the dew off the grass when we set off. By half ten, though, when we seemed to have quartered half the bally forest and the beaters or whatever they call them still hadn't raised an animal, it began to cloud over a bit. Mine Host and the Master called a halt at that time, and we repaired to what they called a hunting lodge – in fact a sort of pavilion among the trees halfway up a hillside – for hot coffee and a snifter. We stayed awhile, since the Other Ranks were having no joy in the way of a target, and I must say that a good deal of the old tipple was quaffed.

Finally, however, the hounds raised a scent and we all remounted and rode off. I say all. Treat the term as relative. Just as I was about to gallop away, practically the last in the line, a peal of girlish laughter caught my ear. I chucked the reins over my steed's noggin, leaped nimbly to the ground, and crept back to the lodge. More laughter, gentlemanly as well. I peered through one of the windows.

Blow me down! What should I see but Uncle Gaston, one of the banker fellows and the Comte de la Ferrière, all of them surrounding a bosomy young huntress, not one of the house party but none the worse for that, whose equestrian attire was strewn mostly on the floor. I say these gentry surrounded the filly; were clamped to her would be a more accurate term. For she too was on the floor . . . and on all fours!

One of the johnnies lay on his back, another knelt in front of her, and good old Uncle G, sly as *ever, was about to creep in the back way. When I tell you that these pillars of society – each sporting a different kind of pillar immodestly projected through his clothing – had each managed that golfer's dream, a hole in one, a person of your agile intelligence, Charlie, will not take long to work out what was happening.*

I toyed with the idea of rapping on the window to ask was this a private club, or could anyone join, but thought better of it when I realised that there was, in a manner of speaking, no room (no, not even standing room!) – or not in any way or place that I could countenance. In any case, at about that time the lady suffered what appeared to be an attack of St Vitus' Dance, and collapsed with a glad cry to the floor – leaving the team shooting, as you might say, blind. I was reminded of that old story about the fellow who bought a canary, 'which, for reasons that should be obvious to readers of the Bible, he called Onan.'

The hunt was up and in full cry now – mine too – so I rode off following the cry of the horn (no comments please). But it had started to rain, the yelp of the hounds was fading instead of getting louder, and at length I twigged that I was off the bally track altogether, hemmed in by one of those spinneys you have to ride around, only to find yourself facing another. Only this time I was facing another of these little pavilions. There were horses tethered outside, so I thought I'd nip in and ask, which way did they go?

I nipped . . . but not entirely in.

More fun and games, you see! I told you it was one of those days.

It was a keyhole this time, but I had to see. Because there were no less than four ladies in a small anteroom at the back of the this cabin. The

Baroness, the Comtesse, Mlle Dorziat and a fellow countrywoman, the show-jumping gel, Miss Dawn Broad. They say a Miss is as good as a mile, Charlie – but if goodness is the key, I'd say Miss B would be rated about fifteen feet.

She was directing what looked like some kind of ritual game, a sort of fleshly musical chairs. Two of the women, you see, were stripped to the waist, and the other two naked from the waist down! Miss Broad and the Baroness were in the latter category; Dagmar and Dorziat in the other.

If you have your ready-reckoner handy, you will quickly find out (going back to our bottom-and-top jingle) that this arrangement frees two pussies, four knockers, a quartet of mouths and no less than eight hands available for manipulative purposes.

Beware the treat that you haven't earned, Charlie! I suppose I had seen about half of the permutations (we won't even talk of combinations) possible when the roof fell in. That's what I thought anyway. Actually, my Dutch partner of the previous night had stolen up behind and leaped on my back. I was face down, flat on the floor!

She kicked open the door and called the others out.

Crikey, you never heard such a dressing down!

Intruder, eavesdropper, spy, voyeur, filthy lecher, dirty old man . . . you write the words: you won't find any I wasn't called.

They dragged me inside and four of them sat on me while the fifth dragged off the Champney boots and breeches. Miss Broad gave me six of the best with her riding crop. It hurt, too: it was just like being back at school, in old Bimmer's study. But the worst thing was, I felt so silly, with JT on display in front of all those girls. Worse still, the old fellow had his own ideas and was suddenly up and raring to go. I ask you!

This was when the Dutch lady took a hand. I'd thought, in view of our relationship the previous night, that she'd be the one to go easy on me a bit. But not a bit of it. She didn't seem interested in Hector any more. Only in the fact that I'd been caught out.

'You're going to be punished,' she said. 'You deserve it. Very well, you think you're such a stud, such a godsend to hungry women. Now we're going to make you prove it . . . and if you have been lying or exaggerating, it will be the worse for you.'

I didn't catch on, of course. Not until they began to draw lots.

The actress lost – or won, according to your point of view.

They had a gold half-hunter out and I was going to have to make good my boasts. About timing, I mean.

I shrugged. The Old Retainer was ready and eager. Why not?

So I gave it to Mademoiselle Dorziat while the others stood round in a circle, clapping in time to my thrusts and chanting: One, two, three, four; dirty man outside the door.

Four and a half minutes. Not my best, but not bad – in the circs. But they were laughing, all of them. Dammit, they were laughing. And it was only then that I realised the punishment part.

I had to prove myself, as it were, five times . . .

It was dusk when I got away. And the fifth was fourteen and a half minutes.

Charlie, it's late: I have to change and crawl down to dinner. You will have to wait until my next – or until I see you – for the saga of Miss

Broad and the Master's groom, which I witnessed on my way back to the manor. Or the episode of the peeping-tom butler and the Baroness in the bath, which happened after I arrived.

Meanwhile, dear boy, keep your fingers crossed, and pray on my behalf for a quick return to the three-minute egg!!

All best wishes from your chum

Hector

CHAPTER TWENTY

The rain had stopped but the sky was still menacing and there was a chill wind blowing by the time the members of the hunt returned to the manor.

Paul Mackenzie was among the guests gathered in the stable yard when the riders trotted in. Hot punch was to be served in front of a log fire in the house's stone-flagged entrance hall, and there was for a few minutes a considerable crowd thronging the yard as the hounds were led away to be kennelled, the local horsemen and horse-women dismounted to exchange greetings with the house guests, and stable lads dodged in and out to take charge of the mounts offered by Robert Laforge. Half a dozen estate workers staggered through the archway carrying a hurdle loaded with the carcase of a stag.

'An impressive brute: and a fine day's sport, eh?' a voice said behind Paul. He turned around. Gaston Despierre stood there with a satisfied smile on his face, rubbing together his cold hands.

Paul glanced at the dead beast, at the cart on the far side of the arch that had conveyed it from its forest home. Congealed blood clotted the soft nostrils, matted the flank, striped the lolling tongue. The eyes, saucer-large and luminous in life, had glazed over and stared sightlessly at the stormy sky. 'I am sorry, sir, but I cannot agree with your definition of sport,' he said. 'For me, this is something matching two individuals –

or teams of individuals – in some kind of contest with clearly defined rules. And if there be an element of risk, at least it is shared equally by both sides.'

'Oh,' the surgeon said loftily, 'so you're one of the new breed of namby-pamby, so-called reformers, are you? Well, that may go in your country, but things are very different here. If England has renounced the manly sports–'

'On the contrary, sir. There are just as many – shall we say brutish? – people in my country as there are here, just as many misguided folk who find their pleasure, if that be the word, in the slaughter of defenceless animals as there are anywhere in Europe. The hunting tradition – permissible perhaps when the hunter is in need of food, unacceptable when it serves no other purpose than to confirm man's arrogant belief in his superiority – such a tradition dies hard, alas.'

'And I suppose,' the surgeon sneered, 'that you would term careering around a track at fifty miles per hour in a machine . . . a sport?'

'At least there is an element of risk. And a certain amount of skill is required.'

On the far side of the courtyard Robert Laforge, hearing raised voices, moved to lend support to his brother-in-law – and then, remembering that Mata Hari had yet to prove the worth of her information, and seeing who the other party to the argument was, thought better of it. He might yet need to remain on friendly terms with the young fool. He went indoors to see about the punch. 'I see very little skill involved,' Paul said hotly, 'sitting on a horse to watch a pack of deliberately starved dogs tear a defenceless, terrified animal to pieces!'

'Bravo!' a female voice called from the other side of the yard.

Turning on his heel to stalk away from the angry surgeon, Paul was astonished to see that his champion was none other than Camille! Not only that; she smiled at him as he strode past . . .

Not quite sure how far it was safe to go, he permitted himself a half smile and a polite nod as he returned to the house, followed by disapproving murmurs from some of the other hunters who had overheard the heated exchange.

But his pulses were racing. The blood sang behind his eyes. She had spoken up in his favour. She had even smiled. At him. Personally!

If that wasn't a break in the ice . . . !

Joyfully, he ran up the stairs to his room. Details and drawings of the Laforge anti-rust process, including the precise formula of the bitumen-based spray, were safely copied into one of his note-books. Now he must keep his promise and return the 'borrowed' file to Agathe Laforge before her husband went to his dressing-room-study to change for dinner.

Agathe herself was already in evening dress – swathed in dark crimson and gold lamé. Her handsome face was subtly painted and her eyes shone. In the bosomy, waisted robe, with a certain haughty tilt to her head she looked, Paul thought, quite magnificent.

Clearly, the thought that she had betrayed one of her erring husband's professional secrets – added to the physical ecstasy she had shared with Paul and the fact that the husband had been audibly cuckolded the night before – had more than restored her confidence. At last, she felt, the score had been evened a little!

'You're a dear boy,' she said, touching his cheek with a gloved hand. 'You must come again, next time you visit this country.' She smiled. 'Without any . . . obligation!'

'M-madame,' Paul stammered, at a loss for words. 'That is to say, Agathe . . . I don't know what . . . I don't know how I can ever thank you. M-m-my father will be . . .'

He handed her the file.

And then, flushing, he added awkwardly: 'And as for last night and this afternoon, you were absolutely stunning. That is to say–'

She stopped him with a forefinger across his lips. 'You don't have to say it. We both know how it was. Let us put it down, in the nicest possible way to . . . shall we say experience?'

Most of the house party was reunited for cocktails in the Chinese room at seven o'clock. There were a number of absentees. Despierre had to return to Paris because he had an operation early the following morning. Milady and Nellie went with him: they too had business to attend to, in the Rue St André-des-Arts. Delgado was on duty in the printshop of his newspaper, readying Monday's edition; Dorziat had an early rehearsal. Robert Laforge offered to drive them both: armed with the metallurgical information supplied by Mata Hari, he was anxious to discuss matters with his technical director at the Le Bourget factory.

The farewell-and-thank-you encounter between Milady and her hostess in the entrance hall of the Manor was, in the words of the Baroness Gisela von Zwickenheim, 'a leedle frosty, no?'

Paul Mackenzie was sampling a new apéritif called Dubonnet when Camille walked straight up to him, smiled, and said without any pre-amble: 'Monsieur Mackenzie, it seems that I owe you an apology. I can only plead that my behaviour was due, in every sense of the word, to ignorance.'

For the second time he was astonished. 'Really,' he said, 'Mademoiselle, there is no need, I assure you . . . rather it is I who should beg your pardon. The blame is mine for too readily assuming that what one expects to be true *is* true. It appears that a gross piece of misrepresentation took place, and it is to my shame that I did not realize this and accosted you in the mistaken belief that – er – that you had been part of proceedings of which in fact, as you say, you were totally ignorant. You were entirely justified in reacting the way you did.' He gulped down the remainder of his apéritif, temporarily winded after this peroration.

Camille was still smiling. She laid a hand on his arm. 'I am familiar now with the *histoire* in all its ramifications and misunderstandings,' she said. 'Like all comedies of mistaken identity, it calls to mind our dramatist, Monsieur Feydeau. I understand that you were courteous enough to send me a letter, thanking me for whatever I had been able to achieve in the matter of the Poiret costume ball?'

'That is so.'

'And that you had the grace to accompany the letter with flowers and offer to escort me to the ball yourself?'

Paul inclined his head.

'Well, as you must know by now, I never got the letter. Or the flowers. Nor, in fact, did I even go to the ball.'

Paul nodded again. 'But *I* got a reply to the letter – and an invitation to meet somebody – somebody I naturally assumed to be you – at this masked ball. I . . . I do not think I need to say more than that.' He paused, and then added nevertheless: 'One should perhaps remember that the 'correspondence', such as it was, was conducted only by means of initials, rather than actual names.'

'Exactly.' It was the young woman's turn to nod. 'It *could* have been a genuine mistake, of course. But it wasn't. My room-mate as you may know, has the same initials as myself. She has in fact confessed the whole thing; she was a very naughty girl.'

Camille beckoned a passing footman, removed two glasses from his tray and handed one to Paul. She seemed a little embarrassed. 'Our concierge,' she resumed, 'was going to do exactly as you asked. Only I was late home that day, she had to go out, and Corinne arrived first. She was told the letter and the flowers were for me, said she would give them to me . . . but didn't. She answered your letter herself.'

Holding one full and one empty glass, Paul felt suddenly clumsy and gauche. He looked around the big room, hoping to find a piece of *chinoiserie* with a flat top, where he could put one down. De la Ferrière, the bankers and Dr Azad were discussing politics around the only vacant table in the room. The *Amazones* were in front of the lacquered and inlaid sideboard. Mata Hari was deep in conversation with the artillery General. Muzzle brakes, penetration capability and spades on each trail were among the terms Paul heard bandied about between them. He turned the other way.

Hector Champney was standing by the double doors talking to Bertrand Laforge and Corinne. The girl's back was studiously turned on Paul and her room-mate. There was no sign of Tom Crawford.

Paul saw a carved octagonal stool in red and gold that was temporarily unoccupied. He set his empty glass down and turned back to Camille. He wondered how much, if any, of Corinne's 'confession' had been centred on the nightlong activity in Poiret's lumber room. Given Camille's reputation as a prude, he imagined the full story would very much have devalued him in her eyes. But if she did know, there was certainly no sign of it now: the beautiful blonde's smile was warm and friendly. 'I much admired your courageous stand against the hunters, and especially that odious Despierre,' she said. 'Also your remarks on animals and their right to live, at lunchtime.'

Paul was about to frame a suitable reply when Serafini, followed by Agathe Laforge, came into the room to announce that dinner was served, 'My goodness, Serafini,' the woman exclaimed, 'whatever have you been doing to your eye?'

In truth, the major-domo was sporting an indisputable 'shiner' together with a swollen lip. 'An argument, Madame, with a cupboard door that should not have been open,' Serafini replied stiffly.

'Don't believe a word of it,' Bertrand whispered to Paul as they moved towards the dining room. 'The rascal was *inside* the cupboard, spying on Tom and Yvette, one of our housemaids. Tom was dipping the old wick, you know, when he caught Serafini at it!'

On account of the absentees, Agathe Laforge had rearranged the seating plan around the refectory table. Tactfully, she had placed Paul next to Camille. 'You don't think,' he grinned, picking up her silver fork, 'that this should be under lock and key?'

Camille blushed scarlet. 'That was unforgivable of me,' she said in a low voice.

'Frankly, Mademoiselle,' Paul said in a moment of daring, 'there is very little, if anything, for which I would not forgive *you* . . . provided I was allowed to be close enough to forgive!'

Camille laughed, forgetting her discomfiture. 'From a woman's point of view,' said she, 'such a rash promise, so sweeping a statement, would seem an ideal base for a long and enduring friendship!'

CHAPTER TWENTY-ONE

Tom Crawford was late for dinner. Apologising to his hostess, on whose right he had been placed, he bent over, kissed her hand, and murmured: 'I intend to steal, for professional reasons and only temporarily of course, one of your servants. The . . . negotiations . . . I am afraid took longer than I bargained for.'

'Really, Monsieur Crawford? On whom, pray, did your choice fall?' Agathe Laforge smiled. 'And am I permitted to inquire why?'

'But of course. I have been having some difficulty with the third figure for the allegorical trio I am executing for your husband. Your chambermaid Yvette – Yvette Tambay, is it? – would be perfect as a model for the lower part of the 'S' figure. But even more importantly for me, she is the ideal I have been seeking for my next work.'

'Indeed, Monsieur Crawford? And what will that be?'

'For the summer exhibition at the Fine Arts Academy; an over-lifesize figure, allegorical again, which I shall call "Harvest". The young lady in question has precisely the kind of ripeness – a certain generosity, if I may be allowed the term, of figure – that I require.'

'How interesting,' Agathe said.

'Initially just clay and plaster, of course. But if it is a success I shall fine-work the plaster and have it cast in bronze.'

'A nude, naturally?'

'Er – yes. Garlanded with flowers and a sheaf of corn on one shoulder. That sort of thing.'

'Perhaps I could persuade my husband to commission a bronze,' Agathe Laforge mused. 'He is fond of nudes. Something of an expert by now, I fancy.'

The Comte de la Ferrière, sitting on her left, gave a sudden snort of laughter.

'How long will you want the girl?' Agathe asked.

'For the *maquette*, perhaps a week; several weeks, probably, once I start work on the full-size work. If you agree, of course – and naturally I shall pay her.'

'Just so long as I have her back before the Season starts,' said Mme Laforge.

Further down the table, Paul Mackenzie and Camille Dufour, to their mutual delight, were finding that they had many tastes in common. The girl was fascinated by motor cars, excited by the idea of speed and thrilled by Paul's descriptions of sprints and hill-climbs in which, driving one of his father's machines, he had competed. For his part, Paul was enthralled with her account of the dazzling world of high fashion, and the lengths to which the rich and notorious would go to outdo one another in that ephemeral field.

In truth, these enthusiasms formed merely a façade behind which their joy in each other could develop.

The game soup, the entrée and the fluffy *quenelles* of freshwater pike, together with the lemon-flavoured water ice that followed them, passed almost without notice, so intense was their absorption. It was only when Paul was paying polite – if fleeting – attention to the local lawyer's wife who sat on his other side that he spared a thought for the food. The main course was about to be served. He had awaited it with some trepidation – for it would have been embarrassing to say the least, in view of his outburst in the stable yard, if his hostess had chosen to serve venison, the fruit of some previous stag hunt!

Fortunately Serafini, scowling at the sideboard, was preparing to carve roast ducklings.

Switching his gaze back to his companion, Paul intercepted a brilliant, conspiratorial smile from Corinne, who was sitting next to Bertrand on the other side of the table. Clearly, she knew now that he knew.

Before he could riposte, she had looked swiftly away to murmur something to the young man. But Paul permitted himself a covert glance before he concentrated all his attention once more on Camille.

The memory of that titanic night was still fresh in his mind, and, yes – registering the fleshy curves that thrust out the swathes of green silk below the neck of her dress, the sculptured smoothness of those bare arms – he could believe that this in fact had been the white body threshing beneath him in the changing light of the room above the Faubourg St Honoré. That the feet hidden beneath the table were those which had locked behind his hips during those hours of ecstasy.

But, thrilling though that had been, how could he – how could he possibly – have confused that body (just a tiny bit, he could see now, too curved and too fleshy) with the exquisite perfection of the blonde beauty sitting next to him now?

Beside the thoroughbred, Derby-winner racehorse lines of Camille, her room-mate could match only the slightly less refined lineaments of a steeplechaser, or even – Paul repressed a smile at the thought – a hunter!

The way women so often do, Camille picked up the subject of his reflections instantly (perhaps she had sensed the start of that smile, so rapidly suppressed). She said: 'You must not blame Corinne, you know, for what happened. It is in her nature, you see . . . to be, well, I suppose you could say inquisitive. About men, I mean.'

'Yes, but–'

'She is driven by some force, something almost outside herself, to try and try and try again – in the search,

I imagine, for some mythical ideal she hopes one day to find.'

Privately, Paul thought this a slightly euphemistic way of describing a man-mad female whose nymphomaniac urges led her to haul anything wearing trousers into bed with her as quickly as possible. But all he said was: 'You are very generous. Considering the damage she could have caused – and did indeed cause – in our case.'

'She is my friend,' Camille said simply.

'That is exactly the reaction, warm, and forgiving, that I would expect from you,' said Paul. 'You really are a very special person.'

'And the reaction you would expect from me at a masked ball' – she was looking down at her plate – 'that would be . . . warm . . . too?'

He felt the blood rising to his face. His throat was suddenly constricted. 'You know, don't you?' he said.

'I know Corinne.'

'Yes, very well . . . but you must think . . . you must surely feel: how dare this man, this stranger, this *foreigner*, assume that I will behave in . . . in a certain way the very first time he meets me. Because after all,' Paul said wretchedly, 'I did believe it was you.'

He swallowed. 'My only excuse, my explanation if you prefer, is that I didn't actually know you. I had never spoken to you. We had never met. You were just - well, to use your word, something ideal I had seen in the distance and very much wanted to see nearer. If I had met you, and seen you as you are, I would never have made such an assumption. I would never have presumed . . .' His voice died away.

'But you would have tried?'

'Yes,' he said hoarsely. 'To be honest, I would have tried – once, anyway.' He dared to look up and meet her gaze. She was smiling.

'Well, at least that is flattering,' she said.

'How do you . . . what is your own . . . I mean what do you really think about such things?' he asked.

'I do not like being taken for granted,' said Camille. 'Morally, although my mother would be appalled to hear me say so, I cannot find it in me to criticise Corinne or her way of life. Like all of us, she is searching. But, to borrow one of your English proverbs, she leaps before she looks. I prefer not only to look before I leap, but also to make sure, quite sure, that the jump is one I really wish to make. Corinne is able to backtrack and have a second, third, fourth, fifth go at the hurdle; I allow myself only a single attempt.'

'You want to be certain that everything is *right* before you commit yourself – is that it?' Paul asked.

'There would be no point whatever to the institution of marriage otherwise,' said Camille.

At the far end of the table there was a burst of laughter from a group around Dagmar van den Bergh. The English horsewoman, Dawn Broad, and Gisela von Zwickenheim were separated from the Comtesse, sitting opposite her hostess, by Dr Azad and the local lawyer. The merriment seemed to have been caused by an innocent remark of Miss Broad's.

'I only said,' she complained, colouring slightly, 'that the difference between a French sausage and a good old British banger is the fact that we use preservatives in ours.'

More laughter, in which the rest of the table now joined. It was Azad, dabbing a tear from his eye with a corner of his napkin, who finally said: 'Perhaps, as a medical man, I may venture to correct you, Mademoiselle. There are words in our two languages which look the same but have different meanings. In French, a preservative is an article made in rubber and used – as we say in my profession – for the purpose of contraception.'

Agathe Laforge pushed back her chair and rose to

her feet. 'I think,' she said demurely, 'that this would be – shall I say? – a fitting time for the ladies to retire to what my mother would have called the *with*drawing room . . .'

CHAPTER TWENTY-TWO

Half a dozen local landowners and their wives, some of whom had ridden with the hunt, joined the party at the Manor for coffee and brandy. Agathe Laforge had organised the same small group of musicians, and there was dancing in the ballroom from ten o'clock until midnight.

Apart from a duty dance with Bertrand and another with Hector Champney, Camille allowed her whole programme to be filled by Paul. But it was not until seventy minutes of polkas, veletas and figure dances had passed – she had just extricated herself from Champney's bruising, pumphandling hold – that the couple were able to recapture the near-intimacy they had shared at the dinner table.

The band was playing one of the new, daring slow waltzes which, like the forbidden tango, permitted physical contact between the dancers. Camille wore a powder-blue silk dress with a tightfitting bodice which flared out into a scalloped basque covering her slender hips. Through the thin material of his white glove and the rich, sensuous sheen of the heavy silk, Paul could feel the muscles of her back as he swung her into each turn. The waist might be small and the fitting close, but there was no corset here to constrict and imprison the flesh of that pliant young body. He tightened his grip slightly, relieved to experience no flinching away on her part but rather a minute, if discernible, return of the pressure as she leaned back against his arm.

He looked into her eyes . . . smiling eyes, their blue intensified by the colour of her gown as they spun slowly past the musicians on their dais beneath the glittering chandeliers. And this time there could be no mistake: there was definitely a knee pressing against the inside of his leg as they reversed!

He held her glance. The smile extended to her mouth. The hand resting on his upper arm moved up and around to cradle his neck; the delicate fingers he clasped gripped his own more firmly.

Oblivious to the world around them, still locked in each other's eyes, they made a dreamlike circuit of the dance floor.

Other couples floated past; fragments of conversation hung in the air.

'Naturally, if your husband decides on a public flotation of his company shares . . .' (One of the bankers to Agathe Laforge).

'. . . with the servants' wages disgracefully high . . .' (A local landowner).

'. . . at least fifteen hands, with a white blaze, and his fetlocks . . .' (Dawn Broad to the Comte de la Ferrière).

'With a howitzer or mortar, of course, the trajectory is much more . . .' (The artilleryman to Mata Hari).

Hector Champney, leaning against a doorway that led into the library, was confiding in Bertrand. 'Frankly, old boy, those two birds I met on the barge – haw! – those are the ones I want to see again before I go back to the jolly old sceptred isle, what!'

Dagmar and Gisela von Zwickenheim, flouting convention by dancing together, eddied past. 'I am desolated, *Liebchen*,' the Baroness was saying, 'that I have to return to Wiesbaden for a week. But you *will* try to get this Lebérigot – such a promising lady! – to visit us again, no?'

'I already have her promise,' the Comtesse said.

Paul and Camille neither saw nor heard any of it.

'I wonder,' he said under cover of the applause as the waltz ended, 'whether we should not be antisocial and sit the next one out? There are so many things I want to say to you.'

'Oh, yes,' she replied – the voice a little breathy – 'and so very many things I want to hear. Could you find . . . do you think you might be able to suggest a place where we should be undisturbed and alone?'

'Champagne!' Camille exclaimed. 'My goodness! However did you get it in your room?'

'I hopped out while you were dancing with Champney,' Paul said. 'Tom Crawford has a yen for one of the girls who works here, and through his good offices I slipped her a few francs to do the necessary.'

'That was very clever. And very thoughtful. Even if–'

'Don't tell me! I assumed. I took you for granted. In view of the message I received previously from your eyes, I thought I was justified! Don't tell me I was mistaken?'

'I shall tell you no such thing,' said Camille.

Each of them was in that heart-stopping, almost breathless state that precedes some momentous event that is anticipated, expected, never explicitly stated or foretold, but nevertheless occurs as inexorably as the day follows the night. For a moment they stood on either side of the wide bed, each of them at a loss for words. As in all Agathe Laforge's guest rooms, a fire burned brightly in the grate. Footsteps, hurried, a little furtive, passed the door. They heard whispered voices. Bertrand and Corinne.

'You don't mind too much . . . about Corinne?' Paul blurted out.

'I don't want to think about it. Or talk about it,' said Camille.

For a moment he was silent, staring at the champagne bottle in its three-legged ice bucket, at the silver tray and glasses on the table. He took the bottle and began unwrapping the gold foil. Each of them had already drunk a fair amount, before, during and after dinner, not really noticing when the footmen refilled their glasses. Paul could scarcely remember by what stratagem he had finally cajoled the girl – most unexpectedly, surprising even himself – up to his room. Perhaps she had not after all needed too much coaxing. Nor could he recall, the dare having been accepted, why it was that they had considered it more seemly to go to his room rather than hers. It was the release, the joy of the agreement that remained uppermost in his mind.

Now, however, everything was crystal clear. Camille unpinned a brooch from her dress. He sprang the champagne cork, poured the frothing wine into their two glasses.

'This is the first time I've done this, you know,' she said in a conversational voice. And then, before he could reply: 'Actually, that is not true. I did once. When I was seventeen. But never again since then.'

'And I suppose,' Paul said, 'that the man was inconsiderate, selfish, brutal even . . . and put you off the whole idea for life?'

'Not at all. I thought it was wonderful. Like most young girls I had been curious, intensely so. This was a boy of my own age; we decided to . . . experiment together. We only had the one chance before he went away. His parents were leaving our village to live in Alsace. We wrote once or twice but I never saw him again.'

'But you found the experience . . .?'

'I found it so wonderful that I decided, then and there, that it must never on any account be wasted; I must never throw it away, never take it for granted, never *soil* it with anything that was not worthwhile. I had to be sure – I told you – I had to be sure, before I allowed myself to surrender to that kind of joy, that the time, the place and the person were *right*.'

'And you *are* sure? And this *is* right?' Paul asked huskily.

'I am sure. It is right.'

He strode around the bed and kissed her then.

Often enough, in romantic novels, he had read the phrase, 'she melted in his arms'. Now, for the first time, he knew what it really meant.

As their lips met, her own arms stole softly around his neck and, within the clasp of his embrace, she seemed to subside, suddenly boneless, so that the entire length of her body was draped languorously against him, flesh to clothed flesh in one pulsating unity.

The lips clung, softly, tenderly, perhaps a little stiff at first on her part, and then relaxing, languidly parting so that the point of a questing tongue could probe. And penetrate.

Against the pressure of her bosom, Paul could feel his own heart thumping wildly. His pulses hammered. He was aware that for some time now the part of him most eager for contact, stiffened and rigid with desire, had been aching almost painfully. Now he could feel it imprinted against the flesh of his own belly under the soft insistence of the girl's abdomen.

Suddenly, generously, Camille's mouth opened wide. There was an abrupt expulsion of air through her nose, and her hips trembled against his hardness as her tongue speared forward to meet the invasion of her mouth. The two tongues wrestled and writhed, interlaced in the hot, wet cavern of their mutual need. The palms of her hands clasped the back of Paul's head, drawing him steadily closer, closer, exacting a deeper penetration of her mouth that was only a foretaste of that other, expected, violation of her body that was to come.

His hands clenched on the small, taut curves of her bottom, reciprocating the pressure . . . and this time he felt a gentle but definite thrust of her hips, squirming her loins against his maleness.

When at last they broke apart, each was quite breathless. Paul felt the backs of his knees trembling.

'I want to . . . to lie down with you,' Camille whispered, the voice, even at that low pitch, a trifle unsteady. 'But I'm shy; I'm still a little embarrassed. Would you mind . . . could you please put out the lights?'

'Of course.' He hurried to the switches by the door. The room, plunged suddenly into darkness, reassembled itself slowly in the warm, shadowed glow of light from the fire.

The decision was unspoken, but it was taken, mutually and simultaneously, just the same. It was time to remove all artificial barriers impeding their togetherness.

Off with the clothes!

Paul saw in the faint, pulsing illumination that she was reaching behind her to unfasten some clasp at the back of her dress. He moved forward with outstretched arms, anxious to help, but she shook her head and held up one hand. 'No. Not this time. Next time perhaps. Another time, anyway.'

He nodded his acceptance and turned away, the blood racing through his veins at the thought of the continuation implied in her words. Keeping his back tactfully turned to her, he took off his own clothes. When he swung around, she was lying flat on her back in the bed with the covers drawn up to her chin.

Wordlessly, he approached, the firelight casting a giant, shafted shadow on the wall behind the bed.

Camille's eyes were enormous in the suffused radiance brightening the gloom that flooded the further reaches of the bedroom.

Her pale hair, unpinned, haloed the face staring up

from the pillows. She smiled, raising the bedclothes so that he could slip in beside her.

Paul stretched out the length of his body, all at once agonizingly aware that he must be tender, compassionate, considerate and gentle, so that nothing untoward or clumsy should mar the magic of this moment. The responsibility seemed suddenly frightening. What should he do first? How far dare he go before . . .?

He need not have worried. Placing a tentative hand on her hip, he felt her turn swiftly to face him. And then the whole long, cool, sculptured glory of her was pressed to his body. The springy hairs covering the mound between her thighs grazed the stiffened and throbbing staff of his manhood.

They kissed again, the hands now exploring, probing, stroking. He could feel her heartbeat against the hair on his chest. His nostrils were beguiled by the musky, perfumed scent of her.

His fingertips caressed her hip, moved over the swell of one buttock to traverse the tiny ridges of her spine and then contoured the delicate curve of a breast. She shifted in his embrace, moaning softly under his mouth. Her hands, locked behind his waist, separated to clutch up the flesh in the small of his back.

So far Paul had not ventured to approach either her secret place or the small stiff buds tipping her breasts. He allowed one finger now to meander back across the taut, flat plane of her belly, circle the hollow below her hip bone, and explore lazily the crease of her thigh.

Camille's response was electric. She caught her breath, rolled slightly away from him, so that her breasts and pelvis drew apart from his body, and brought one hand around from behind his back to seize the distended shaft that had been grinding against her loins.

Feeling those cool fingers wrap around his throbbing maleness, Paul uttered a gasp of excitement. The thrill was almost more than he could bear. He flexed his hips, thrusting a knee between her thighs.

'Aaah!' she breathed . . . her legs parted slightly to admit the knee . . . 'Oh, my goodness: it's so big, so hard!'

The fingers grasping him tightened; almost unconsciously, the hand began to move, rolling the outer layer of skin up and down the shaft, palming the velvet tip. 'Come to me, Paul,' she whispered.

He tensed. One hand had already found its way to the soft, furred cushion of flesh above those secret lips so firmly closed over the treasure he had for so long wanted to possess. But now the lips were parting; his forefinger slid between them, warm and wet in the welcoming folds. He raised the upper half of his body, supporting himself on one elbow. He flung aside the covers. 'Now!' murmured Camille.

She spread her legs wide. And suddenly, effortlessly, he was sinking between them, the holding hand coaxing his stiffness, nudging, probing as she arched herself up from the mattress to meet him.

Easily, naturally, with the most normal movement in the world, he was inside her; as silkily as an index slipping into the finger of a glove, his tight and throbbing penis was engulfed, swallowed in the hot moist clasp of her body.

For a moment he lay still, his every nerve highstrung and thrilled to the magic of flesh on flesh – the soft belly beneath him, the tender breasts squashed under his chest, the hands now kneading the muscles of his back. Then he raised his head and stared down into her face. 'This is real, isn't it?' he murmured. 'This is it.'

'Yes,' she said. 'This is real.'

He lowered his lips to kiss her. As their tongues met, the ridged muscles of her secret passage clamped even more tightly around his hardness, and he began a slow, dreamlike oscillation of the hips, sliding out of her and then pushing back in with a powerful but gentle insistence that soon had Camille's hips arching off the bed to meet each thrust.

Silently, they settled into this steady, compulsive rhythm, the two reciprocating bodies functioning as a single, balanced entity. Paul was lost in a world of sensation; every nerve in his being – or so it seemed to him – was concentrating its reflexes in the shimmering ... burning ... forceful ... plunges ... and withdrawals, at the fiery point of his pounding loins.

And then, one by one, the mundane evidence of his other senses intruded: the crackling mutter of the fire; the dancing, ruddy light that chased fleeting, non-existent expressions across Camille's serene features; her quickened breath, hot and winey against his ear; a crease in the bed-sheet that was grazing his knees; and above all the suck and slap and squelch of lusting flesh and the vibrant quiver of the body beneath his hands.

A piece of coal fell out of the fire and crashed to the hearth, sending a sudden burst of flame to brighten the gloom. Footsteps creaked past outside the door (in fact Serafini, furious that the couple had come to one of the few rooms he had not equipped with a spyhole – and that the doors in this oldest part of the house were too thick to allow a sound to escape – on the way to his solitary bachelor bed).

The breasts crowning the girl's heaving chest were grinding more quickly against the form bearing her down into the mattress. Paul sensed an occasional quake somewhere between her hips; a spasm contracting from time to time the muscles gripping his shaft. And the plunging movement of his own body was becoming erratic, the thrusts sometimes harder, deeper, sometimes almost hesitant as the fluttering sinews of buttocks and pelvis broke the rhythm to send him surging forwards on the crest of that wave whose inexorable progress ends on the shore of ecstasy.

Their coupling accelerated. Camille's breath grew hoarse. Hips and bellies slammed together. The whole of Paul's self centred on the piston point of his fiery loins. And then, as a low shuddering shook the body of the girl, pulses hammered, hearts stopped, breath was stifled and . . .

The wave broke.

Over the thundering of surf in his ears, Paul dimly heard his own voice rapturously cry out over the mewling groans of his partner's release. And then the words huskily murmured, almost growled, against the sweat on his shoulder; 'My man . . . my own!'

Later, after they had drunk their untasted champagne and Paul had refilled the glasses, Camille switched on the lights again.

She took great pleasure in his body, admiring the muscular lines of his lean frame, marvelling at those parts of him which had instilled in her such joy. '*Oh, mais qu'il est beau, qu'il est beau!* How handsome he is!' she crooned, stroking the proof of his virility.

Paul himself was in a transport of delight. He had been so dazzled by the sheer *fact* of Camille, by the realization that here, now, in this room at this time, he was to enjoy that ideal so long cherished, so often despaired of, that he had somehow neglected to revel in the details of her actual appearance: he had overlooked the parts in favour of the whole. But now, after the sublime, almost mystic, experience of that first encounter, he was free to indulge his eyes.

Camille was of medium height, with a splendid upright carriage, a long straight nose and chiselled, curling lips of infinite promise. Her blue eyes were fringed by long blonde lashes, and her hair, tumbled now about her shoulders in a pale cloud, was naturally wavy. A haughty, almost disdainful chin completed the delicate oval of her patrician face.

Seeing her naked now, Paul allowed his gaze to roam from the sculptured symmetry of a slender waist and hips, past the enticing thicket of hair between her thighs and the exquisite taper of long legs, to the narrowed elegance of her feet. Bluish veins webbed the fragile tendons rayed beneath the skin from ankle to toes. Sitting on the edge of the bed, he leaned over and kissed the toes one by one.

She leaned back on the pillows, her eyes half closed, smiling dreamily. Over the rim of his champagne glass, Paul eyed her shoulders and breasts – small and perfectly formed, the taut little mounds tipped by rosy nipples that were still swollen with desire. Cool fingers fondled the wrinkled sac below his cock, massaging the tender glands within. Her eyes opened wide and she raised her head. 'My, how quickly he grows!' she said, stretching across her other hand to hold the lengthening, already stiffening stalk. Slowly, eyes gleaming in the bright light, she pumped him up, kneading the tumescent flesh to throbbing hardness, milking him forcefully now to the point where the blood-engorged head was purplish and distended, and the veins stood out against the rigid shaft.

Paul breathed hard. He could feel his heart thumping against his chest. On the bed beside him, the young woman stretched voluptuously, squirming her hips, languorously inviting him with the whole length of her supple body. She eased open her legs. Already, between pink lips half parted in anticipation, he could see that a single pearl of moisture glistened. With an inarticulate cry, he tore himself from her grasp and sprang onto the bed, lowering his head to her loins in tribute to the perfection of such a jewel, spearing his tongue through to the tender bud sprouting beneath it.

Camille moaned, thrusting up her hips to meet the lapping, sucking, probing invasion of his lips and tongue, writhing with lascivious pleasure as he explored the folds of her secret lips, jerking galvanically each time he penetrated the dark depths beyond or took between his teeth the fleshy button on which each fibre and nerve end in her body was concentrated. 'Oh, God,' she panted, 'I knew . . . I always knew, it had to be like this!'

Through Paul's impassioned kissing flowed the entire flood of his devotion to the ideal she represented. He raised his head and moved swiftly up to smother her belly, her neck, her shoulders and armpits, and especially the firm swell of her small, delicious breasts with adoring kisses. 'My dearest love, my own princess,' he gasped, 'I never thought . . . I never hoped . . . you are so wonderfully, so marvellously–'

'Hush!' she whispered. 'I want you back inside me.'

The natural curiosity she had confessed to – Paul discovered as the night wore on – allied to an extraordinary, instinctive sexuality that mixed ritual and drama with pure lust, combined to produce in her a partner whose adventurousness few men even dream of, let alone experience.

She was under him, over him, fingers sometimes even inside him, licking, sucking, tonguing, caressing. The brush of a satined breast across the hairs of his thigh, the sudden thrust of a warm belly against his hip, the manipulations of those inquisitive hands over his secret parts, raised the young Englishman to such a pitch of sensual awareness, so quivering a thrill of pure excitement, that each time her now practised fingers guided him inside the scalding haven of her belly the relentless approach of a shared climax was no more than the resolution of some cosmic law ordained before their birth and destined to continue for ever.

It was after the hot spurts of his love and devotion had for the third time provoked in her the shuddering sighs of ecstasy that he whispered; 'You said at dinner time that there was no point to the institution of marriage unless you knew everything was *right* before you committed yourself. Well . . . isn't everything right here?'

She clasped him agonizingly close. 'Yes,' she murmured, small white teeth nibbling at his ear lobe. 'Everything is right.'

'Then would you be prepared to commit yourself to that institution – with me? Would you consent to marry me, my love?'

'Yes,' Camille said, wrapping her arms even more tightly around him, 'I think that would be right too . . .'

CREMORNE GARDENS

ANONYMOUS

**An erotic romp from the
libidinous age of the Victorians**

*UPSTAIRS, DOWNSTAIRS ...
IN MY LADY'S CHAMBER*

Cast into confusion by the wholesale defection of their
domestic staff, the nubile daughters of Sir Paul Arkley are
forced to throw themselves on the mercy of the handsome
young gardener Bob Goggin. And Bob, in turn, is only
too happy to throw himself on the luscious and oh-so-
grateful form of the delicious Penny.

Meanwhile, in the Mayfair mansion of Count Gewirtz of
Galicia, the former Arkley employees prepare a feast
intended to further the Count's erotic education of the
voluptuous singer Važelina Volpe – and destined to
degenerate into the kind of wild and secret orgy for which
the denizens of Cremorne Gardens are justly famous ...

*Here are forbidden extracts drawn from the notorious
chronicles of the Cremorne – a society of hedonists and
debauchees, united in their common aim to glorify the
pleasures of the flesh!*

FICTION/EROTICA   0 7472 3433 7